SEC
REV

ROW
2

SEAT
ID

The **Death and Life**
of **Mal Evans**

A Novel

D1059738

The Death and Life of Mal Evans
A Novel
by Peter Lee

Avony Publishing, LLC

Lawrenceville, Georgia

This novel is a work of fiction. Any references to historical events, real people (living or dead) or to real places are intended only to give the novel context in a historical reality. Other names, characters, places, events and incidents are either the product of the author's imagination or are used in a fictitious manner. Any resemblance to actual persons is entirely coincidental. Some names and identifying details have been changed to protect the privacy of individuals.

Copyright © 2015 by Peter M. Lee. All Rights Reserved.

Cover design © 2015 by Christina Lingga.

Book layout and design by Rebecca Shaw.

Printed in the United States of America

ISBN: 978-0-9965127-1-8

MOBI eISBN: 978-0-9965127-3-2

EPUB eISBN: 978-0-9965127-0-1

∞ This paper meets the requirements of ANSI/NISO Z39.48-1992
(Permanence of Paper)

The **Death and Life** of **Mal Evans**

A Novel

Peter Lee

AVONY **PUBLISHING**
LLC

Dedication

To Mal Evans, who deserves the title of the Fifth Beatle as much as anyone, and whose memoirs would have been a fascinating read for all Beatles fans.

1

5 January 1976

I didn't think they would shoot. In fact, I may not have even noticed that they were pointing their guns at me.

But who could blame them? My girlfriend probably told the police dispatcher that I was high on Valium, paranoid and delusional, and severely depressed. I'm a big man (well over six feet), and I had a gun drawn on them—if you want to call an air rifle a gun. I'm sure the Los Angeles Police Academy trained its cadets to shoot whenever a large, crazed man is pointing any gun at them. There's no time to ask whether it's a shotgun or a water pistol. But I meant no harm to anyone, ever. I'm pretty timid, actually. My friends call me the "Gentle Giant."

I took Valium tonight because I was getting that feeling again—the feeling that I was disappearing. Drugs bring the real Mal Evans back. My faults fade away, and for those few hours, at least, I am the old Mal, talking and laughing. Tonight, though, it didn't work.

I had made the mistake of taking stock of my life; here I was on the other side of the planet from the U.K., sharing a flat with a woman who was not my wife, strung out and despondent while my wife and kids went on with their lives back home. I'm barely making ends meet. Too bad it took possession of an air rifle—can its pellets even penetrate a person's skin?—for people to pay attention and take me seriously. And as it turns out, they have taken me too seriously.

My breath is coming in short gasps. A process as natural as breathing is no longer automatic, and my head is swirling; I have to tell myself to breathe—in, out, in, out—as the air rushes out of my lungs and forces me to inhale again. I am sprawled on the floor next to the kitchen table, staring up at two police officers in the doorway, who are still aiming their pistols at me. *What, six shots weren't enough?* I begin to notice strange things: how the tiles on the ceiling create a checkerboard pattern, a soothing, consistent pattern across the apartment; how it is starting to look like a floor, with the chandelier standing upright like a fountain, and I am walking across the ceiling. The surreal picture makes my head spin even more.

I smell gunpowder.

An empty beer bottle that had rolled under the couch months ago is still there.

Now there is only silence in the room, but my ears are ringing from the sound of the shots. Every so often, I hear the wails and screams from my girlfriend, who is still downstairs.

My God. I'm dying.

My first thought after realizing this is almost silly: Will my death make the newspapers? At one point my death may have garnered a story in the *Daily Mail*, only because of my association with four boys from Liverpool. But now, six years after the group broke up, will anyone back home in England know what happened? Will anyone even care? I was so close to fame again; my memoir, *Living the Beatles Legend*, was nearing completion and would put me on firm financial footing—at least I hoped it would.

The second thought is of my wife and kids. Isn't that strange, almost selfish? I realise now that I'll never see Mimi again. Sure, she had asked for a divorce a month ago, so it's not as if I would ever hold her again. But the kids. Shouldn't I be thinking about what they will do without me, how they will cope, who would be there to give them advice about life?

No. Instead, I feel relief.

Mimi's request for a divorce was probably ten years too late. I have been in Los Angeles, off and on, for a few years, and my visits to the family have come less often. I think the last time I saw them was at a spring festival in Liverpool about eight months ago—a sunny day when the kids were happy, where the calliope chugged its nostalgic tunes, and we ate mounds of fudge until our stomachs ached. Mimi looked sad and tired, however. With each visit, our conversations were more forced and were limited to the kids' activities. We didn't even ask how each other was doing anymore.

I regret the fact that I have wasted thirteen years of her life; I hope my death will free her from the pain of those years. I'm sure she has regretted ever meeting me, her only happiness these years being our two kids. But even they are a reminder of the choice she made in me, how our relationship changed her life forever. How many nights did she sleep alone, having no idea where I was or what I was doing? How many birthdays and anniversaries did I forget while I was traversing the globe, either on tour or on holiday with the group? I could barely support my family on my measly salary while with the group (£38 a week), and in the few things I could give them—my love, my presence, my attention—I failed miserably. I had treated Mimi and the kids as a second option, knowing they would always be there if I wanted to go back. Now that's impossible.

I still love Mimi just as much as I did when we were first married back in 1961. But in reality, from the minute I heard the Beatles playing in the Cavern Club the next year, I had a new love interest. She never asked me about other women, but I doubt that she would have been as jealous of them as she was of John, Paul, George and Ringo. They were more of a threat than a one-night stand would have ever been.

Now I will give her the separation she desperately needs without all the messy court papers and negotiations. That's the way the Beatles had broken up, and it had been hell to watch. Mimi will not have to endure that. She can get on with her life, and I will be just a thirteen-year interruption.

One of the officers tells the other to go radio the incident to headquarters and to try to console my girlfriend. His gun is still aimed at me while he issues the commands (as if I were going anywhere). The etching on his badge reads "G TAYLOR" in ordinary block letters.

He is my killer. He's the man who will end my life.

I wonder what he's thinking, what the G in his first name stands for. I wonder where he lives, whether he has children, whether he honestly thinks I am a threat, and whether he is as shocked as I am at what just happened. I'm forty years old, and it's all for naught.

This is not the way my life was supposed to turn out.

Six years ago I was in the thick of what rock critics are now calling a revolution in music. I spent my days with the most popular—and arguably the best—rock and roll band in the history of the world. What's more, these geniuses, these pop gods, they accepted me. I would like to think that they were even my friends. They could do nothing without me. I took care of their instruments, hand-picked fans to go backstage for their nightly shag, and saw to their every need: a guitar pick, socks, even a cup of milk. And when I walked outside with them, when I prepared their gear on stage, people looked at me with awe and respect, knowing that I was one of them. I was *somebody* then.

People know me, but they don't realise it. My story and contributions have always been missing from the Beatles saga, but I've been with them almost since the beginning—before Ed Sullivan, before their first single in England, even before Ringo joined the group. I'm on some of the most famous Beatles recordings. I sang and played the bass drum on "Yellow Submarine." I looked high and low for the sound effects used in that song—whistles, bells, chains, straws to blow bubbles in water—anything that sounded nautical. I played trumpet on "Helter Skelter," helped play that endless final chord on the piano for "A Day in the Life," played the harmonica, kazoo, and organ on "Being for the Benefit of Mr. Kite!". (Hell, I even helped Paul write "Sergeant Pepper's Lonely Hearts Club Band.")

I shovelled a bucket of gravel on "You Know My Name (Look up the Number)." I was the silver hammer on "Maxwell's

Silver Hammer," striking an anvil in time with the beat. I was the swimmer who kept appearing at different times during the movie "Help!", asking where the white cliffs of Dover were. I'm in photos—a hulking figure with glasses, usually lurking in the background. I was always bending over, looking away from the camera as if I were caught off guard. I was probably busy with something, and no one ever asked me to pose for a photo. I often was just hidden from view—still there, just out of the frame.

I was always there.

Now, I'm lying on the floor of a flat in Los Angeles—half a world away from the U.K.—strung out, yelling a stream of obscenities at the police in between wheezes, and staring at that damn checkerboard pattern on the ceiling (or is it a floor?), all with four bullet holes in my body.

"Do you know what you've just done?" I scream. "I'm Mal Evans! *The* Mal Evans!"

This is not the way my life was supposed to turn out.

Honestly, they needed me, but I needed them more. In 1970, when Paul announced that he was leaving the group, I feared the worst. It was like a divorce—complete with court proceedings, shouting matches and hurt feelings. I was the child left to suffer, and after years of public quarrelling, of gossip and innuendo, of catfights played out in letters to the editor and talk show interviews, I knew they would never reunite. And I tried to make it on my own, I really did. I produced some albums, and I continued to hang out with the lads and other celebrities, but I was in over my head. I fell deeper in debt and more unstable month after month, year after year.

People have asked me over the years, "Why did the Beatles break up?" Depending on my mood, I have given different answers: money issues, spouses, just growing apart. Most accept my answer as the gospel truth, but for the longest time, I had no idea why they split. I sat and watched everything unravel before my eyes, powerless to do anything. But after six years of analysing that last year we were all together, I had finally pinpointed a day when everything began to fall apart: September 13, 1969.

It all started with one of John's daft ideas. A promoter had called him asking him to come to the Rock 'n' Roll Revival Festival in Toronto as a guest of honour. But John felt cocky. He believed that he could throw a band together in a few hours, get on a plane and play in front of thousands of fans. He told them he would come, but only if he could perform. The promoter was no idiot; he agreed at once. I'm sure he called the local newspapers and music publications in a matter of seconds.

As soon as he hung up the phone, John realised that he was in trouble. He began calling everyone he knew—everyone except Paul, George, and Ringo, of course. They were already walking on eggshells around each other at this point, and John's ego was too big to share the spotlight. He convinced his friend Klaus Voorman to play bass, and a session drummer named Alan White agreed to perform as well. He tried to call Eric Clapton, but Eric was nowhere to be found. Frantic, he had me ring Eric's house. It felt as if I were on that phone for hours, just listening to it buzz. But just as I was about to give up, the gardener answered. I put John on the phone, and after several minutes of pleading, he convinced the gardener to wake Eric, who was in a deep sleep. Eric stumbled to the phone and agreed to join us at the airport in an hour.

Having had only twenty-four hours to practise, John and the band were not at their best. But Eric Clapton saved the day with his superb guitar playing, boosting John's confidence. The concert was a success, and on the plane ride back from Toronto, John told the band's manager, Allen Klein, that he was quitting the group. Paul was the first Beatle to acknowledge it publicly some seven months later, but John was the first. He'll tell you that, too.

I remember how relieved I was that Eric was able to come, and how proud I was of my part in helping him get to Toronto. Now, lying on the floor of my flat, I know that I was no saviour. In fact, *I* was the cause of the Beatles' breakup. If only I hadn't told John about the gardener, if only I had hung up the phone before he answered. It took me six years to die after the Beatles broke up —much longer than I had thought it would take. But as soon as Paul announced that the Beatles were no more, I knew that I would not survive.

The end is near; the room begins to swirl. Or maybe it's my head spinning, I can't tell. The smell of gunpowder fades away, as do the police. I see only the checkerboard tiles moving apart, and a light shining down like a spotlight on me. Don't all those near-death experiences talk about a light?

I brace for whatever death may bring. But instead, I hear a familiar voice say, "Not yet, Mal. Hang on. I want to show you another path." I can't place the voice, but it's so inviting, so reassuring. I reach out and grasp a hand.

2

The bright, blinding light dims, and I'm sitting in an expansive, wood panelled room. A beautiful bay window stretches out in front of me, with a view of a formal garden. A fireplace is to my right, and hanging over the mantle is a framed photo of a nude John Lennon and his wife, Yoko Ono. I remember: It's the cover of their controversial avant-garde album *Unfinished Music No. 1: Two Virgins* LP, released back in 1968. I'm sitting on a black leather sofa with a telephone receiver at my ear, listening to a steady buzz.

I haven't been in this room since John and Yoko moved out. It's Tittenhurst Park, a Georgian mansion in Ascot, their home until they moved to New York in 1971.

How did I get here? I feel my chest for bullet holes, for the blood spurting out of me, but find a dry turtleneck shirt. There is no pain; granted, there was none before, but there is no shock, no breathing problems. I feel . . . normal.

"Dammit!"

The voice is to my left, and it belongs to John, who slams his own telephone receiver onto the base. But he doesn't look anything like the John Lennon I last saw, in the autumn of 1975—clean shaven with shoulder-length hair, holding little Sean in his arms. Now his hair is splayed down his back, and he's sporting a long beard and moustache, as he did on 1969's *Abbey Road* album cover.

"What the fuck are we supposed to do, Yoko? I can't get anybody on the phone. Nobody knows where he is." Yoko, in the kitchen nursing a glass of wine, says nothing. "I never should have signed up for this. It's gonna blow up in my face."

So this is what it's like to be dead. I remember John singing something like this in "She Said She Said," the psychedelic cut from their album *Revolver.* Am I getting a glimpse of my past before I go to heaven, or hell, or purgatory, or wherever it is people go after their life ends? What part of my life will I experience next? *The Ed Sullivan Show*? The filming of *Magical Mystery Tour*? The unplanned concert on the freezing roof of the Apple offices?

But those aren't images flashing before my eyes. Instead, this one recollection is lumbering by in real time. I'm Ebenezer Scrooge with the Ghost of Christmas Past, but I don't just *see* the old me. I can *feel* the telephone receiver in my hand. My clothes—an olive green turtleneck and dark nylon pants—are clothes that I vaguely remember owning a long time ago, but different from the brown corduroy suit I was wearing earlier this evening at my flat in L.A. I touch my face; my contact lenses are gone, replaced by the old bulky black glasses I used to wear. I've been clean-shaven for a few years; now my goatee is back. I am the old me.

I spot a newspaper beside the telephone. The date: September 12, 1969.

What the hell?

The receiver slips from my shaking hands, clattering to the wooden floor. A wave of nausea hits me. I need a drink.

"Mal. Mal! You dumb nit! Pick up the fuckin' phone! And don't put it down until Eric answers!"

Before I even think about it, I pick up the phone as I always did when John or one of the others yelled at me. But then it hits me: I'm real. I'm visible. *I'm here.* My mind tracks back to this particular time in my life—I do remember this happening. I remember John telling Yoko that it was going to blow up in his face.

Klaus Voorman, a bass player and friend of the Beatles from Germany—*looking so young!*—walks into the kitchen and hits his head on an open cabinet door, cursing uncontrollably. *That happened too.* I remember all of this; I've replayed the scene dozens of times in my head, wishing it had ended differently, that John had not gone out on his own, that the foursome would still be together.

As if on cue, someone picks up on the other end of the line. "'Ello, Eric's house."

It's Eric's gardener. I'm about to wake Eric up and kill the Beatles.

"Hello? Anyone there?"

Now is my chance to change music history. I can't hang up, or else John will see me. Slowly I depress the buttons on the cradle, the receiver still pasted to my ear, and the line goes dead.

Eric will not appear in Toronto.

John walks over and echoes the gardener's question. "Anyone there?"

I try to steady my voice. "Er . . . no one. Must be on holiday."

"Jesus! Stay on the line just in case. Meanwhile, we'll start plan B . . . Yoko, what the hell is Plan B?"

13 September 1969
Toronto, Canada

The vast locker room of Varsity Stadium is spartan in its makeup: concrete walls, concrete floors, wooden benches, lockers. The air is filled with cigarette smoke, threatening to overpower the lavatory deodorizer. John is to my left, crouching over a dank toilet. He is dressed all in white, a blinding contrast with the dull grey floors and walls. His body convulses in a long series of dry heaves, as if he's trying to purge some demon that has possessed him. On the other side of the toilet, Yoko sits like a statue on the floor, calmly smoking a cigarette. She is the yin to John's yang; dressed all in black, her long raven hair falls down her chest and is camouflaged amongst her clothes. A few yards away, Klaus Voorman is pacing the floor like a prisoner waiting for the gallows. Alan White is sitting in a chair glaring at Klaus, trying to will him to stop. A rockabilly tune blasts through the cement walls as if the walls didn't exist, the walking bass line buzzing the beer bottles on the sinks.

Eric Clapton is not here.

I haven't had time to find out why I'm here, but I'm not sure what I could do to learn—go to a priest? A psychic? A psychiatrist? For the past 24 hours, I've been trying to organise this impromptu appearance at the Rock 'n' Roll Revival Festival; Plan B, it turns out, is to play with the original lineup—minus Eric. I have absently collected all the gear, arranged hotel accommodations and made last-minute arrangements for the concert, just as I did last time. Several people have asked me if I'm okay, that I seem out of sorts. They have no idea why; to them I'm just the same old Mal Evans from the day before—just distracted.

I haven't slept at all; in fact, I'm afraid that if I were to lay my head down to sleep, as the old prayer says, I would die before I woke. Now is the first time I've had to sit without having to do anything since my return to 1969. I need to discover what's going on before this dream ends—if it is a dream.

I can't process it: *I am alive.* No bullet holes, no police officer, no checkerboard ceiling. Time is moving as it is supposed to, second by second. But every time I start to think about the possibilities, my head starts spinning. I can change—I *have* changed—events. If things happen the way I want them to, this concert will be a disaster and the Beatles will not break up. I light a cigarette and take a few drags from it, hoping that the smoke will clear my head. I wait for clarity.

Someone clears his voice. A young man, looking both nervous and eager at the same time, is standing at the door to the locker room. He searches the room for John, recognises Yoko, and then sees the figure kneeling in front of the toilet. "You're on in 15 minutes, Mr. Lennon," he stammers.

"Bugger off!" John yells, ending his outburst in a series of coughs and retches. The young man's eyes widen and he turns and runs.

The John Lennon I remember from that night, not to mention countless nights of performing through the years, is not here. He always got nervous before a concert, many times to the point of vomiting. But it was never like this. Tonight, he is a shadow of his former self, a ghost of a person. Gone is the braggadocio, the swagger replaced by uncertainty. He just can't pull himself together. He tries to light a cigarette, but it keeps slipping through his shaking hands. He's drinking anything in sight—soda, scotch, wine—to calm his stomach and nerves, but it comes straight back up, and he runs to the toilet. Yoko sits still and straight beside him, like a queen on her throne, hardly noticing his angst.

The strains of "Tutti Frutti" are now pelting through the walls; Little Richard, one of John's boyhood idols, is playing the last song of his set. John's nausea gives way to panic. "What are we doing here, Yoko? What was I thinking? An instant band? I must have been off me rocker."

Yoko, sitting on the floor, is unfazed. "It doesn't matter if you play well," she says, her staccato voice barely registering above the music. "Remember, it's the spontaneity, the raw sound that truly represents the Plastic Ono Band." I don't think she's talking to anyone in particular. "We will be the only one in the world playing those songs in that way at that time. It will be marvellous," she says, emphasizing the last phrase.

(I never quite understood their vision for this "Plastic Ono Band," a band made up of anybody at any one time. Yoko's original idea for the band was four plastic stands with tape recorders on them. It had seemed to me like another one of their stunts, like the time they stayed in bed all day during their honeymoon and invited the press to interview them during their "bed-in for peace." That was John and Yoko. We just shook our heads and moved on.)

"I can't do this without Eric. Where the fuck is he?" John throws an empty beer bottle to the concrete floor, and the bottle shatters in every direction. I know where Eric is, but more importantly, I know where he isn't. I have no idea what will happen, whether my tinkering with this event in music history will have any effect whatsoever. Maybe John will go out there and dazzle everyone without Eric. John will be the only guitar player; he is good, but not great by any means. Should I break a guitar string, create a short in an amplifier, to complete the sabotage?

I look up, the room silent again with only the bass lines buzzing away through the concrete. Alan is tapping out a cadence on the back of a metal folding chair with his fingers while Klaus is taking a profound interest in the business section of the Toronto newspaper. The soft, reluctant knock on the door is a welcome distraction. It's time. John bends over the toilet and heaves once again in reply.

I instinctively go into helper mode as I did six years ago, taking on my former job as Beatle roadie and helping set up the band's instruments. This is my exceptional ability, one of the few things I excel at. Anybody can fetch a soda for someone; it takes a special type of person to set up the instruments in just the way a performer likes it. It's a mindless task to me, something I had done countless times before when the Beatles were on tour, but something mindless is just what I need.

The stage is black, lit only by the thousands of cigarette lighters the crowd are holding while the people whistle their impatience. They are not as frenzied as they were back during Beatlemania. Back then, I couldn't hear a thing for all the screams, and usually had to spend part of my time keeping fans off the stage. But this crowd is more alive. They are poised and expectant: this is a monumental moment, a time they can tell their children about, when they saw a Beatle perform for the first time away from his band mates.

I am screaming on the inside as I lead the Plastic Ono Band onto the stage. The air is crisp but not too cold, adding to the excitement. The spotlights fire up, the crowd roars, and there's John, temporarily blinded as the lights sear into his retina. He looks as if his head is going to explode. He glances to his left at Yoko, who is sitting under a large piece of canvas. *Why the hell is she under there?* His gaze moves to Klaus—another familiar face, but not one that he usually sees on stage. Alan White is unknown to him. John is searching for familiarity, but the look on his face says he is finding very little.

"We've, uh, never played together before, so we're just goin' to play some stuff," he sputters, almost apologetically, before launching into the band's first hastily rehearsed number, the 1950s Carl Perkins song "Blue Suede Shoes."

I know from the opening bars that the set will be different from last time; back then, the band had made some mistakes, but it had sounded more cohesive and energetic. And seeing John Lennon and Eric Clapton on the same stage had been breathtaking. This time, though, the group stumbles through the song. John's voice is faltering and flat; he can't remember the chords and lyrics, and without Eric Clapton to cover for him, the mistakes are evident. At one point he begins making up words to the song before resorting to unintelligible syllables.

About halfway through the set, Yoko emerges from the canvas to accompany John on "Yer Blues," a song from the Beatles' *White Album*. Holding the lyrics to the song, she screeches incoherently with an almost inhuman quality. God! Why does she need lyrics for *that*? Alan White is performing admirably, holding the beat well, but he has to adjust his playing to different tempos created by the other band members. Klaus shakes his head; he knows it's going badly, and he looks offstage at me, almost pleading for help with his eyes. But aside from pulling the plugs from their amplifiers, I am powerless. And if I were able to do something, I don't know if I would.

The crowd seems excited at seeing a living legend onstage, and I think that John might actually get away with it. But as the set limps along, enthusiasm turns to confusion. This is John Lennon, composer of "Lucy in the Sky with Diamonds" and "Revolution"? The cheering subsides, replaced by catcalls and requests for old Beatles numbers.

John stops playing in the middle of "Yer Blues" and admonishes the crowd. "Give us a fuckin' break! We've only rehearsed once!" A heckler from the front row answers, "It shows!" and causes a ripple of laughter throughout the first few rows. *My God, they're laughing at a Beatle.*

John's latest composition, an ode to his heroin addiction called "Cold Turkey," is a mixed blessing; the performance is disastrous, but since the crowd has never heard it before, his flubs go unnoticed. But when Yoko begins a set of her own compositions, yowling incoherent syllables into a microphone as feedback roars from John's electric guitar, the catcalls grow to a chorus of boos. An empty beer can flies out of the crowd and lands at Yoko's feet. *Now they're throwing things at them!* That hasn't happened since their all-night shows in Hamburg in 1960—before they were gods—and those people were too drunk to know any better.

Yoko ducks as another beer can whizzes past her head. Fearing for their safety, John throws down his guitar, grabs Yoko and stomps offstage, raising his middle finger to the crowd. I run out, dodging a hail of cups and cans to move all the gear offstage as quickly as possible, leaving Jim Morrison and the Doors behind to save the festival. It's dangerously close to becoming a riot.

When I catch up with John backstage, he's creating a riot of his own, slinging chairs, trays of food, and instruments in every direction, yelling and cursing at anyone within earshot. "I'm a *Beatle*, fer Chrissakes!" he screams. "There's a certain standard I've got to live up to, and we just made total arses of ourselves!" No one disagrees with him, and no one dares to argue or even speak to him. Meanwhile, Yoko is chastising the promoter for the less-than-ideal conditions and the sound equipment, calling him an amateur and threatening to ruin his name in the music business. The promoter stammers, apologizing as fast as the accusations come out of Yoko's mouth.

John's mood, however, turns from rage to depression, and he sneaks off into the dark depths of the stadium. Forty-five minutes later, as crews begin to dismantle the equipment and clean up, he is back in the locker room, sitting on the floor with his head in his hands, looking like a defeated athlete. Yoko sits in the corner, expressionless, smoking another cigarette.

This is not the way it was before. The music then was only marginally better with Eric Clapton, and there were some boos as Yoko began her set, but Clapton gave the band more legitimacy, as if they were some supergroup. John's confidence was high, and the crowd went crazy for him. Before, he had shown that he could do it alone, that he didn't need the others. Now, it's painfully apparent that he needs something else besides a makeshift band.

* * *

14 September 1969

The plane ride back to England is quiet; no one is speaking to John except Yoko, who sits beside him and occasionally whispers encouragement in his ear. I'm sure in some way this has been a success to her; the crowd's rage, such a strong, raw emotion, is what she wants her art to accomplish. But John is in no mood to have his ego boosted or see what happened on that stage as a successful display of art. Instead of celebrating his new-found freedom, he is limping home, his journey away from the Beatles' nest beaten back with boos and catcalls. This concert was to be a test for how a solo career would go; if successful, he was planning to announce to the other Beatles his intention of quitting the band. Now, judging from the looks of him, he doesn't seem too sure.

What was going on with the Beatles before the Toronto concert? From what I recall, at that time John's heart just wasn't in the Beatles anymore. I had seen his face less and less around the Apple offices, and when he had shown up, his attitude was indifferent at best. Somehow, it wasn't enough for him. He hated the confines of the band, hated making three-minute pop songs with the same three guys. Even the thrill of touring, with adoring female fans throwing themselves at him at every stop, had ceased back in 1966 when they couldn't even hear themselves sing and play over the screaming crowds. They had begun to spend most of their time together in the studio or in business meetings, and I think Paul's sometimes overbearing attitude was grating on John. Making music had become a *business*.

In the old days, "Yeah, Yeah, Yeah" had been enough, but as the Four grew older, they also grew further apart. All four had gotten married—John twice already—and both John and Ringo had children. Paul's first child with his wife, Linda, was due any day now. They had all bought separate houses—a far cry from their days in Hamburg, when they all slept like puppies on top of each other in one dingy room.

I watch Yoko with profound interest. Her eyes are shut, and she looks calm, as if she's not even on the plane with us. She seems so out of place; I never fully got used to having her around. But when John got involved with Yoko around 1968, his life changed forever. She was exciting, controversial and unusual. Making music with her was so different from Paul's sometimes formulaic pop songs. The couple had released a few albums that consisted mostly of noise, tape loops and screaming, and it was like nothing John had experienced before. He was intrigued and excited; maybe this new sound was the future of music. Why limit himself to constant time signatures and scales, the same chords repeated in a different order? Why work so hard to make his music sound so predictable and rehearsed? So many more musical possibilities lay undiscovered and untried.

But the Toronto concert seemed to be a failure. And John Lennon was not used to failure. *I'm a Beatle, fer chrissakes!* Those words still rang in my ears. Despite his cockiness and independence, that still meant something to him. Even if he didn't like it, that label was something he could never rid himself of. Now, as the plane cuts through the black night outside, he is coming back to England, defeated.

For the moment, at least, the Beatles are still together. I lean back in my seat and finally sleep.

* * *

It takes me a moment to remember where I lived in 1969, and when I pull into the drive at one o'clock in the morning I hope that it's the right place. I find that the keys in my pocket fit the lock in the front door, and breathing a sigh of relief, I step in quietly, hoping that my heart does not sound as loud as it feels.

Even though it's dark, I still know where all the furniture is. I see the outlines of toys on the floor and know exactly what they are, when the kids got them. Their presence is welcoming, so familiar and friendly that I stop, basking in the comfort that I have missed for so long. This is my house—*our* house. The 1970s had been so intimidating and unfamiliar, with me traveling like a gypsy from flat to flat, sometimes staying with friends for weeks on end. But now I am safe. Now I am coming home.

I sneak into the kids' rooms, seeing them not as pre-adolescents anymore but as small children once again. Thomas, now seven years old, is breathing heavily, his hair plastered to his head in sweat. He must be having a bad dream. I pull the covers around him and scratch his back; he shudders once, then his breathing becomes more normal.

I travel to Susan's room. She is only three—my God, I had forgotten how fragile and pretty she was at that age—and sleeps with her face pressed on her hands as if in prayer. Her papa is with her again. I reach down and give her a kiss. She doesn't stir.

Mimi, my darling Mimi, is in our bed, *our* bed, snoring away, still with her day clothes on and still above the sheets. A romance novel lies beside her. I stare at her for what seems like hours, fighting the urge to wake her, hug her, and tell her how much I love her.

Her face is younger now, with fewer wrinkles and bags under her eyes, many of which were caused by the stress of being married to me, I'm sure. It's closer to the face I first saw at the funfair in New Brighton in 1961. We fell in love immediately, and after that we spent almost every minute together, catching the latest movie at the theatre, grabbing fish and chips at the local pub, taking a walk (and stealing a few kisses) in Old Nick's Caves at Sexton Park. Later that year, after we were married, Thomas was born; five years later we had Susan. We bought a house and a car.

Then during my lunch hour one day, I dropped into the Cavern Club and heard the Beatles play for the first time, and all of our lives changed. I became friends with the band, offered to handle their gear for them, and over the next six months, I worked less and less at the Post Office and eventually quit to work full-time for the four. Coming in at one a.m.—and later—was typical for me during the 1960s.

She stirs as I ease myself into bed. "Oh, you're back. Where have you been?"

I try to sound as normal as possible, almost bored. "Trip to Toronto. John performed at a festival there."

"It's been a few days. You could have called."

To tell the truth, I didn't want to call her. It would have been too much of a shock to hear her voice. "Sorry, luv. I've been working nonstop."

She doesn't answer, and soon the light snoring resumes. She must be tired. I wonder how many loads of laundry she washed today, how many dishes she washed while I was gone. She has always been here, letting me live my fantasy with the Beatles across the globe. I look at her face again, and this time I see the faint beginnings of those stress-related wrinkles. It has already begun – the deterioration caused by my absence and recklessness. Then the urge hits me: *Don't go back to them! You have your life again—live it without them! Get your job back at the Post Office and live a normal life. She deserves it.* But the thought passes quickly. When I place my head on the pillow, I am already looking forward to the day when I have a chance to see the Beatles all together again.

3

16 September 1969

Funny thing about places. The same thing rarely happens twice during our lifetime, and people come in and out of our lives so often that the next time we say goodbye to someone may be the last time we ever see them. But we can always go back to the place where something happened, and the memories come flooding back. You can visit your childhood home and find the exact spot where you skinned your knee at the age of five, and the pain and fear instantly fill your head. You can go back to the site of your old high school – the building doesn't even have to be there—and see where you received your first kiss. And your toes still curl.

The memories slam into me as I walk into the Apple offices at 3 Savile Row for the first time in six years. A Georgian townhouse, it had been the home of Lord Nelson's Lady Hamilton and most recently the property of entertainment magnate Jack Hilton. When the Beatles bought it for £500,000, they turned it into their office and kept most of the historical construction. Everyone, everything, is just as I remembered it; the ornate mouldings and fireplaces, the stark white walls contrasting with the apple-green carpet and the occasional gold record or framed photo of a band, and the controlled chaos of the Apple staff—phones ringing, typewriters clacking away, and continuous movement—staff revolving in and out of doors, handing memos back and forth, greeting visitors as they enter, and carrying cups of coffee and lunches to management.

My memories are now alive and playing out in front of me once again. This office was my home away from home; being there at the nerve centre, the home of the Beatles, had given me strength. I see friends, old and new: the switchboard operator, Laurie McCaffrey, who's been with the Beatles as long as I have; Neil Aspinall, my fellow roadie turned Apple executive, whom I have also known since the beginning of Beatlemania, talking with Derek Taylor, the press officer; Paul McCartney, dressed in a suit but no tie, listening intently to Derek and Neil's discussion; Ringo Starr—dear Ringo—sitting on a desk chatting up a beautiful secretary; and George Harrison in the corner of the room with a sitar, absorbed in tuning the Indian instrument's numerous strings. (I never was able to tune it for him before rehearsals.) Like John, he is no longer clean shaven. His long hair and goatee are the way they were in 1969.

I never thought I would see this again. Tears blur my vision, and they soon grow into heaves of sobbing. I turn away.

"Mal, what the hell happened in Toronto, I didn't even know he was going, I can't control him every minute of the day," Derek says in his nonstop tone, cigarette smoke billowing from his mouth. He's just as I remember him, all gentleman, dressed in a suit, but always looking as if he were involved in something of vital importance. "Christ knows I try, but here you go off with him and don't even call, and now we've got reporters calling from ev—"

"Hey mate, what's wrong?" Neil asks, putting a hand on my shoulder as if I were unstable. "Bad news?"

Ringo turns from his flirting, furrows his brow in concern but doesn't skip a beat. "Mal, I know working here is bad, but it'll be okay."

I take a few deep breaths and try to regain my composure, waving off tissues and glasses of water. Unable to think of any excuse for sobbing like this, I leave their questions unanswered and follow Ringo into an office, where he is looking for some LPs.

"Everything okay, Mal?" he asks.

I look around to make sure no one else can hear me. "I dunno, Ringo. Things have been really strange the past few days."

"Not any stranger than usual, I hope. Although a trip across the pond with John and Yoko can be pretty wild."

"Yeah . . . A *lot* stranger. Look, have you ever experienced *déjà vu?*"

"Haven't we had this conversation before, Mal?"

My heart skips a beat. "Really?"

"It's a joke, mate. I've never seen you before in my life. What do you mean?"

"I—I just feel like I've lived all this already. Like I've got a second go at this part of my life, and it's all happening again. Does that make any sense?"

Ringo whistles. "Whoa, Mal, I'll have whatever you're having. How much is it? Do you smoke it?"

I laugh, pat him on the back, and walk away, swearing not to talk to anyone about this ever again. I sound completely daft.

* * *

I have finally gotten used to being back in 1969, but that gives me more time to try and make sense of things. Is all this actually happening, and those awful 1970s were just a nightmare? So far I had lived through only six of those years, but it already has to rank as one of the worst decades in recent memory: Watergate in the United States, Labour's inability to stop inflation, power outages. It hasn't been a fun ride.

It's as if I am in purgatory, some sort of suspended animation, a final punishment before my judgment. Or, as George would probably say, I'm caught in some cosmic loop, not really dying but living another life, reincarnated in an alternate universe where the same things are happening, only a little differently. Will I die another way, only to re-emerge at a different time in my life, working things out and fixing the countless errors I made until I get everything right? Surely I must have done something wrong to deserve this.

George, who had become more spiritual since the Beatles' trip to India in 1968, taught me that we were all part of some cycle of birth, suffering, death and rebirth—I think he called it *samsara*. "I'm just passing through this world right now," he would tell me. I always thought the things he learned from the Maharishi in India or from his Hari Krishna brethren were just spiritual babble. Now I am starting to question who, or where, or when I am.

For the most part, things are the same as they were six years earlier. It's like watching a rerun on the telly: I vaguely remember events as they occur, but I can't predict it minute by minute. I have spent my days running errands, doing the same things I had done many times before. I forgot how much I had loved the excitement of the record business when I wasn't actually in charge, and I was for a few years. I hated making decisions on what songs other bands were going to record, I hated mixing and producing songs. I am back at my more mundane duties, but I'm good at them, and I relish the routine. It stabilises me.

Every so often, though, something *weird* happens that doesn't match my recollections. Paul or George will say something that doesn't sound quite right; I expect an argument to erupt, but it doesn't; or Ringo tells a story I know I have never heard before. None of it will change the course of history, mind you, but I wonder, *why?* Did the Toronto concert change everything, or is it just a momentary blip in the historical timeline, one that is bound to unfold no matter what some crafty time traveller does to change things? Am I in some bizarre warp in time that is setting off a chain of new events—kind of like the theory that a butterfly flapping its wings on one side of the world can cause a tornado 5,000 miles away? But one thing is for sure: the Toronto concert did end differently, and other things are different, too.

Maybe I have received a second chance. Maybe the last six years were a dream—one long dream after a night of binge drinking, and I now have awakened knowing what I need to do to correct my errant ways. This seems so real—I sleep and wake up every day, just as I always have. I taste food, I wince when I accidentally hit my head on something, I laugh at a good joke, I get drunk after a long day at work, and it all goes so slowly. I am *alive*.

When our lives come to an end, don't we wonder where the time went? What value did our lives have? What mark did we leave on this world? Was it all worth it? By then, of course, it's too late, and we end up fatally wounded on the floor of some flat, wishing we could turn the clock back. Our mark is nonexistent, and people continue to live their lives not knowing or caring whether we are here or dead. Our lives didn't matter at all.

But what could we have done to change that? There are four billion people on the planet, and a precious few leave their marks on it. And even if we had the potential or the luck to be famous or change the world, who's to say we would take advantage of it? We live our lives half asleep, noticing little, and forget most of what we do notice. The people we see, the conversations we hear, the books we read—everything gets filed away somewhere in the deep recesses of our brain, all but forgotten. What may have seemed like a pivotal moment in our lives at the time—or what is the funniest joke we've ever heard—will disappear.

But this time, now, I notice everything: the placement of every item on the administrative assistant's desk, the puff of every cigarette Paul takes, the jingle of every commercial on the telly. I listen closely to everything said, remember the funny jokes, and commit to memory every measure of every song my friends play.

This time, I am not missing a single moment.

4 November 1969

Screams come from outside the Apple offices. I am chatting with one of the secretaries in the reception area when I hear them. It's the Apple Scruffs—a group of fans whose sole purpose is to hang out at the Savile Row office and Abbey Road studios, hoping to steal a glimpse or even get an autograph of one of the Beatles. They are the eyes and ears of all Beatles fans, the front line of information. In fact, they've been here so long that we know most of them by name. Something bizarre must be happening, I think, to provoke such a response from the seasoned veterans.

Through the curtain I see John and Yoko emerging from their limousine parked in front of the building. We haven't seen him here for about six weeks—ever since the Toronto debacle. I had stopped by their home at Tittenhurst a few times to deliver papers to sign, but always left them at the front door because they wouldn't answer. A few days later, an assistant would tell me to come pick them up. There were rumours that John was strung out on heroin; knowing that he had done that the first time around, I didn't doubt this.

To my surprise I see that the Apple Scruffs are crowding around John, and he has stopped to sign a few autographs. Oblivious to the crowd, Yoko waits patiently for him. I hurry into the inner sanctum of the Apple offices, where the other three Beatles are in a business meeting in the conference room. "Um, guys . . . you'd better come take a look," I say. "It's John."

Ringo and George dash into the hall. I turn to follow them and glance back at Paul, who stays behind, smoking a cigarette and looking tense, even annoyed. I catch up with the other two as George peers out the window. "Bloody hell," he mutters. "The prodigal son returns."

This should be good, I say to myself.

John marches up the steps two at a time. Cracking the door open, he waves at George and Ringo. "'Ullo, mates, let's make a record and show those bastards we've still got it. Who's in?" he says, without any explanation of where he has been the last few months. His long hair and beard have been shaved off, revealing a stubbled head, and he looks frail. But there is a note of defiance in his voice. "Is the other one around too? The cute one? Bring him along—I'll meet you at the studio." He turns back around and gets into his limousine, Yoko trailing behind him. As we stare after him from the front steps, he lowers the window and yells, "Last one there is a rotten eggie!" George and Ringo look at each other and shrug.

That's all I need; I return to the conference room and in a shaky voice tell Paul that John wants to meet us at the studio. He rolls his eyes, but stabs his cigarette into the ashtray and collects his things. I grab my coat and keys and pull a car around to the front; within a few minutes, the three come down the steps, Paul taking up the rear.

My heart is racing as I speed the three miles to EMI Studio located on Abbey Road—the site of the famous album cover in which the four walked in single file across the street. *This has never happened. I might hear the beginnings of a new Beatles album.* The history books will tell you that the last time the Beatles were ever in the studio together was August 20, 1969, when they were putting the finishing touches on the song "I Want You (She's So Heavy)," which appeared on the album *Abbey*

Road. It was another eight months before Paul left the Beatles—and about three weeks before John's concert in Toronto.

Now it's November, *Abbey Road* has been released to critical acclaim again, and they're returning to the studio. I have no idea what might come out of their heads; John and Paul may take a new turn—start playing R&B music, or write "Philadelphia Freedom" before Elton John does. I might be ripping a hole in the space-time continuum. But I don't care. I'm ready for anything.

The guys are nervous. Ringo chatters away idly; George is sceptical but curious; Paul stares out the window, biting his fingernails and saying nothing.

At Abbey Road, we find John in a rehearsal room, sitting at the piano and tapping his foot impatiently. He begins playing, and from the sound of the first two notes that emerge from the piano, I know that "Instant Karma!" is about to become a Beatles song instead of John's first solo single and his declaration of independence. John runs through the song, showing them how to play it—"It's really simple, mates, just A, F-sharp minor . . ." Meanwhile, I have found an EMI assistant to make sure a studio is available and to secure an engineer. Now I head into our rented storage area to get a few guitars and a drum kit for the boys to use. One hour later, after a few rehearsals, Ringo pronounces it good enough for a single.

"Let's put it down on tape right now! 'Instant Karma!', instant single," John says.

George agrees, but Paul is silent.

"Well, Paul, whaddya think?" John asks, peering over his spectacles.

Paul avoids his gaze. "It's good, John, really good. But don't you think we need to practise it more? I was thinking of some overdubbed harmonies, and I think I could work out a better bass line."

"Nah. The sooner we get this down, the better. I want it to sound fresh. Too much planning's gonna ruin it."

Paul shakes his head.

"Oh, come on, Paul!" John says. "I thought you liked that rough, demo sound. That's what you were looking for with *Get Back.*" *Get Back* was the Beatles' attempt last year at a spontaneous, studio session album and movie—a fly-on-the-wall approach to recording that made the band uncomfortable. The sound quality and performances were sub-par, and mixes of the album proved to be unusable. The group had recently decided to scrap the project, releasing "Let It Be"/ "Across the Universe" and "Get Back"/ "The Long and Winding Road" as singles.

Paul laughs. "Yeah, and you saw how successful that was. We're not at our best when we try to pound something out."

George pipes up. "Let's go ahead and do it today. I hear Phil Spector's in town. Let's see if he can sit in on the session, smooth out the rough edges." Spector, who made such girl groups as the Ronettes and the Crystals famous, met the Beatles before their U.S. invasion in 1964. I remember John saying once that if they ever used anybody besides their long-time producer George Martin for directing their recording sessions, it would be Phil.

John loves the idea. Paul, of course, has other ideas.

"I dunno. I mean, we know how to do this. Let's produce it ourselves, make a go of it. Besides, I've heard Phil can be difficult to work with."

"Look, Paul, we're getting Phil," says George. "We need some new life in our sound, and he's just the guy to do it."

Paul is silent. I'm shocked by George's boldness; in fact, I think George may even have surprised himself. The public knew him as "the Quiet One," and it was true in the studio as well. It's a side of him I rarely see, but it comes across effectively. A little more subdued, Paul still offers suggestions on how to improve the song. John ignores them.

An hour passes, and John says he wants a break. He gets up to go to the toilet, and Paul sweeps over to the piano to take his place. "Hey guys, as long as we're here, I have a song I'd like to try out. I think it's pretty good—maybe A-side material, too."

John turns around, snorts and shuts the door. "Okay, Macca, let's hear your masterpiece."

Paul hammers out a sketchy draft of a piece that I remember was his solo single "Another Day." It's a sweet, innocuous song, typical McCartney—a gorgeous, simple melody with substandard lyrics. As he plays the last chords of the song, John stares at him in stunned silence.

"That's it? '*Dum dum dee doodle doo*?' John asks, referencing the nonsensical chorus. "C'mon. Seriously, that's not it, is it?"

Paul's face reddens. "Well, it's still got some rough edges, but I think we can work on it some."

"That's a nice B-side, Paul. But that's no single." John turns to George and Ringo. "What do you think?"

After a few seconds, Ringo mumbles, "I liked John's better."

George nods his assent. "You can't have all the A-sides, Paul."

"Well, there you have it," John says, satisfied at the outcome. Paul is outvoted again, and the three proceed to begin preparations for laying down tracks for "Instant Karma!" After being outvoted a second time that day, Paul decides to take a cigarette break, exiting the rehearsal room and slamming the door behind him.

John laughs. "Paul's gone to pout. He's gonna hold his breath until he turns blue in the face." George snickers, and the two whisper amongst themselves, no doubt poking fun at the absent Beatle. I remind myself to check on Paul later, but I'm so busy readying the instruments and performing sound checks that I forget. It's only when I notice Ringo looking out the door like a worried parent that I realise Paul isn't back.

Ringo walks over to me. "Mal, be a good boy and go check on Paul, will you?"

I walk out the back exit to a landing where the boys usually take a breather or a smoke, but he's not there. I check with the receptionist.

"Have you seen Paul?"

"Yes. He asked for a driver to take him home. He left about ten minutes ago."

Uh oh. I go in to tell the others the news, expecting my fantasy Beatles session to end just as it's starting.

"Fuck 'im," John bellows. "We don't need 'im." And so the sessions for "Instant Karma!" begin. John calls Klaus Voorman to step in for Paul on bass guitar for the session; it's the first time Paul has not played on a group recording, from what I can remember.

Studio Two at Abbey Road. I spent countless nights here. In fact, I know the entire building by heart, testing unlocked doors during breaks in recording, venturing into restricted access areas. Studio Two was another home. With the recording consoles high above the floor of the studio, you felt like a god up there, looking down on the recording artists. A small stairway ran down the right side of the wall to the expansive parquet floor, which sometimes was filled with instruments and engineers but was mostly empty today. I was always surprised that such a tight, compact sound could come from such a cavernous hall. The acoustic tiling on the walls helped, I'm sure, as well as engineer Geoff Emerick's innovative recording techniques.

Recording sessions can be maddening—plenty of hurry up and wait goes on. I restring guitars, fetch drinks and food for the guys, and then sit and wait for a few hours while the lads discuss changes to the song or instruments. And then I start the process over. But I'm a part of a Beatles recording session again, just like old times. That is, until Phil arrives.

Phil Spector is one part greatness and two parts worm. His pasty white skin contrasts his dark suit, sunglasses and shock of dark hair swooping down his forehead. He's not intimidated at all by the presence of the Beatles, and why should he? He's worked with the Righteous Brothers and Ike and Tina Turner and has been a part of dozens of number one hits. His "Wall of Sound" production technique, which employed many instruments playing the same thing to create more of a dense, layered effect, made records on lo-fi equipment sound like you were in a concert hall.

He doesn't bother to say hello to anyone; instead, he points to Geoff Emerick, the Beatles' sound engineer who is behind the control panel, snaps his fingers, and makes a gesture with his thumb to get out of the chair. Geoff starts to say something but thinks otherwise and obeys. Phil then rattles off a list of things he needs from Geoff: "Gimme four session guitarists, two drummers, three—no, make that four keyboard players. And book an orchestra to keep on standby." Geoff starts to open his mouth again, wondering where we're going to find an entire orchestra on such short notice, but Phil has moved on. He motions to me. "You, big guy. Courvoisier, and keep it coming." I guess he can tell that I'm the errand boy. And that's pretty much all I do for the next hour: fill his glass at an alarming pace. I am scared of him. I'm walking on eggshells, trying to anticipate his next tirade or impossible demand.

His odd production tricks emerge soon enough. Once the session musicians arrive, he sends them in like a coach substituting football players, telling them to all play the same thing at once, over and over until it sounds in unison. He tells Ringo to lay a towel over one of his drums to dampen the sound, going through different types until the right towel achieves the desired result. But some twelve hours later when he plays the completed version back to John, George, and Ringo, they are astounded.

"It's fantastic!" John exclaims. Spector has made John's voice stronger, almost godlike, enhancing it with an echo that goes on forever—something that the self-conscious John had always pleaded with George Martin to do.

It's a new Beatles single. But without Paul it sounds incomplete.

4

5 November 1969

I am dreaming—at least I think it's a dream—of Officer G Taylor lowering his pistol at me and pulling the trigger. I am trapped, my arms chained to a wall within Studio Two at Abbey Road. He smiles menacingly at me, his eyes drilling holes into my skull.

He pulls the trigger. *Click.* He pulls again. *Click.*

And then he starts laughing as his finger pulls the trigger again. "*Bam! Bam! Bam! Bam!*" The muzzle flashes again and again, and the noises sound so close, so real. I had convinced myself that the last six years of my life were one long dream. *So why am I having dreams of old dreams?*

I bolt upright. The sounds *are* real. Someone is knocking on a door. It takes me a few seconds to figure out that I'm on the sofa in the lobby at Abbey Road. We had finished at three a.m. the night before, and I had to help clean up after that, so I crashed here. I think it was about five thirty a.m. when I collapsed. I look at my watch; it's eight thirty a.m. Paul and his wife, Linda, are at the door, waving at me.

Linda has been married to Paul for almost a year now. I didn't like her at first, and I don't know why; maybe it was because she was American, or maybe it was because of my distrust of letting yet another person into the inner circle. I also suspect it was because I fancied his old girlfriend, Jane Asher. But I grew to like Linda; she was one of the few people who asked how I was and how my family was. She carries herself with a quiet dignity, her long blonde hair framing a natural beauty that never needs makeup.

"Jesus, Mal, you look like hell," Paul says, smiling as I unlock the door for them. I mumble my assent.

"What are you doing here so bright and early?" I ask.

"I wanna get an early start for the recording session today—that is, unless you did it without me yesterday." He laughs.

"Er . . ." I don't know what else to say. The silence is deafening.

"You're kidding," Paul says, mostly to himself.

"Um, no, they played until three this morning. Klaus was here. You just left without telling anyone . . ."

"Get me a sound engineer in here. *Now.*" Paul brushes past me, storms into Studio One, the other main studio at Abbey Road, and slams the door. Linda smiles almost apologetically and follows him into the studio.

That's strike three against Paul. He and John had recorded together without the other two, but the Beatles had never recorded a song without him being present for at least part of the session. Now they were saying to him, *We don't need you!* I ring Geoff Emerick, who has had about as much sleep as I have.

"Whaddyawant, Mal?" he says, half asleep.

"I'm sorry to bug ya, Geoff. Paul's in the studio. He's pissed off, and he wants to record."

Geoff yawns. "Jesus. I wish these blokes would all kiss and make up. Babysitting two groups is too much work."

About an hour later, with a groggy and grumpy Geoff Emerick at the helm, Paul begins to lay down tracks for "Another Day." He plays all the instruments—guitar, keyboards and even drums, and he and Linda provide the vocals. Later in the day, Ringo walks into the studio and sees Paul with his headphones on, playing drums.

"Oh, he's off doin' everything himself again," Ringo complains, and he walks out. I know Ringo will call John and George; at least I don't have to tell them.

* * *

With Paul's recording session, what I had hoped would be a quick drive home after some shut-eye has turned into another full day. I finally arrive home about one a.m.—after 48 hours away from my family without so much as a phone call to them, 48 hours with only three hours of sleep. Sneaking into the pitch black bedroom, I stub my toe on the bed post and curse.

Mimi looks up, startled, sees it's me, and sighs. She rolls over and doesn't speak until I climb into bed. I know I'm in the kennel. But why? Is it a general reason or something more specific?

"You missed Thomas's school play yesterday. And you didn't even call." Silence. "He's crushed, Mal. He kept looking for you during the whole performance."

My heart sinks. I touch my right index finger and feel the string still tied around it. Strings do no good if you don't notice them, and I completely forgot both it and my son's play. I try to say something—anything—that can somehow make it better. But nothing comes to mind. I have let down the family again.

I swore that this time will be different, that I would change for the better, but all my time and energy are being spent trying to keep the band together and happy, or at least civil with each other. As far as my family is concerned, nothing has changed. I am still the same old Mal, the same old father: absent and a constant disappointment.

I roll away from Mimi. Within seconds, I am asleep.

* * *

You'd think that reliving an era over would give you some advantage over others, as if you possessed some superpower. I knew in advance that the Conservatives would win the election of 1970 and that Edward Heath would be named prime minister. I won a few wagers on that one and made a handsome profit. More often than not, though, my memory fails me. I have tried to remember events as they originally happened in 1969 and 1970, thinking that I can exert some small influence, or at least profit off a few football games. But Liverpool FC still finished fifth in the league in 1970, despite my many attempts to contact Bill Shankly and tell him to play Ed Hall more.

Wagering on individual games was no good; most of the time I had forgotten who won the game, and my success rate was about fifty percent. I guess I didn't pay much attention to anything during the 1970s; I can't even tell you much of what I did during that time.

Other times I remember events too late. When the bodies of two children were found in Essex in June, I wept, recalling the tragedy when it happened the first time and cursing myself for forgetting it. I could have found the kids, warned their parents, and told them never to leave their sides. Or another lost opportunity: I wanted to go to Colombia in May and see if England's football coach Bobby Moore really stole that bracelet while at the World Cup, but my duties with the Beatles prevented me from going. I am reliving history, yet it is passing me by again.

The only power I have is with my mates. The first time around, on April 10, 1970, Paul released a solo album called *McCartney* and announced the end of the Beatles the same day. Back then, no one was speaking to each other except through insults and allegations in the media. We all knew Paul was releasing the album, but no one knew he was announcing the split. Now they are a group again.

Except for John's frequent absences, things are tense but good. There are no solo albums, no bombshell announcement in the works, no lawsuits, and the band is still together. I try to stay positive around them, telling jokes and trying to keep the mood upbeat. I play mediator when an argument arises, mending any wound that occurs to keep it from festering and killing the group. And deep down, I wonder if they will reward me by somehow getting together in the studio again to create another new masterpiece as God intended—or at least as I intended.

5 March 1970

The tension in the control room at Studio One is thick as Paul plays "Another Day" for John, George, and Ringo, still hoping for an A-side. He drums along with his fingers, at times singing along with the tape, apparently pleased with himself and the result. Neil, manager Allen Klein and Geoff are in the studio to share in the awkwardness, and they don't seem to know what to say to Paul. I'm out of place, knowing that they aren't really seeking my opinion. But watching the other Beatles' reaction provides plenty of entertainment. George and John raise their eyebrows at Paul's refusal to include them in the recording. Paul's nonsense vocalisms stay in the song, and John stifles a laugh when he hears them. His eyes widen, though, when he hears a female voice on the tape. "What the hell? Is that *Linda?*" Paul's jaw clenches; he merely nods his affirmative. Through the rest of the song, John stares a hole through Paul's skull as if he is trying to force Paul to respond. Paul looks straight ahead. I don't know why John was so upset; Yoko had contributed background vocals on "Birthday" and even had a solo in "The Continuing Story of Bungalow Bill."

After the recording stops, John responds: "Nice B-side, Paul. Our work is done."

"C'mon, at least think about a double A-side for this. It'll help the single overall," Paul pleads.

Klein then speaks—nobody referred to him as Allen, or Mr. Klein, only "Klein." He was brought in last year from New York to help stop Apple's financial bleeding; and from the start he angered everyone with his confrontational personality and flippant way of firing faithful employees whom he saw as a threat to his authority. He is a loose cannon, and he's one that I have no influence over. I've even heard that he tried to get rid of me a few times, but Neil and George talked him out of it.

"John's is more up-tempo, Paul. Yours just don't have the hard edge that people like nowadays." He emphasizes his point by stabbing the air with his cigar. Klein is a businessman, not a musician. This is not his territory, but that doesn't stop him from evaluating Paul's song.

Paul's face reddens. "Who gives a bloody hell what *you* think, Klein?" he yells. "You handle our business, not our songs, so shut up." He brushes past me toward the door. "Do whatever you want, mates!" And with that, he walks out.

Klein shrugs. "You heard him. Let's do this!"

I think about following Paul, but it's no use. The damage is done. *You're doing swell, Mal. They're disintegrating again before your eyes, and you're doing nothing about it. You're just as helpless as you were the first time.*

Village Voice

March 21, 1970

"Instant Karma!" – The Beatles

"Instant Karma!" is an instant classic for the Beatles. It's another upbeat anthem in the mold of "Revolution" and "All You Need is Love," with a similar mantra. Ringo Starr's drumming is brought to the forefront on this single, delivering a rolling tempo to the piano-driven song.

The B-side, a melodic ditty called "Another Day," is a charming if innocuous mid-tempo number that brings to mind "Obla-Di, Obla Da" – and that could be a good and bad thing.

5

25 May 1970

I have been waiting for this day for an eternity.

The Beatles are starting sessions for a new album, and I have done very little to facilitate it. I am at the helm of a runaway train, but for now it is heading straight, and I dare not touch any controls for fear the train might somehow veer off course, derail and crash.

After the last recording session, Paul stewed for a few weeks, then saw the success of "Instant Karma!" and ate his humble pie graciously, sending John a congratulatory telegram when it hit number one worldwide. A few days later, he was back at the Apple offices. All seems well now; I do my job as I always have, but I still secretly watch every move of the four, not wanting to let them out of my sight for fear that they will do something that will jeopardise their relationship. And I honestly have no idea what I am looking for. With each new threat, I try to change the subject or distract the parties involved, but my negotiating skills are about as weak as my leadership skills. I am always anxious and alert when Yoko or Linda is with the Beatles; their presence seems to bring out the worst in the group. I also pay attention to Allen Klein. He can set Paul off with just one sentence—as he did during the debut of "Another Day."

Today, I am once again preparing the studio for Phil Spector, bringing in boxes of Courvoisier and putting away anything that is fragile or valuable. Phil is known for his temper, and things tend to break within a three-foot radius of his presence. But John, George and Ringo were so elated with the results of Phil's production after the last session that they asked him to come back and help record the album. Paul hated the sound of "Instant Karma!"—he told me that he thought it sounded like it had been recorded in a cave—but I think he has agreed to continue, hoping that Phil will slip up and go out of control. He wants to be there to pick up the pieces and prove himself right.

Unlike the session for "Instant Karma!", Paul has shown up along with everyone else as they begin auditions for new material, but I can tell he has an agenda; he is anxiously tapping his feet during the catered breakfast I have brought in this morning. Once we begin eating, he gulps down his coffee and starts urging his mates to start auditioning new songs for the album. I think he's going to try to reassert himself as the leader of the group.

Before each album, the four play rough demos, sketches and ideas for songs. If the members embrace the song, they continue development, with input from all sides. Disinterest or disagreement about a song usually means that they won't use it. It's a good way of weeding out bad ideas and substandard material. In the past, it had been mostly John and Paul debuting material, but the last few auditions had George debuting more material—songs that rivalled the Lennon/McCartney magic.

At times, my job is herding preschoolers; one member runs off, and I get three together, only to have someone else run off for a smoke. I retrieve the runaway only to find two others missing. After about 45 minutes, my patience wearing thin, I finally get the entire group in the rehearsal room. Just as Paul is about to begin, though, George runs over, grabs his guitar, and makes an announcement.

"I'd like to play a few things for you," he says, smiling. John steals a glance at Paul, who looks surprised. Usually Paul or John began the sessions; George's songwriting prowess was still not considered to be as high as theirs. But he had started to make himself known; "While My Guitar Gently Weeps" was a standout track on 1968's *White Album*, and arguably the two best songs on *Abbey Road* were his: "Something" and "Here Comes the Sun." Today, he plays *seven* complete songs for them. I recognise all of them; some were auditioned or written during previous recording sessions but were not fully developed, such as "All Things Must Pass." He plays the slow, majestic ballad, and Paul nods his approval. "I always liked that one, George. You gonna give it another go?"

"Depends on whether you let me." *Whoa*, I think. *Paul offers an olive branch, and George swats him with it.* Phil Spector, who had walked in during the performance, begins to throw out ideas. "That's the closing song, George. I can add strings, some brass. It'll be a great curtain call."

Another tune of George's, an acoustic skiffle homage to the fans outside called "Apple Scruffs," is upbeat and sounds like a

Lennon/McCartney original. John even takes out a harmonica and plays an improvisational accompaniment. I can tell that it's going to make the cut as well. That should be it for him; usually, John and Paul dominated albums with their songs and made room for two George compositions. But he keeps playing, his confidence growing with each demo, and I smile at his newfound talent. He is coming into his own as a songwriter, possibly becoming as good as his two famous bandmates.

George adjusts his guitar strap and announces the last song to the group. "I call this one my 'Ode to God,' " he says. John and Paul eye each other when they hear the description—George's involvement in the Hare Krishna religious movement has been growing deeper, and in the past they had tried to stay away from religion in their music. They had previously vetoed some of George's songs because of their religious overtones. But when he starts playing the opening chorus to the song, "My Sweet Lord," John starts laughing uncontrollably.

George stops playing. "What is it?"

"Don't you hear it?"

George doesn't answer, so John picks up his guitar. "What's it in, E minor?"

He doesn't wait for an answer.

"It's the same bloody song! He's So Fine! The Chiffons!" John exclaims. "Phil, you produced it, didn't you?"

Phil grins but says, "That's okay. We can tweak it enough to avoid a lawsuit."

"I don't know. It sounds an awful lot like 'He's So Fine,' " Paul says. "You probably didn't even know you were doing it. But I'd stay away from that one, George."

Paul's tone sounds condescending, and I'm not the only one who notices. George is fuming silently over Paul's words. I forgot that the first time I went through the 1970s, George released the song on his first solo album and was hit with that same lawsuit. Without the others to bounce ideas off of, no one recognised the similarities to "He's So Fine." George denied the charges then, saying it came from an old out-of-copyright spiritual called "Oh Happy Day," but to hear John play the Chiffons song right after "My Sweet Lord" was damning evidence. Leave it to the Beatles to weed that one out and avoid legal trouble. The audition format worked again.

Paul finally has his turn and is eager to re-establish his musical dominance. He takes an acoustic guitar and plays a leftover from the *White Album* sessions called "Junk," a bittersweet waltz. This selection, which didn't pass the auditions for the previous albums, evokes groans from the others.

"C'mon Paul, we've heard that before and it didn't make the cut," John complains. "What else do you have?"

"Sorry, mates. Thought I'd give it another go. That song has grown on me." He then demos a song called "Every Night," a soothing acoustic ballad whose chorus evokes the *Abbey Road* cut "You Never Give Me Your Money." Again there are more syllables instead of words in the chorus—this time it's oooh's and aaah's. The band says nothing—not necessarily a bad thing, but their silence is unnerving, and Paul looks worried. Desperate to impress them, he walks over to the grand piano and begins playing another ballad: "Maybe I'm Amazed." Here it is—Paul's shining moment as a solo artist, from his first solo album—being played before me as a piano demo. *And it might even become a Beatle song.* Hearing this song must confirm my suspicion that I have died and gone to heaven. All of the words aren't there—he hums a few parts of the verses, and I want to blurt out the lyrics for him.

Paul's song is again met with silence, but then it is followed by clapping throughout the studio. A handful of engineers and studio assistants are gathered by the doorway staring in awe. As the applause dies down, Paul tries to be nonchalant, but I can tell he's pleased. "Now there's the Macca we've missed," John whispers. It sends chills down my spine.

John's auditions leave the group dumbfounded. They're a mixture of screams and noise, with the words focusing mostly on drugs and politics, and Yoko accompanying him on vocals. His first number is "Cold Turkey," the stark testimony on heroin addiction that he had debuted at the Toronto Rock 'n' Roll Revival. It sounds a bit more polished than it did back in September, but it's not the performance that causes a stir.

Paul shakes his head. "Too controversial, John. We don't need that now."

John rolls his eyes and tries another one, a folk number called "Working Class Hero." Its overtones are purely political, and when John says "fucking" in the second verse, Paul interrupts him.

"No way, man. That's a sure-fire ban from the BBC."

"Oh, c'mon Paul!" John said. "The Beeb would ban 'Mary Had a Little Lamb.' That's never stopped us before."

I snicker. "What's so funny, Mal?" Paul asks. I am the only person in the room who knows that in 1972, in response to a song of his that the BBC banned, Paul released a version of "Mary Had a Little Lamb." I hang my head, holding up my hand as if to apologize. There's no way to explain that.

"What else do you have?" George chimes in.

John walks over to an electric guitar and after fiddling with the knobs of the amplifier, starts creating awful feedback with the guitar. Yoko closes her eyes and begins howling.

After fifteen seconds, George has had enough. He runs over to John's amplifier and yanks the cord, interrupting the performance. The reverb and feedback take several seconds to clear the amp, and the cymbals in the room continue to ring. "What the hell was that?" he yells.

John stops playing. Yoko opens her eyes. "I call it 'Don't Worry, Kyoko, Mummy's Only Looking for Her Hand in the Snow,' " she says, almost whispering.

Ringo mumbles, "It sounds like someone just chopped Mummy's hand off."

Paul begins laughing, but George is incensed. "Yoko, you do know that the Beatles are four guys—me, Paul, Ringo and John?" I am stunned; George has never stood up to John in this way. In fact, John was once George's mentor of sorts. I wonder what bizarre turn of events is unfolding before me.

Yoko doesn't answer George, but John jumps in to defend her. "Don't you realise that there is no John anymore? There's just Johnandyoko! She's just as much a Beatle as I am!"

"Oh great, John. And we can have a song from Georgeandpattie! Or let's hear something from Johnandjulian," George cracks, referring to John's estranged six-year-old son from his first marriage. "Paul already got away with it, but we're not doing that anymore."

At that, John has had enough. "Piss off, all of yeh!" he yells, picking up his coat and turning to leave, with Yoko glaring at George as she follows John. Panicking, I try to think of some way to change the subject, or to recommend a perfect compromise that will calm everyone down and allow the demos to continue.

As John flings open the door, I blurt, "Hey, don't you want to hear Ringo's song?"

Ringo looks horror stricken, then looks accusingly at George, who seems puzzled. I worry that I have my dates confused, that Ringo hadn't written a song yet, until Ringo asks, "Mal, how did you know I was working on a song?"

I search desperately for an answer until John saves me. Staring blankly at Ringo, he calmly says, "Well, well, Master Starkey, let's hear it."

Until now, Ringo had written only two songs that the Beatles recorded and released—"Don't Pass Me By" from *The White Album* and "Octopus' Garden" from *Abbey Road*. He knew his songwriting ability was substandard; he was given one song per album, and he usually either sang a song written by one of the others or did a cover of someone else's song. I knew what the others didn't; by this time in my old life, he had written a very good song. I hoped that in this new world, he had done the same thing. I was taking a gamble.

Ringo still looks at me dumbfounded as George readies his guitar and begins to accompany the drummer. Ringo breaks into "It Don't Come Easy", which was a smash hit from 1973 in my previous life. He finishes the song, and John and Paul look at each other and laugh. Paul shakes his head. "Ringo, Ringo, Ringo!"

Ringo looks crestfallen, thinking Paul is patronising him again. "What was wrong with it? Does it sound like a Supremes song or something?"

Paul stares at him. "What's wrong with it is that I'm not going to get an A-side again. That's our first single, mate!"

Ringo looks stunned, and John adds, "You've come a long way, Richie. That was fantastic!" George winks at Ringo, who has never had such praise as a songwriter.

I am proud of Ringo. He was always the one who gave his all to the band, loved by all, but was seen as the one who rode on the coattails of the other three. His 1973 album, *Ringo,* was the closest thing to a Beatles reunion we ever had, with the other three contributing songs, instrumentation or vocals on various songs. "It Don't Come Easy" was on that album, so it's only fitting that it should be included as a Beatles song now. I also silently thank him; his song has provided some much-needed levity to the session, and may have even saved the album, which, based on the auditions, is in jeopardy even before rehearsals begin.

News of the World

29 May 1970

BEATLES TO RECORD AGAIN?

Yes, Beatle fans, it's true: Sources close to the Fab Four tell us that John, Paul, George and Ringo are busy writing and rehearsing songs for a new album, slated to be released later this year.

"They're really motivated to get the creative juices flowing again," the source told us. Renowned American producer Phil Spector, who produced the last Beatles single "Instant Karma!", has been spotted at the studio as well, leading some to wonder if he will helm the soundboard for the album.

No details have emerged on the album's name or any potential tracks.

6

17 June 1970

"Where's John?"

It's a familiar question the past few days. I've made repeated attempts to call him at his house, with no answer. This is the fifth day in a row he hasn't shown up; we have tried to record around him, hoping that he'll come in later to fill in some vocals and, of course, record his songs as well. So far we've only heard one song, an acoustic ballad called "Look at Me." We don't even know if he's planning anything more.

This time it's Phil Spector asking the question; you know it's bad when the chronically absent producer is asking where someone is. I promise to make another call and pick up one of the phones in the control room.

The phone rings and rings; finally a housekeeper answers.

"Yes, I'm looking for John. This is Mal calling from the recording studio."

"Sorry, he's not here."

"Well, do you know where I could reach him?"

"I'm not supposed to say . . ."

"Look, we need to know. He's supposed to be here recording. We're worried. Do you want to delay a Beatles recording session?"

The housekeeper sighs. "Try the Inn at the Park."

* * *

"Mum! Mum! Come back! Oh, Jesus God, come back, Mum!"

John's at the Inn, all right. After driving over to the hotel and dropping a few quid among the staff, I find him in a suite, huddled on a mattress placed on the floor, crying and rocking back and forth, his knees tucked up under his chin. He looks seven years old. There are no lights; next to the mattress is a man seated in a chair, taking detailed notes in a spiral-bound notebook by what little light is coming through the window. All I see of his silhouette are locks of curly hair. In a soft voice, he is asking John questions—almost whispering: "Where is she, John? Why did she leave you alone? Let it out, son, let it out." It's like an exorcism; John is now rolling over on his side, screaming, as his face, covered with tears, turns beet red.

"I don't know! I don't know! She's not moving! Wake up Mum! Wake up..." He trails off in silent heaves; it seems as if he takes forever to breathe again, and then he gasps for breath so he can wail for another thirty seconds.

One of John and Yoko's assistants, May Pang, is waiting in an adjoining room. May looks like a college student, she's so young, but her round spectacles, not unlike John's, add an air of professionalism to her. She motions to me, with her finger next to her lips.

"What the hell is going on?" I whisper.

May rolls her eyes. "Primal therapy."

"What?"

She hands me a book: *The Primal Scream* by Dr. Arthur Janov, a psychotherapist. A look at the back of the book confirms that the curly-headed person is Dr. Janov. "John's trying something new. This Dr. Janov is taking him back to his childhood, thinks John's parents didn't give him enough love. He thinks that if you get a person to give their 'primal scream' and release all that pain from his childhood, you'll cure him."

Oddly enough, this made sense. John barely knew his father, who left him when John was still a boy, and his mother, Julia, was often absent while he was growing up; his Aunt Mimi raised him. Just when he was beginning to bond with Julia when he was around the age of 18, she was hit by a car and killed. Since then, he was always searching for a new parent. First it was the group's manager, Brian Epstein; in 1968 it was the Maharishi; in 1969 it was heroin. Yoko had now taken up the role; John even called her "Mother." But it was clear he was still looking for something else.

"Where's Yoko?" I ask.

"She's screaming too, in another room. He's keeping them separated on purpose."

Smart man. Divide and conquer.

"So how long is he gonna be here? We're waiting for him at the studio."

An almost inhuman shriek emanates from the room next door. May shrugs. "Your guess is as good as mine. Could be weeks."

Not the answer I want to hear.

* * *

5 July 1970

John has finally shown up at a rehearsal—at least his body has. It's eleven thirty at night, and I'm cleaning up from the day's activities. Ringo is half asleep, drunk on the couch in the control room. Geoff Emerick is listening to the tapes from the previous session. John stumbles in looking disoriented, and says very little. Yoko is with him. He goes down the stairs to the floor of the studio and has a seat at the piano, Yoko sitting to his right as he begins to play. Geoff quickly readies a blank tape, checks the microphone levels and starts recording; otherwise, we might have missed the only take of "Isolation."

I see and hear the same despair that I saw in the hotel room a few weeks ago, but it's more subdued and morose. "Isolation" is slow and pensive, but lashes out in anger during the chorus. It's as if I have heard a whole new version of the song, which was on his first solo album in my old life; I now understand the meaning behind the lyrics. John is indeed alone, isolated from his band, his family and perhaps, even his wife. The last chords fade out, eliciting a response from Ringo, who wakes up when he hears the new song.

"Jesus, John, You got me all depressed now," he yells down to the studio floor.

John says, "Add a little percussion, will ya, Ringo? But not too much. Really punch that chorus."

He then launches into another piano ballad, "Oh My Love." It's sweeter and more loving than "Isolation," but it still shows a vulnerable John Lennon. In this song everything—his mind, his eyes, his heart—is clear. *Maybe Janov's therapy did some good.*

As the night wears on, the songs pour out of him, and all of us, including John, grow weary. He stumbles through "Jealous Guy," based on a demo he had made during the Beatles' trip to India in 1968. Again, it's an admittance, even a repentance to Yoko for feelings he's had in the past. It takes him several takes to get through it. He offers no direction aside from the occasional "I'm gonna do it again." At five a.m. he gets up, walks up the stairs and out of the studio without saying a word to anyone.

"What the hell was that?" Geoff asks.

Phil Spector shakes his head. "The first one was good, but we're going to have to work on the rest of those."

I groan. That means more recording sessions, more stringed musicians, and more Courvoisier.

* * *

19 August 1970

It's taken almost three months, but finally things have spun beyond my control.

I'm in the control room of Studio One, watching George and Paul yell at each other as they have never done before. Paul—

the mild-mannered, courteous Paul—is throwing things, and George is close to violence. I see his clenched fists and wonder where the quiet Beatle, the meditating, self-actualizing Beatle, has gone.

Recording a Beatles album has never taken this long. George Martin, the ever-organized, meticulous producer, is not at the helm, and the group has missed his regimented approach to recording. He had a schedule and stuck to it. Without him, things just aren't getting done. Phil Spector is living up to his reputation, and his behaviour is becoming more erratic. Last week he declared all the recordings substandard and threw the masters in the rubbish bin. Geoff and I saved them at the last minute from the janitorial staff.

Paul's micro-managing has become almost obsessive-compulsive; he spent three weeks recording "The Back Seat of My Car," preferring to score the orchestral part of the mini-medley without Phil. Phil came back and recorded another version. I have no idea which one will end up on the album. John's absence has doubled George's guitar work, but instead of complaining George has preferred to remain quiet.

Now his pot is finally boiling over. He had already recorded "All Things Must Pass" and "Apple Scruffs" but today Paul discovered that George was working on a third piece, a ballad called "Isn't It a Pity."

"Er, aren't you're done, George? You can stop recording. You have your quota already. Good job," Paul says. I swallow hard; knowing George, he will not accept this statement quietly. And I am correct.

"Excuse me, Paul, but who said you and John have to have all the space on an album?"

Paul laughs. "Well, George, that's just the way it's always been. Every album, two songs for you. Until recently, your songs just haven't been up to standard."

George fires back as if he has been rehearsing this argument for years. "Well, now they are! 'Something' and 'Here Comes the Sun' were better than anything you had on *Abbey Road*. Hell, it was the best stuff on the album."

Paul stares at George, dumbfounded. "What do you want? *Equal footing?*"

"Yes! I dare to request equal footing with the sacred Lennon/McCartney songwriting legends. Look, John obviously doesn't care about this record. He's not even here. And my stuff is better than most of what you've got. I want four songs."

"Oh, of course, George." Paul looks over at Ringo. "What about you, Ringo? Do you want four, too?" Ringo knows better than to get involved and does not answer, preferring to play with the wing nut on his high hat. "And shall we give Yoko four as well? Let's make a triple album, George."

When George blows his top, we are all taken aback. "I've had enough of your decision making, Paul! It was you who got us into that *Magical Mystery Tour* mess, and it was you who thought it would be a good idea to record those awful rehearsals for *Get Back*. You've tried to take control of this album, and it's a bloody mess." He walks over to Paul calmly but with authority. Pointing a finger at him, he says, "I just don't trust your judgment anymore. It's time for you to get the hell out of the way." George throws down his guitar, and the strings twang in response as he walks out of the studio.

Paul looks stunned by the outburst. He clears his throat and asks, "Does anybody have anything else to say?"

Without a beat, Ringo says, "No, I think George just said enough for all of us."

I'm not quite sure how to take this development. Fights are bad; fights are always bad in this new world of mine. Fights mean conflict, and conflict signals cracks in the group, leading to a breakup, and then I'll be back where I started—or ended. But this fight . . . George just declared his ability and talent as an equal, vital member of the Beatles. He had stood up to Paul once during the *Get Back* sessions, but this time, he asserted control. And with no one to back him up, Paul is speechless. He is used to ribbing and confrontation from John, but now George has become bold enough to question him, and I think it's thrown him for a loop.

7

If I didn't know any better, I'd think that I was attending a recording session for a George Harrison solo album. George is no longer the quiet Beatle; with John continuing to show up only occasionally, and Paul keeping to himself after the outburst, George has found himself the *de facto* leader of the group.

He has made his presence known. He's given Phil Spector more leeway to produce the material, and Phil's grandiose production has added even more time and money to the project. Fed up with the griping and the tense atmosphere in the studio, George has unearthed a song he had written during the *Get Back* sessions titled "Wah-Wah." The song was the result of the frustration George had with the group and the headaches that the latest recording sessions brought ("wah-wah" was a pedal for a guitar, but it was also a slang term for "headache"). He has added "Isn't It a Pity" and turned it into a seven-minute epic piece that recalled "Hey Jude" (no doubt to show Paul that he could create an epic masterpiece as well). Phil has composed yet another orchestral arrangement to accompany the song, which Phil says will end Side 1. George's song tally is now four, more than Paul's or John's so far. Two of those songs are the finale to both sides of the album.

I have heard all of these songs performed by each Beatle on various solo albums, but now they are *Beatles* songs. Granted, these songs are among the best of their solo work—they knew somehow to keep their subpar material at home. But in some indescribable way, the songs sound more important, more valid. At times, it was almost as if the Four have waved magic wands and made the songs even better. Although most of the guys are recording by themselves, there are subtle differences from the solo versions. "Every Night," which was on Paul's first solo album, now features three-part harmony with the help of John and George, and Paul lends his voice to "It Don't Come Easy" while adding a more intricate bass line—a definite improvement over the original. George has added an emotional guitar solo to "Maybe I'm Amazed" that is simply better than the one Paul performed on his solo album. The good songs have become great, and the great songs are now heavenly.

* * *

10 September 1970

Paul is in a bad mood. This album has taken its toll on everyone; we're now four months into the recording sessions. Most of the others have completed their work—Phil has worked some magic on John's recordings—but Paul continues to struggle with his songs. Having withdrawn "Junk" from the potential track list, he has three songs in the bag: "Maybe I'm Amazed," "Every Night" and "The Back Seat of My Car." His latest problem is a song he's calling "Too Many People." As is usual for him, he has the music completed, but the words are not coming.

Paul, Geoff and I are having snacks in the break room. Geoff and I are seated, trying to enjoy our sandwiches, but Paul is pacing nonstop, smoking a cigarette.

"Damn it, I don't know what's wrong with me. I've never had this kind of block before," he says.

"Well, you usually have John to bounce things off of," Geoff points out.

"What? You think I can't write a song myself, Geoff? I can write better stuff than John ever dreamed of writing. And you can tell him that, too." Geoff looks at me as if he just dropped a priceless vase. Paul kicks an empty beer can that's fallen under the table, and I dutifully go to pick it up. "Besides, where the hell is he?"

I shrug. "Last I heard he and Yoko were planting flowers at a military base."

"Those two can't focus on the music. That's what we're here for, aren't we? Not planting bloody flowers and chanting peace mantras. They're *always* off doing their thing, having bed-ins, preaching their sermons . . ." His voice trails off as an idea strikes him, and the words strike a dreadful chord in me. Once again, I've remembered something two seconds too late. The lyrics to the original song, from his second solo album *Ram*, referred to people who were constantly preaching their beliefs and philosophy to others. Paul admitted that the line was an indirect attack on John and Yoko's activism, and it caused a further schism between the two.

I urge him to take a break, get inspiration from somewhere, but he waves me off and begins scribbling away on a sheet of paper.

Sure enough, thirty minutes later, he begins recording the vocals to "Too Many People," complete with most of the offending lyrics that I remember. He takes a shot at George's inclusion of four songs on the record, complaining that too many people are trying to get their share of the pie. I sit on the stairs, head in my heads, waiting for him to finish. When he takes off the headphones, satisfied with the track, I try one more time to get him to reconsider as he goes past me up to the control room.

"Please Paul, you don't want to piss off John in the condition he's in. Why don't you sleep on it for the night?"

Paul shakes his head, looking defiant, not even looking back. "No, Mal. This is exactly what I want to say. I've done it. Let the chips fall."

He then adds, "And oh, Mal—don't tell anyone about this."

* * *

14 September 1970

I keep the secret, but it doesn't matter. John and Yoko, having completed their Primal Scream therapy, come into the studio in the morning—the earliest I've ever seen them here—and John asks to hear the final version of the album. I try to act unconcerned about it, but I take my time, hoping he'll change his mind, get distracted or fall asleep; I get the master tapes and set them up, fiddling with the machine as much as possible, but it's inevitable. I hope that somehow, the song is different, that some gnome has entered the studio while I was away and erased the song.

The tape begins to play.

It doesn't take long; "Too Many People" is the opening cut. John listens closely, and when he hears the offending lyric, he tells me to stop it and replay it. Then he asks me to replay the entire song—three times. He doesn't say a word, but I can tell he's furious; he copies the lyrics down as the song plays, bearing down so hard on the paper that I can hear the pencil scribbles and the dots punctuating the ends of the sentences.

When the song ends, he looks at me.

"Did you know about this, Mal?"

"News to me. First time I've heard it," I lie. I need to stay on John's good side.

He slams the pencil down, takes the sheet of paper and goes into an office to find a phone.

It's no mystery whom he's calling. He has the call on the speakerphone, and after a few rings, Paul answers, but John doesn't even bother to say hello.

"You didn't think I'd notice, Paul?" he screams.

"What are you talking about?" Paul asks.

"You know goddamn well what. Take it out. Now!"

"You know we can't do that, John. We're sending the record off to be pressed tomorrow, EMI's waiting, and we have a schedule to meet. And if you came to the studio every once in a while, you could've objected a little earlier."

"You really wanna play that way? Haven't you learned never to cross me?" Silence from Paul. "Okay, Macca, fine. Have it your way. But you're gonna regret this. If you think there are too many people around, consider this the end of our relationship. Have a nice life." John ends the call by picking up the phone and slinging it across the room. Two EMI staffers duck just in time to miss the unit flying over their heads. It crashes into the walls, sending plaster chips flying in all directions as the bell rings a final dying note.

And that's how I witnessed the Beatles breaking up for a second time.

* * *

15 November 1970

I am embracing my copy of *Everest*, the thirteenth studio album by the Beatles, marvelling at the cover like it was from another planet. Most people know of those iconic album covers that represented the Beatles— *Sergeant Pepper*'s collage of cardboard cutouts, the White Album's simple blank cover, the four walking across the street on *Abbey Road*—but here is a new one that will now take its place among them: a photograph of a pack of Everest cigarettes, Geoff Emerick's favourite brand to smoke. The four had talked early on about traveling to Nepal to get a picture of them near Mount Everest, but since that was impossible now, Apple publicist Derek Taylor dug up some photos of the mountain for the back. It was only the second album that didn't feature the band's faces on it.

My God, what an album. They came together just long enough, some of them only half trying, and they had created a masterpiece. They brought their best and left the rest at home. "Maybe I'm Amazed" is here, but the other impromptu jam sessions that spoiled Paul's debut album certainly aren't. "Jealous Guy" is here, but the harsh, unmelodic rants of songs emanating from John's therapy such as "Mother" and "God" are gone. George's best songs make the cut, but you don't have to listen to George's triple album to get through it all.

Still, though, they couldn't keep themselves from tearing each other to shreds. The record went to press with the offending lyrics, but no one except John, Yoko, and George noticed. John's paranoia got the best of him, and he and Yoko poured through the rest of Paul's songs, finding what they believed to be other veiled references to them.

The track list is perfect. I couldn't have dreamed up a better one. I wonder if history will agree.

For immediate release

16 November 1970

Contact: Derek Taylor

BEATLES REVEAL INTIMATE SIDE WITH EVEREST

The world's greatest pop band have stripped away more than their instruments with their latest album, Everest, offering a rare glimpse into the members' hopes, fears and memories.

The Beatles' thirteenth album is highly personal — many songs feature solo performances—

but it is perhaps their most collaborative release to date. John Lennon, Paul McCartney and George Harrison have penned an equal number of songs, while the first single, "It Don't Come Easy," was written and sung by drummer Ringo Starr.

Many songs feature a testimonial or confession by their writer. Both Lennon and McCartney have written love songs to their wives, and Harrison sings of the "Apple Scruffs," the loyal legion of fans who gather outside the band's offices. Other songs' titles are self-explanatory: Harrison's "Isn't It a Pity" is a heartbreaking lament, and Lennon's "Isolation" is a painful, lonely soliloquy.

Legendary producer Phil Spector is at the helm for most of the album. At times he gives cuts a touch of majesty, as with the closing cut, "All Things Must Pass." But other times he lets the artists be themselves, stripped away and intimate. The result is a truly intimate portrait of a band growing more mature, wiser and heartfelt.

Track list:

Side A

1. "Too Many People" (McCartney): McCartney performed and produced this haunting, sometimes angry track.

2. "It Don't Come Easy" (Starr): Although backed by the other three Beatles, the group's first single from the album is all Ringo Starr.

3. "Every Night" (McCartney): McCartney's acoustic ballad is an ode to family life and features three-part harmony by the band.

4. "Oh My Love" (Lennon): Lennon's first song on the album is a tender love song to his wife, Yoko Ono. His lyrics are direct but honest and loving.

5. "Apple Scruffs" (Harrison): Another acoustic but upbeat song, punctuated by some harmonica playing by Lennon, recalls early Bob Dylan. The chorus features some of the best harmonies sung by the Beatles to date.

6. "Isolation" (Lennon): Moody, cynical, and powerful, Lennon's second cut alternates between calmness and chaos.

7. "Isn't it a Pity" (Harrison): Harrison's second track serves as the magnum opus of Side A, timing in at over seven minutes. It is sweeping and sad, epic in scope, recalling "Hey Jude."

Side B

1. "Wah-Wah" (Harrison): Backed by a horn section, Harrison steals the show with an opening guitar riff that sets an energetic pace to Side B.

2. "Look at Me" (Lennon): An introspective acoustic ballad from Lennon that recalls his White Album tribute to his mother, "Julia."

3. "Maybe I'm Amazed" (McCartney): Another instant classic from McCartney, this piano-based ballad is punctuated by Starr's emphatic drumming and a heart-wrenching guitar solo by Harrison.

4. "Jealous Guy" (Lennon): A song that dates back to the Beatles' trip to India in 1968, it has been remade into a classic Beatles tune. It shows a side of Lennon rarely seen—vulnerable, sweet and apologetic.

5. "The Back Seat of My Car" (McCartney): McCartney creates a mini-medley of songs that seem instantly recognizable.

6. "All Things Must Pass" (Harrison): Another instant classic from Harrison to close the album. Acoustic guitars are mixed with Phil Spector's Wall of Sound orchestra. A wistful end to a bittersweet album.

####

Melody Maker

16 November 1970

Beatles Return to Form with *Everest*

After rumours of infighting, of growing tension and rifts between the members of the greatest group on the planet, fans have been wondering if *Abbey Road* and the two subsequent singles, "Let It Be" and "Get Back," were the last material we'd ever hear from the Beatles.

But why should we doubt the four men from Liverpool? The Beatles are back with a monumental album that, track for track, may be their best yet.

This time, the album is a true ensemble effort, with George Harrison boasting as many songs as Lennon and McCartney. The standout track, in fact, belongs to our beloved Ringo Starr, whose catchy tune "It Don't Come Easy" was written by him and sounds ready for "Top of the Pops." Paul McCartney has picked up from where he left off with "Let it Be," creating a beautiful ballad called "Maybe I'm Amazed," which sounds like an extension of the former hit single.

Lennon and McCartney have loosened the reins on Harrison, and he excels. His ballads "All Things Must Pass" and "Isn't It a Pity" set the tone for what is, as a whole, a rather sombre record. The group has ditched longtime producer George Martin in favour of American Phil Spector, whose "Wall of Sound" production is sometimes obtrusive but often perfect. On "Apple Scruffs," Harrison channels the spirit of Bob Dylan, as John Lennon accompanies Harrison's acoustic guitar on harmonica.

The Beatles are mellowing with age; seven of the 12

tracks feature an acoustic guitar prominently, and two others are piano-based. But they also seem to be second-guessing themselves, looking back on mistakes and trying to rationalise their intents. Lennon confesses that he doesn't mean to hurt his lover in "Jealous Guy," a tender ballad whose roots hearken back to the Beatles' visit to India in 1968. Harrison laments breaking each other's hearts and causing pain on "Isn't It a Pity."

At other times, they reveal fragility; Lennon asks who he is supposed to be in "Look at Me," which recalls an earlier ballad, "Julia." He tries to tear down his brash, bold public persona on "Isolation" by confessing that, unbeknownst to everyone, he is actually afraid. Likewise, McCartney suggests in "Maybe I'm Amazed" that he is lonely and doesn't know what's going on.

A closer look at this album, though, shows signs that the group is drifting apart. For the first time, Lennon and McCartney's songs are attributed solely to the principal songwriter, not to Lennon/McCartney as a duo. McCartney has produced several of his songs himself, while the others have chosen Spector. In fact, at times, *Everest* sounds as if McCartney is playing in one room and everyone else is in another. One wonders whether these changes lend further credence to rumours that the band is near the breaking point.

If they are, Harrison is giving the eulogy." Isn't it a Pity" pulls at the heartstrings as he admits how we sometimes hurt each other. In the final track, "All Things Must Pass," Harrison seems to have created an epitaph. Horns accompany the grand finale as Harrison reminds us that even sunshine doesn't last. Some things are merely temporary (even the Beatles?). All things do have an end.

The only quibble is with Lennon, who has given us a half-hearted attempt. He has either grown soft, or, given his new-found job as activist/performance artist with his wife, Yoko Ono, he *doesn't care* anymore. All four of his songs are ballads, and in his best offering, "Jealous Guy," the *de facto* poet of the group whistles the bridge. That's not to say that his songs are inferior; "Isolation" is despondent and powerful, and like many of his previous ballads ("Julia," "Don't Let Me Down"), all are heartfelt. It seems, though, that he is holding something back.

The Beatles may be fracturing, but all the parts are there. If the sun is setting on the Fab Four, it's one hell of a send-off.

The Daily Mail

17 November 1970

JOHN QUITS THE BEATLES

The day Beatles fans found a new album in record bins, John Lennon told reporters he has had enough of his bandmates and is leaving what is arguably the most popular and successful rock group of all time.

Lennon told *The Daily Mail* that growing tension with his songwriting partner Paul McCartney led to the split. "I just couldn't work with a lying, back-stabbing p---- anymore," he said.

According to Lennon, the opening track from *Everest*, "Too Many People," contains multiple jabs at him and his wife, Yoko Ono.

"There are too many references to Yoko and me with our peace movement," Lennon said. "Paul's too scared to confront me directly, so he puts it in a song without my knowledge and tells everybody how angry he is at our activism."

Lennon said McCartney tried to dominate the recording sessions for the album and when he didn't get his way, "he'd just go off and do his own thing."

When asked for a comment, McCartney said Lennon had not talked to him about leaving the group. "It's news to me. I don't know what's gotten into him, but I'm not walking away."

While not denying that the lyrics were about the Lennons, McCartney said he meant no harm. "We always deal with our grievances and problems through songwriting. This is nothing new."

The other members of the Beatles, George Harrison and Ringo Starr, could not be reached for comment.

Lennon said he was not open to a reconciliation. "Why bother? We haven't been a group for five years. We've just been putting out albums for your benefit. Ringo quit once, and so did George. I'm just the first to tell you about it."

8

21 December 1970

In a way, it was unbelievable that they stayed together for eight years. Their personalities and egos were like oil and water, but the fans, their old manager Brian Epstein, George Martin, EMI, and especially me—we kept stirring the glass for as long as possible. I'm starting to believe that it was bound to happen. I could play this era over one hundred times and come up with the same result. John and Paul always seemed to be five minutes away from boiling over. Add a newly inspired George to the mix, and it became even more volatile. And when you had four distinct personalities living out their lives in the public eye and then cramming themselves into a studio for hours on end, something was going to blow.

I tried so hard to prevent it from happening a second time. I had finally convinced myself that *Everest,* my newly created extension of the Beatles phenomenon, was a way for the universe to somehow correct a huge mistake. Somewhere out there, there was a world where things went right—wars never happened, people never got sick, and good bands stayed together.

What did we gain from the Beatles breaking up the first time? Paul and George's constant stream of mainly mediocre albums? John's heroin addiction? In my previous life, I searched long and hard for that reason, trying to find a bit of happiness in the four after the breakup, or seeing the good that they had done as solo artists, but it just wasn't there. John had an up-and-down relationship with Yoko (even left her at one point), drank way too much, and took an ungodly amount of drugs. His music was hit and miss. Ditto for Ringo. George couldn't follow up on early success and lost his wife, Pattie—the object of his hit "Something"—to Eric Clapton. Paul married Linda and had kids, but their new band Wings, despite some successes, were mostly a critical failure, and the group had a revolving door of members entering and exiting the band. It seemed he was trying to prove to everyone that he didn't need the Beatles. But every album was proof that he did, and he never could find the right combination to replace John, George and Ringo.

I have never become truly comfortable in this second world. I have been fearful of waking up from this fantastic dream (if it is a dream), of doing something that would set off a series of events that would demolish it. For if that world crumbled, so would I. In this new life I had a base, a purpose, but when I read that headline in the Daily Mail, my entire soul trembled. I felt the demons of chaos and uncertainty start to creep up, and I feared that it was only a matter of time before I would slip into the old way of life that had put me on the floor of that Los Angeles apartment.

I'm now sitting in one of the Apple Corps executive offices, which also serves as a common room for many Apple insiders. It's decorated all in white—white walls, chairs, desks and throw pillows—and almost blinding, as if someone has sucked all of the hues out of the room, leaving a blank colouring book page with only lines and shapes.

My life is like that room. The dream of the Beatles being a cohesive group is now over, and I am panicking. I tried to see if Paul was remorseful in any way, but he was too angry to listen. I have just returned from John's house, after yet another effort to extend an olive branch. Everything that came out of my mouth was a lie: that Paul regretted using the lyrics, that he didn't mean it, that he wanted to apologise. It was desperate, I know. But it did no good. John wouldn't entertain any idea of a ceasefire and threw me out of his house—the first time he had ever done that.

The other three probably breathed a sigh of relief when John said he was quitting the group. George and Paul were now free to make their own music, with no filters from the rest of the group, and Ringo was happy to be away from the stress that had been mounting among the members.

I've failed. I swore things in my life would be different the second time around. My wife, my kids, and any long-term career hopes fell by the wayside as I tried to fix the one thing I truly cared about. And, as it turned out, I couldn't do much. I was as powerless this time as I was the first time.

I look around, hoping to see someone walk in, but no one is there. The office is quiet, almost tomb-like. I walk over to the window and see a mother pushing a pram down the street, occasionally making faces at her baby. She's probably twenty-five, and I know she has grown up listening to the music of the Beatles. How does she feel about the breakup? Life for her is moving on; she's off on a walk, or running errands, or visiting a friend.

Inside the Apple offices, though, life is at a standstill. No office chatter, no jokes, no Derek Taylor rambling on. I am alone.

* * *

3 June 1971

John, Yoko and Allen Klein are huddled in a rehearsal room at Abbey Road, and they are up to no good. An unwitting Paul McCartney is their victim. They're writing lyrics to a new song called "How Do You Sleep?" for John's first solo album.

"Put something in there about how he can't write music. Hit him where it hurts," Klein says. "How 'bout something like, 'Yesterday' was the only good song you had." My annoyance at Klein grows even more. You could call Paul overbearing, controlling and annoying, but how can anyone say that he can't write? That was unfair and untrue.

John loves it, though, and writes it down. "You know he says it came to him in a dream. Can you believe that? I bet he heard it somewhere else and stole it." He snaps his fingers. "What about, 'I know you ripped that off – and that's so sad?'" Klein roars with laughter. That's it. I have to say something.

"Er, John, I think you may be going a little overboard here," I suggest.

John turns, his face filled with rage, and I think he is going to strangle me on the spot. But Ringo, whom John has asked to be a session drummer for his album, comes to my defence. "Yeah,

John, knock it off. That's just not nice. Bygones." Thankfully, Ringo could somehow get through to John when no one else could. John turns away from me, snickering like a twelve-year-old. Klein suggests a line making fun of Paul's song "Another Day," and John agrees.

"Brilliant, Klein, brilliant!" he hoots. "Dum, dum, de doodle doo," he sings mockingly. My stomach turns. The new lyric is a little better than "I know you ripped that off," but not by much. The song will drive a wedge further between the two. John hums Paul's ditty over the next few hours, exaggerating the nonsensical lyrics and laughing after every recitation. But I find it interesting that he can't get the tune out of his head. That's the way a McCartney song can get to you. No one in the studio is humming "How Do You Sleep?"

Sounds

8 July 1971

Lennon Misses the Mark with *Primal Scream*

If you thought that John Lennon's media salvo when quitting the Beatles was the end of the war of words, guess again. *Primal Scream,* the new double album from Lennon and his wife, Yoko Ono, is a shockingly frank manifesto from them. God, capitalism and his former songwriting partner Paul McCartney are all targets. And the couple don't hold back.

Lennon has used Phil Spector again to produce this album, having most recently recruited Spector to helm the Beatles' last album, *Everest.* But he apparently told Spector to tone down his trademark Wall of Sound production and instead opted for a stripped-down sound. The result? John Lennon, laid bare for all to see. He is bitter, airing out his grievances one by one. The music matches his honesty, with most songs featuring just an acoustic guitar.

Lennon proclaims that he doesn't believe in the Beatles in the track "God," in which he proclaims that the Creator is only a concept that causes us pain. On "Mother," Lennon cries out for his parents, who left him at an early age; it sounds as if he is in a therapy session.

Lennon saves his sharpest words for McCartney." How Do You Sleep?" is a song whose sole purpose, it seems, is to launch a personal attack against his former bandmate. He likens McCartney's music to elevator music and suggests that McCartney's only success was the group's hit "Yesterday."

Primal Scream took only two weeks to record; unfortunately, it shows. We have always known that Paul was the tunesmith, and John was the poet. With *Primal Scream*, that is painfully apparent. The lyrics are powerful, but the songs lack the musicality of his songs with the Beatles. "Cold Turkey" and "Working Class Hero" both drone with little, if any, chord changes. And at times, even the lyrics are heavy-handed. Lennon's sloganeering and preachy attitude sometimes wear thin.

But the real downfall of *Primal Scream* is that it's a double album, and Ono performs half the songs. With such enigmatic titles as "Greenfield Morning I Pushed an Empty Baby Carriage All over the City," "AOS," "Open Your Box," and "Don't Worry, Kyoko (Mummy's Only Looking for Her Hand in the Snow)," you expect some bizarre music, and at least Ono delivers at that level. Some, unfortunately, are unlistenable. There is no melody, and Ono replaces that musical concept with screeching and incoherent noises.

John has told the world that he is now Johnandyoko, but we'd like to listen to John's music only— without the personal attacks and preachiness.

* * *

9 July 1971

"How can he say that about me?" Paul asks. We're in Paul's office at Savile Row, and he and Linda are listening to John's satiric "How Do You Sleep?" for the first time. I think he is both angered and shaken by it. "How can he say that about my music?"

Linda massages his back. "Who cares what he thinks? He's just blowing off some steam. We all know you're the best. You know you're the best." Linda was always his advocate, at times his cheerleader. But I'm not sure Paul is buying it.

"'Yesterday' was the only hit I had? He knows I can rock as well as he can. How about 'Helter Skelter?' " He sounds as if he's trying to rebut an argument in a debate. "I mean, I know he hasn't liked some of my ballads, but I never criticised 'Julia' or 'In My Life.' We all have a soft side. In fact, this album of his is pretty laid back. If it weren't for the lyrics . . ." He stops himself from saying it would sound like one of his ballads.

I feel sorry for Paul. He's like a wounded puppy, painfully vulnerable. Even though they were equals, John was always the popular, edgy kid whom everyone wanted to please and emulate. Having John as the artist and the poet meant that Paul was middle of the road; to be mocked by John Lennon was tantamount to being told you were a fool. With this record, Paul felt as if John was dulling some of his shine.

And while I always questioned Linda's involvement in Paul's music in my previous life—she played keyboards and sang weak and often out-of-tune backup vocals in Wings – I see that her encouragement is actually hurting Paul's music. Paul always needed a censor, and Linda's endorsements made him oblivious to any tracks of lower quality.

He stops the record, takes it from the phonograph player, and breaks it over his knee. "Here Mal," he says, tossing the pieces to me. "Send these to John."

I don't know if he means it, but after Paul leaves, I toss the pieces in the rubbish bin. John and Paul are miles apart already, and this gesture will do nothing to mend fences.

* * *

1 August 1971

I think my work for the Beatles has hit an all-time low.

In the past I have run inane errands for them—fetching socks for John, finding paper cups so they can drink some milk, made guitar picks from plastic spoons. But this trumps them all. I'm walking in a quiet neighbourhood in Greenwich with a shovel and a paper bag, looking for dog shit. Dog shit.

I've been doing this for four hours now; I have ten bags of it in the boot of my car, and the smell is making me gag. It's for a new project for John and Yoko. Their response to the negative reviews of *Primal Scream* was to rent an art studio and paper it with reviews of the album. The next phase was to litter the walls with rubbish and animal faeces. I collected garbage as well earlier in the day, which had turned acrid in the hot sun and had seeped onto the surface of my car's boot. It will need a serious cleaning after this. So will I.

I start to follow a woman walking her poodle down a back street, hoping for a new deposit. She notices me and quickens her pace. I am about to turn around when I see the dog stop and brace to defecate on a grassy area. I walk up to the woman, now alarmed and pulling her dog, who is frantically trying to finish its business. I scoop up the poo into a bag, and the woman's eyes grow larger. She is almost running away by the time I move on. Yes, a giant six foot four inch man is picking up your dog's poo. Move along, nothing to see here.

When I return to the studio, John and Yoko are tacking the last bit of trash on the wall; I see soiled diapers, beans, used condoms, and banana peels covering the walls. A horde of photographers with handkerchiefs over their noses are taking photos while John empties the bags of faeces against the walls. A chorus of moans erupts as a new stench enters the room.

All the while, John and Yoko are silent. Playing in the background is the album *Primal Scream*; apparently, John is acting out the rage and frustration of the music, while forcing the press to listen, winning the battle with just the music.

My job is not yet done. After a slight pause to let the photographers finish, the two begin yelling and screaming, tearing everything off the walls and creating a bigger mess. As the reporters rush out of the room, John hands me a broom and a shovel and orders me to tote everything out onto the sidewalk. The worst day ever gets even worse.

It takes me about thirty minutes to take it all outside. John and Yoko then douse the garbage with petrol and set it aflame. Over the roar of the flames, John exclaims to the few reporters left, "Yes, the critics' reviews are garbage and shite, but they are just words." Yoko adds, "Words are short-lived and forgettable. Like this rubbish and faeces, they will be ashes soon." Too bad John doesn't heed his own advice when it comes to Paul's words. But then he often lived by double standards.

The Johnandyoko soliloquy marks the end of their performance/press conference, and it's a good thing; the police have just shown up and are writing citations to the two for disrupting traffic and burning items in a public place without a permit. I'm sure there were other things they could have been cited for—public health hazards, improper disposal of waste. Within an hour, all of the commotion has died down. And guess who has to clean up the aftermath?

I find a broom and start collecting the excrement for a second time. God, I hope no one that I know sees me doing this; I must look like a parolee or homeless person trying to make a shilling. But the only person I see is a street preacher walking down the sidewalk across the street. Seeing me, he points a finger and yells, "Repent! Repent! Jesus knows your sin!"

I shake my head and keep sweeping. If Jesus knows my sin, he is making me pay for it today.

* * *

I am floating high above Liverpool in some kind of limbo. It's a typical day in my hometown: The milkman is dropping off a few bottles at the local bakery and chats with the florist next door, trying to make an impression. Scores of workers trudge down toward the docks, ready to start their day. A policeman directs them across the main intersections. On Mathew Street the local pub is just closing up after a long evening. The owner kicks the last drunk out and locks the door behind him.

The Cavern Club is just a few doors down. The familiar sounds of "Roll over Beethoven" waft up to me. *They're here!* I think, recalling how the Chuck Berry tune was a favourite of the Fab Four. I descend rapidly, but when I open the door to the club and walk in, the music stops, replaced by the drumbeat of my heavy footsteps on the wooden floor of the dark hallway. A light clicks on, revealing the blue-black shine of a revolver barrel just inches away from my face, and above that barrel, the leering smile of a police officer. A name tag, glaringly white against his dark uniform, reads "G TAYLOR."

The muzzle flashes and cracks in my face, and a bullet slowly spins toward my eyes.

I wake up in a cold sweat, breathing heavily. It's the same dream. Three times in the past three weeks. I touch my head, searching for a bullet hole, and to my relief find only sweat. But as I take my hands away, I notice dark flecks of something on my fingers. I turn on the bedside lamp and look at my hands, and my fears are confirmed.

There's not much there. But it looks like blood.

I search my head for a wound but find nothing. I have no idea how the blood got there, but I know I will not sleep again tonight.

9

19 November 1971

"Mal, big wonderful Mal, you have saved me from famine,"
says George Harrison with a smile. I've just brought tea and
sandwiches into the studio for everyone. I know EMI Records'
canteen inside and out; after all, I've been making refreshments
for the guys for eight years. Usually they barely even grunted
their approval, but this time George, surrounded by a different
lot, is thankful, even gracious. He and the rest of his entourage
dive into the sandwiches, and I beam with pride.

I can't remember ever having so much fun recording an
album. George has been in the studio for three months now,
and the atmosphere is so relaxed. I believe that this has been his
dream; free from his mentors, he has blossomed as a songwriter.
Until the 1966 album *Revolver*, George had been considered an
inferior songwriter by John and Paul, both in the quality and
quantity of his contributions, but over the past few years he has
hit his stride. And he's reaching his creative peak.

In making his first solo pop album, George has plenty of
help. Eric Clapton and Ringo are talking on the steps to the

control room, each with a beer in hand. A couple of members of Badfinger, a group I discovered and signed to Apple Records (my one proud achievement in the music business), are jamming in one of the corners of the studio. The only person here I don't like is Phil Spector, who is producing the album yet again. He's as eccentric as always, but at least his presence lends to the all-star quality of the company. Yesterday, Bob Dylan, who has co-written a couple of tunes with George, was in the studio, and last week I saw Mick Jagger and Keith Moon, the drummer for the Who.

It's wonderful. I don't want to leave Abbey Road because I don't want to miss anyone coming by; everyone treats me like one of the guys. I find plenty of things to do; in the middle of dinner with Mimi and the kids, I remember that I need to do something, and head back to the studio just to see what's happening. I don't want the sessions—or this feeling—to end.

After an hour of talking, laughing and eating, George takes charge. "Okay, everybody, grab a guitar. It's time to play." No one grumbles. They all *want* to be here. And I can't wait to hear what he has in store for us.

Billboard

February 18, 1972

Harrison shines with debut solo album

George Harrison has always been known as the quiet Beatle, the second tier of Beatledom, the little-less-than-fab. But the recent breakup of the group of the century has awakened a slumbering giant: *George*

Harrison, the solo debut from the ex-Beatle, is a majestic masterpiece that calls to mind the best of the 1960s, from Spector's girl groups to The Band, The Stones and yes, the Beatles.

Despite his heavy helping of four songs on *Everest*, Harrison still has many unreleased songs dating all the way back to 1966. They have been collecting dust in the midst of John Lennon and Paul McCartney's songwriting monopoly. The breakup of the Beatles has given Harrison the perfect opportunity to dust off those songs and let them flourish.

The first single from the album, "My Sweet Lord," showcases Harrison's spirituality and guitar playing. It is a remarkable song, led by layers of acoustic guitars, alternating chants of "Hare Krishna" and "Hallelujah" and a marvellous slide guitar solo from Harrison. Eric Clapton, Billy Preston and fellow Beatle Ringo Starr also contribute to the track.

"What is Life" is a rocker with an unforgettable guitar riff, and Phil Spector's production turns it into a flashback to his "Wall of Sound" days with the girl groups.

With this self-titled album, it's clear that George Harrison deserves to stand alongside Lennon and McCartney as their equal. So far, at this early stage in the post-Beatle world, he is surprisingly the most marketable and—dare we say it—talented of the four. His debut album is an instant classic. Grab it now.

The New York Times

February 27, 1972

Ex-Beatle Harrison Hit with Lawsuit

Bright Tunes Inc. yesterday filed suit in federal district court against former Beatle George Harrison, alleging copyright infringement in Mr. Harrison's hit single "My Sweet Lord."

The suit claims that Mr. Harrison plagiarized parts of the melody to the Chiffons' 1963 hit "He's So Fine" and seeks to seize any profits realized from the sale of the single.

According to the lawsuit, Mr. Harrison knowingly used the chorus of "He's So Fine," a three-note phrase that forms the basis of the song, as the basis of the song "My Sweet Lord." Bright Tunes Inc. holds the copyright to "He's So Fine," originally written by Ronald Mack.

A spokesman for Mr. Harrison and Apple Records declined to comment on the lawsuit.

* * *

28 February 1972

I see the stacks of records only five minutes before George does. Upon entering the office Tuesday morning, I am met with thousands of 45 rpm records in stacks five feet high, taking up most of the walking space in the central common area. Most employees seem puzzled, even amused, looking at the towers as if they were a new London tourist attraction; others walk around the stacks, refusing to acknowledge the distraction while doing nothing about it.

"What the hell is this?" I ask a secretary. With a puzzled look she hands a few discs to me. "Five thousand of them," she says blankly. "Delivered here this morning."

Of the five or six records in my hand, the one on top is "My Sweet Lord," but the one just below that is the Chiffons' single, "He's So Fine." Sandwiched in between the two is a handwritten note from John: "Shame shame, Georgie! What did I tell you?" That pattern continues throughout each stack; each grouping is a nasty reminder of the lawsuit.

"Get these out of here, now! Move them into the basement!" I order the staff. I'm surprised at my boldness. They aren't used to taking orders from me, but the urgent tone of my voice makes them move. They have managed to get only a few hundred out of the common area when George walks in with his mentor, an Indian sitar player named Ravi Shankar. Already sullen from the news of the lawsuit, he sees the mass of records and mutters, "Bloody hell . . ."

It doesn't take him long to figure it out, and the usually even-tempered George responds by demolishing the towers of discs, kicking and swinging his arms and sending discs flying across the room as employees duck out of the way. A simple touch on the arm from Ravi stops him, though, and George retreats to his upstairs office with Ravi following closely behind.

"George," I cry after him. "Do you need—"

"Leave me alone, Mal."

A rubbish collector arrives with a bin to dispose of the records. I begin helping in the effort but can't get my mind off George. I inch up the stairs and tiptoe down the hall to his office.

Inside, I hear George, sounding distraught. "I swear, I hadn't thought of that song in years. I wrote it based on a jam session with Billy Preston. If anything, it's a rip-off of that old gospel song, 'Oh Happy Day.'"

Ravi is silent, allowing George to vent.

"They warned me that it sounded like 'He's So Fine.' But I ignored them, believed that I knew better than they did."

I peek into the room. George, his head in his hands, doesn't move for minutes. I have never seen him so exposed, so spiritually naked.

"I don't know, Ravi. I'm spooked. I mean, now that I've heard it, it does sound like 'He's So Fine.' But I swear I had no idea when I was writing it that it was so similar. They warned me, but I just denied it. I thought I had written a classic. Now—now I'm afraid to write anything."

"It will come, George. The songs will flow again."

"I dunno. I tried yesterday. Sat down with a guitar and tried a few things, but all of them sounded like an old Beatles tune or a Clapton song. I think my well is dry. Hell, maybe all of us are out of ideas." He sighs. "They warned me, they warned me," he keeps repeating.

"You might be out of ideas in this type of music," Ravi said, smiling. "But you are still learning the fundamentals of Indian music. It's a whole new experience, and you realise that."

I can see George considering the suggestion. And I know he will do it. Indian music began luring him a few years ago, as if it were calling him from another life. A few of George's contributions to earlier Beatles records featured Indian music.

"I believe that if you explore new sounds, you can find new melodies." Ravi pats George on the knee. "Think about it. Your answer will come to you."

Strawberry Fields Forever fanzine

May 15, 1972

Album Review: 'Bhaja Bhakata-Arati"— George Harrison and Ravi Shankar

Here at *Strawberry Fields Forever*, we focus on Beatles music and any solo music released by the four. Most of the solo material released so far resembles the Beatles in some way, and it's easy for us to bypass the stranger or subpar cuts and be thankful that our Fab Four are still making music, if not together.

That being said, I can tell you that the only reason we're reviewing "Bhaja Bhakata-Arati" is that it features George Harrison. And I honestly can't tell you whether it is good or bad.

There's a lot of Indian music—chanting, sitars, drums, finger cymbals. The title is taken from a popular Indian chant, according to the liner notes. George has co-written a few of the songs, or ragas as they are known in Indian culture, and his friends from the Hare Krishna movement help with the vocals.

It's admirable that George is embracing Eastern music, and I applaud him on his effort. I just don't know if I like it. Buy it if you want to complete your Beatles collection.

* * *

27 March 1972

John is drunk and starting to make an arse of himself. We're at the Park Lane Hotel at a party hosted by EMI. And it's EMI management – lots of cocktail dresses, suits and ties, and waiters walking around with fancy appetizers. You can spot the artists, who aren't wearing fancy clothes. They're here for the label to show off. And the artists don't mind the attention and free drinks.

At first, John didn't want to come, but when he saw the bar, he quickly got over any reluctance, and he has grown louder and ruder with each drink. He has found fellow singer-songwriter Harry Nilsson—not a good sign, since the two have a tendency to toss a few back. Harry is also quite drunk already, and he's urging John on with each drink. Every time they laugh, people turn their heads and murmur nervously. They don't know what to expect, and neither do I. I see R&B musician Billy Preston from across the room. Thank God.

"Billy, great to see you," I say, extending my hand.

"You too, Mal." Billy, sporting a giant Afro now, smiles his wide, gap-toothed grin, the same one that kept the Beatles together during the ill-fated *Get Back* sessions. He had played the organ on a few numbers—you could hear him in the song "Get Back"—and I believe it was his presence that kept them from splitting up, at least that time. You always behave at your best when there's a guest in the house. I should have requested that he be at the *Everest* sessions.

"Working on anything new?" I ask.

"Just session work right now. I hope to start working on something new next month. George has me signed on with Apple for a few more records."

"Do you need any help?" I'm searching for something to do. Anything.

"Yeah, I don't know yet. I'm sure I'll need someone like you around to help. I'll give you a call."

I offer my thanks, but I know that he won't call. Why would he? *Someone like me?* We people are a dime a dozen.

"Are they still keeping you busy running around?"

"All the time, Billy," I lie. "I'm here with John, driving him home whenever he's had enough. Playing babysitter." I roll my eyes as if I'm the grownup, the one minding a thirty-year-old.

Billy raises his eyebrows. "Well, don't look now, but if John's drunk, I don't think you want him talking to that reporter."

My heart skips a beat as I turn around and see John gesticulating wildly at a reporter for the *Daily Mail.* And suddenly I'm in a movie: I'm running in slow motion as I move across the room, knocking over plates of hors d'oeuvres and bumping into famous people in a vain attempt to stop whatever is coming out of John's mouth. Just as I arrive, the hubbub in the room quiets to nothing, and I hear John exclaim, "Of course he knew it! I told George it sounded like 'He's So Fine.' Even played it for him. Amateurish mistake."

As I usher John away from the reporter, I know the damage is done. John babbles aimlessly to anyone and no one, followed by alternate refrains of "He's So Fine" and "My Sweet Lord." I call for our car and shove him in, hoping to stuff all memories of this evening away as well.

The Daily Mail

11 April 1972

Harrison Settles 'My Sweet Lord' Lawsuit

Former Beatle George Harrison yesterday settled a lawsuit with Bright Tunes Ltd., effectively admitting that he plagiarised the tune for his hit single "My Sweet Lord" from the publishing company.

Although terms of the deal were not announced, it is believed that Bright Tunes received the full amount of what they were asking: all profits from the sale of the single, which hit number one worldwide. Bright Tunes owns the rights to "He's So Fine," the song from which Harrison borrowed the melody. All subsequent pressings of the song will credit Ronald Mack as co-writer and cite Bright Tunes as well.

Harrison initially denied the charges, but his attorneys began negotiations with Bright Tunes shortly after Harrison's former band mate, John Lennon, told a *Daily Mail* reporter that Harrison was aware of the similarities between the songs, and that Lennon himself had played the two songs together to demonstrate.

Neither Harrison nor Lennon was available for comment.

* * *

8 June 1972

It's late. Again. And I'm the last one to leave. Funny how one of the least paid people on Apple's staff is the one who works the latest. I guess I bring it on myself; I don't have to be here after everyone else, and it's not as if I will be rewarded with a raise or promotion for my dedication. It's because I don't want to go home.

As I am cleaning up the board room at the Savile Row office and filing papers, Ringo, of all people, walks in. He looks and smells awful, with dishevelled hair and shirt, and a stench that is a blend of whiskey and stale cigarettes. It is the look and smell of despondency.

"Hi Ringo. What are you doing here at this hour?" I really am wondering. I hardly ever see him at the office anymore, and never after two o'clock in the afternoon.

Ringo grunts and throws a newspaper on the table. It's open to a review of his latest album, *Beaucoups of Blues,* an album of country/western classics. It's the second album of cover songs he has recorded since the group broke up. The reviews for the first, an album of standards called *Sentimental Journey,* were scathing, and critics have been no kinder to this album. The headline to this review reads, "More Cover Tunes: Is That All Ringo Has to Offer?"

"Don't listen to 'em Ringo. It's a good album," I say, trying to cheer him up.

He sits down and looks up at me, his eyes red. I can't tell whether it's from lack of sleep, drinking or crying. "Let's not kid ourselves, Mal. I know people call me the luckiest man in the world."

No, that would be me, I think to myself.

"I know I'm lucky to be where I am. Jesus, if Pete Best had been a little better drummer, he'd still be a Beatle, and no one would know who I was. He was the pretty boy, and they threw him out of the group just so I could play drums for them. I'd just be a washed-up drummer for Rory Storm and the Hurricanes if George Martin didn't step in. I mean, who thinks about Rory Storm anymore?"

"But you're a great drummer. They wanted you. And they couldn't have done this without you."

Ringo laughs. "Yeah, they could. Y'know, Paul played drums on a few songs. He didn't even need me. I'm the invisible Beatle sometimes."

I'm not sure what to say. It's as if I were talking to myself.

"Jeez, everybody sees you as one of the guys. John, Paul, George, and Ringo. You're one of the most popular people alive."

"See? I'm always the last one mentioned. Almost an afterthought, really." He gazes at the ceiling as if he is listening for an answer from the heavens. "Mal, you know I'm not one of the guys. You're not, either. Even George feels left out sometimes. But hey, that's just the way it goes."

The gaze lasts for what seems like minutes; then, suddenly, he rises to leave. "Look, I'm proud of what I've done. If this is the end, well, I've had a great time. I don't think I'll survive the decade, but I'll have a hell of a time going downhill, eh?" He winks, and with that, the discussion is over. He puts his self-effacing facade up again, bows and walks out.

The temperature in the board room is stuffy and hot, but I shiver at the encounter.

10

23 October 1972

Something is wrong here.

I'm watching Paul record his first solo album in Studio One. Everything seems fine; he is joking with the engineers, playing piano in between takes, even playing with his kids during some of the longer breaks. But it all is a bit contrived, a bit of bravado.

He mixes the bass for an inane, pointless jam called "Oo You." I am silent, preferring to say nothing instead of something negative, but Linda claps her hands. "I love it, Paul! That sounds so spontaneous!" Paul smiles at the praise; I smile as well, nodding my head in forced agreement. This is the tuneless material that surrounded "Maybe I'm Amazed" on his first solo album back in my former life. And without John to veto it, it's going on the album. That's what it sounded like to me—none of Paul's signature melodies, no memorable lines. He's tearing down the walls of what he has built so well, maybe on purpose.

Sometimes the familiarity is worse. His next song is "Junk," the song that had failed to make it onto the last three Beatles albums. I know now that this will now be a cut on the solo album too, and it reminds me of how lightweight his solo songs could be. John isn't here to block its inclusion, and within minutes, the acoustic guitar track is completed. A Beatle throwaway is now a major track on a solo album, just like that. I shake my head in amazement.

NME

12 December 1972

McCartney Proves You Can't Do it all Alone

McCartney is precisely what you'd expect from former Beatle Paul McCartney—harmless drivel on one end, and unpolished, unfocused prattle on the other. Where the two meet, for a few songs, is the core of what could have been an excellent Beatles album.

Those moments are few and far between. "Uncle Albert/Admiral Halsey" is a mini-medley that is dreamy at times, jaunty at others. And "That Would Be Something" shows that McCartney can take a bluesy lick and turn it into gold.

There's not much there after that. "Junk" is a leftover from an old Beatles album that didn't make the cut. It's catchy, but lacking in substance. The same goes for "The Lovely Linda," a 40-second snippet that indeed sounds lovely but is clearly unfinished. The rest is just filler. It's as if McCartney went into the studio, pressed 'Record' and started playing. He has given no thought to melody, lyrics, production or quality. Other than that, though . . . it's okay.

It's clear that McCartney misses the Lennon in the Lennon/McCartney songwriting team. Without his former songwriting partner reeling him in, his dance-hall, Vaudevillian fantasies are running wild. Listening to the album takes patience, an open mind, and lots of coffee.

* * *

6 December 1972

I'm at a pub in Soho at one in the morning, tired and buzzed. I have spent 18 hours that day running back and forth between the four. I got nine white rose petals for Yoko—I have no idea why she wanted nine white rose petals—put some documents in the post for Paul to read, waited for Who drummer Keith Moon to show up at the Apple office for about two and a half hours (he didn't come), and took one of Ringo's autos into the shop for repairs. I topped it off by helping weed George's gardens and hosting the Hare Krishnas at his house. It's the same type of things that I have always done, but it's for four people, not one group. What have I become?

I thought a few beers would help me relax, but now I regret it. Alcohol always depresses me, and my anger and frustration have given way to pity and despair. It worries me; the last time I felt this way I ended up on the floor of my apartment with four bullet holes in my torso.

Down the counter of the bar, another buzzed patron is staring at me. At first I think he recognises me from my association with the Beatles, but I quickly forget that assumption.

"Hey, you with the glasses," he begins. "You're . . . You're kinda goofy lookin.'"

I ignore him. He starts talking to his friend, who is equally inebriated. "Look at 'im. He's big, but he's got them glasses on. Pansy if you ask me."

His friend starts giggling. "Pansy! Ha ha! Hey pansy, I bet you never beat up anybody in your life. You queer or something?"

My hands clench into fists in response. I've manhandled plenty of pushy fans and reporters during my years with the Beatles, but I hated it every time I had to be tough and threatening. In a way, they were right. I was the Gentle Giant, and I usually shied away from controversy and conflict.

My mind went back to primary school. I was about ten years old but already six inches taller than everyone else. But instead of being an intimidating figure among my smaller classmates, I stuck out and was ridiculed. I cowered away from them when they threw dirt balls at me, did nothing when they stole my glasses and crushed them with their feet, and rolled into a ball whenever they began to punch me for my lunch money. I came home many days either dirty, half blind or penniless and hungry. My father looked at me with disgust and usually administered another beating to me for being so passive. In fact, I think he used the word "pansy."

I pay my tab with the two still yelling at me, but like my younger years, I have tuned it out and am trying to think of better things—something to take me away from the current moment. The problem is, there are no better things that I can think of, and their jeers sting me. A spray of peanuts hit me in the back and I stop. I slowly turn around, and their faces suddenly turn from delight to fear. I see them thinking that maybe they went too far. It's enough satisfaction for me, and

I walk out as they begin to laugh again, though a little more reserved this time.

It's unseasonably warm for December, and the streets are empty save for a few cars parked nearby. The sounds from the pub are now muffled and dim. I stagger down the sidewalk in the vague direction of Savile Row, hoping it will take longer than the twenty-minute trip. I'm in no hurry and am in no condition to drive. If I need to, I will crash in one of the offices.

When John quit the band, I panicked. I believed my life had ended again. But instead, I have found myself busier than ever, dividing my time between the four Beatles. Of course, I did that the first time around, too, but as the four found their independence, got married and had kids, they didn't need me anymore. Instead of being the fifth Beatle, I was a fifth wheel. Now in the back of my mind, I fear that eventually they will find their own niches again, and I will find the pathway back to my death.

And then there are the dreams, becoming more real and more frightening. I don't want to sleep.

Not wanting to see where I am headed, I walk with my head down, studying the cracks that break up the sidewalk, a regular and constant pattern broken only by kerbs and the zig-zag stripes of a pedestrian crosswalk. Sometimes I turn randomly, wondering where it will take me but still not caring to look up.

I almost run into her, catching a flash of red. I look up and hear her exclaim, "Hey, watch where you're going, big guy!"

The red blouse is cut tantalizingly low and is met at her hips by a purple skirt, short and tight. A pair of bright red stilettos at least five inches high completes the wardrobe. Her skin looks pale in the streetlights, and her long auburn hair is brighter than it should be.

"Hi there," she smiles, sizing me up. In a thick Cockney accent, she asks. "Lookin' for a date?"

I want her. I have no idea why; Mimi is waiting at home for me as always, and the lady is not the most attractive prostitute I've ever seen; a cigarette is dangling from her mouth, the makeup is way too thick and artificial, and her eyes are bloodshot with bags underneath them. She may have been strung out right now, or badly in need of cash to get another hit of something. But I need to *feel* something, to do things to her without remorse, to get lost in the moment of pure passion, and to pretend that I am one of the four, who have had countless women throw themselves at them.

I look away, embarrassed, and on instinct reach in my pockets. As usual, they are empty. I spent my last quid on the pints of beer at the pub.

"I've got no money."

She rolls her eyes and turns away.

"Wait," I say. "I—I know the Beatles." It's the ace up my sleeve, and it's enough to make her halt. But her expression is cynical.

"So what?"

I have no idea where I am going with this. "I can take you to their office—3 Savile Row?"

She glances at me sceptically, her eyes narrowed. "Yeah, I know it. Okay, big guy, show me."

Savile Row is a little over half a mile away, but it seems longer as my pace quickens. Unsure of my intentions, she walks a few paces behind me, wondering if I'm going to shove her into a nearby alley and assault her.

" 'Ow do you know them?"

"I'm uh, their personal assistant. Been with them since the early days."

"Never seen you with 'em."

"Well, I'm usually off doing something else. Trust me. They work my arse off." I see how this looks: I know the Beatles, but you never see me. But I know them, believe me. Believe this six foot four inch hulking giant who is walking you to God knows where.

The awkward silences are unnerving; I try to think of something cool or relevant to say, but I come up with nothing. I've never been good at small talk. We finally arrive at the doorstep of 3 Savile Row; I fumble with the keys, trying the first key I find on my ring. It's the wrong one, of course. She is standing even farther away now, arms crossed and worried that she had made a huge mistake following me here. At last I find the right key, and the door opens silently. She gasps, and my confidence rises as we walk into the dark lobby of Apple Corps, Ltd.

The woman is instantly enamoured, running from room to room, touching gold records hanging on the wall, picking up stationery with the Apple Corps logo on it. Usually, I would have worried, but I don't care this evening. The longer we stay, the bolder I get.

After a while I find her in John and Yoko's office, sitting in a chair behind a desk. "So do you really know them? Or are you just the janitor or something?" she asks, looking like a school girl with a crush.

'Know them?" I laugh. "I just came from George's house. Got Ringo's car serviced earlier. I've even sung and played on a couple of their records. 'Yellow Submarine,' 'A Day in the Life' . . ." She is staring at me, trying to picture me in a studio with the Fab Four. However, familiarity is not a must for her. She walks over from behind the desk and starts unbuttoning my shirt. "Any chance of meeting them? Or at least a souvenir?"

"Let's see if we can work something out."

Those are bold words coming from me; in fact, it sounds like someone else is saying them. My thoughts immediately go to Mimi, and I know I can't do anything here. I break down, face in my hands, stammering, "I'm sorry, so sorry," as the woman says, "Er, I think I'll just let myself out, if ya don't mind." She grabs a few souvenirs from a desk, and I hear the door slam as she exits the building.

The Fab Four are staring down at me from a *Rubber Soul* album cover on the wall. Before, I felt sheer desperation and loneliness, and I thought having sex with someone would overcome that. But I wasn't like them. When the four shagged their fans, it was as if they were doing the girls a favour. They could do anything and get anything they wanted. In the past I delivered countless numbers of wide-eyed girls to them, and they had used them and tossed them aside.

But now that the woman is gone, having done nothing to earn the souvenirs she took with her, I know that she has used me instead. I am not their equal. In fact, I'm not equal to most people who would have been in this situation. I stayed true to my marriage – the marriage I have consistently left behind and forgotten. I stay on the sofa, wishing I was back at the pub having peanuts thrown at me.

11

17 March 1973
San Francisco, California

Ravi Shankar speaks with sincerity but bravado, each word delivered with purpose and forethought.

"In 1971, the people of Bangladesh gained their independence from Pakistan. They had won control of the government, but West Pakistan moved quickly to stop their revolution. The military massacred and raped thousands, and destroyed villages."

I have accompanied Ravi and George to a small rally in San Francisco's Golden Gate Park to raise money for the plight in Bangladesh. George's name has drawn hundreds of curious onlookers, but many are just screaming his name or, seeing that he doesn't have a guitar with him, walking away. I am there to help with crowd control, but since the crowd is rather well-behaved and small, I listen to Ravi speak. I may not like his music, but his public speaking style is a different story.

Shankar pauses for effect, then begins speaking to them more earnestly. "As many as three million Bengalis have died. And then, if that were not enough, they were hit by several cyclones, which killed another 500,000 people. Some 10 million refugees have poured into India, and it will cost a million dollars per day to take care of them.

"My friends, I come to you for help. While I speak to you, disease and starvation are continuing to kill thousands of people—every day. I beg you, please spread the word about Bangladesh, and if you can spare some money, help your fellow man. Do not forget about them."

His words are met with heartfelt applause, and I help collect money from those exiting the rally. Many apologetically put coins into the box I am holding; few put dollar bills, and some shrug embarrassingly as they walk by without contributing. In the end, the rally takes in only $2,000. Ravi is pleased, but George looks disappointed.

* * *

I am struck by the contradictions in the flight back to England. We are sipping an expensive brandy on a private jet, equipped with leather seats and a full staff to meet our every need. Indian music plays from a state-of-the-art hi-fi system on the aeroplane. The trip probably cost more than we had raised in San Francisco. But it doesn't faze George, who is brainstorming.

"What you're doing is good, Ravi. But it's just a drop in the bucket."

"Many drops in the bucket will fill the bucket, George. We can feed thousands of people with what we collected today."

"Yeah, but we don't have time for that. Our bucket has a hole in it, and it's leaking out quicker than we can fill it. I mean, there are people dying right now." George scowls, lost in thought, then speaks again. "I've been thinking about this for a while, and I've decided we need more water in the bucket. I want to organise a benefit concert."

Ravi raises his eyebrows.

"You saw those people at the rally. They came to see me, and a lot of them left when they saw I wasn't going to perform. But if we get a lot of big-name performers and charge five pounds a head, we could send all the proceeds to Bangladesh. I'll cover the costs." George leans in closer. "I believe that music can be a positive force, and we should use our fame and influence to help others. Look at how Woodstock brought all those people together to celebrate the ideals of the 1960s. We can do the same thing for Bangladesh."

Ravi smiles. "This is very generous of you, George. I know you have had some problems playing and writing music lately, and for you to perform for this cause is very admirable. Thank you."

George pales in response and shakes his head; Ravi has misunderstood. It has been months since George has even picked up a guitar. "No, Ravi, I'm not playing. I just can't do it."

Shankar looks puzzled. "Then what did you have in mind, George?"

"I have lots of friends, I know lots of people. We can turn this into a festival like Woodstock, only for charity. Bob Dylan, Eric

Clapton, that sort of thing. But don't ask me to go on that stage." A dark cloud passes over George's face, and he does not speak for the rest of the flight.

* * *

2 April 1973

I have been on the phone almost all day; my fingers are sore from dialling, and I am growing hoarse from talking with managers and performers. And I have very little to show for it.

At first, finding performers was easy. Eric Clapton agreed to perform, as did Billy Preston. Even Ringo sounded enthusiastic, promising to play drums and sing "It Don't Come Easy." But not much has happened since then.

"James Taylor is a no," I announce to George, who is making his own phone calls. "Bob Dylan, the Rolling Stones, the Who, Ronnie Spector—they're all sorry, but they can't make it."

"Buggers," George exclaims. "So all we have is Eric, Billy, and Delaney & Bonnie. And Ringo."

A charity concert with Eric and Ringo will generate some ticket sales, but it's not what George was planning. He will have to supplement the main acts with little-known groups, but the fewer recognizable acts there are, the fewer tickets he can sell. And his vision of a massive event that will change millions of lives will not emerge.

I pick up the phone again and dial the number for John Fogerty, Creedence Clearwater Revival's lead singer and manager. After a few rings, he picks up. I'm in luck.

"Hey John, it's Mal Evans."

"Who?"

Dammit. "Um, Mal Evans. With the Beatles. I'm acting as a personal assistant for George Harrison."

"Never heard of you."

Of course not. George is on another phone, pleading with Paul Simon's manager. I hold up the phone to him, but he waves me off.

"Say hello, George," I yell to him

George puts his hand over the mouthpiece. "Hello, George."

I put my ear to the receiver, half expecting to hear a dial tone. At first I hear only silence, but Fogerty finally says, "I have no idea if that's George, but it sounds like something he'd say. What do you want?"

"We're, uh, putting a concert together for the victims of Bangladesh. Eric Clapton is going to be there, and Ringo, and we were wondering if you could get Creedence to make an appearance."

Fogerty chuckles. "What's your name again? Mal?"

"Yeah," I mumble.

"Mal, did you not hear what happened to us in Denver back in May? The crowd threw coins at us. I'm done with concerts, done with Creedence. Got it?"

I thank him for his time. George has ended his call; he looks over at me and I shake my head.

As if he is expecting to be needed, Ravi Shankar walks into the room. "How are we doing?"

George has his head in his hands. "It's not happening, Ravi. We just can't pull enough big names together."

Ravi's expression doesn't change; in fact, his eyes twinkle with an idea.

"You know what people will pay to see. And you have the means to do it."

* * *

7 May 1973

I have a case of ale by my easy chair and a package of crisps in my lap. Mimi is on the loveseat with the kids. It's time for Paul's new BBC television special, called "Heart of the Country." I have no idea what to expect; Paul hasn't contacted me in the last few months, but I know he has been hard at work at his farm in Scotland.

I try not to take his silence personally; Paul has not been in contact with anyone except Neil Aspinall, who worked out a deal with the BBC to air this documentary. But if Paul doesn't need me, I'm down to serving three masters. I'm a little less necessary than I was before.

The show is cute but inane. Paul talks about life on the farm and his many tasks—feeding animals, gardening, building barns. The interviews are interspersed with vignettes of him, Linda and their children playing with the animals and running around the farm. The quality is poor and grainy. It's like watching Paul's home movies.

I suspect he is treating this as a public relations ploy. Look at Paul McCartney: he's easygoing, enjoying life without the Beatles, a normal guy, good with kids and horses. He even gets his hands dirty. But the music . . . I wince when I hear the songs. Paul cannot get away from the ditty and the ballad. Most of the songs have something to do with animals and the farm: "Ram On," "Big Barn Bed," "Little Lamb Dragonfly" and "Single Pigeon." Although the majestic "My Love" is beautiful, it's the only memorable song in the show. Then, with no explanation, two reggae-influenced songs are featured: the droning "C Moon," and a song by Linda called "Seaside Woman."

"Why are they singing a song about the ocean? They're on a farm," my son Thomas asks.

"Well, their farm is close to the ocean," I try to explain.

"But this song sounds like they're in the tropics, and they're all bundled up like it's cold. Why is that?"

Because Linda wrote a song and Paul wanted it in the special. "I don't know, son. You'd have to ask them."

We watch in silence as Paul feeds a baby goat with a bottle. "You should have been in this, Dad. He never asks you to come up anymore, does he?"

I say nothing.

"Are you still important, Dad?"

"It's time for bed, Thomas. Go on, *now*."

. . . It's obvious from the BBC documentary "Heart of the Country" that Paul McCartney has nothing to say. The phrase "Bip Bop," repeated four times in a row, is the first stanza of the song of the same name, while "Ram On" has just two lines of lyrics that are repeated ad nauseam. The one highlight, "My Love," features the word "Wo" repeated in the chorus. He's run out of words – and ideas.

- NME

. . . McCartney believes that anything that comes out of his piano or guitar magically becomes a "Yesterday" or "Hey Jude." And he does tend to churn out charming little musical numbers. But that's all they are—fragments that will quickly be forgotten in six months. It's obvious from his dismal solo album that something is missing from his craft, and without it, he will continue to run in place.

- Rolling Stone

. . . Cute but irrelevant. Kind of like Paul himself.

-Creem

* * *

28 May 1973

Paul's farm is breathtaking: rolling green hills and very few trees, with sheep dotting the pastures. His television special didn't do it justice. The dirt road I'm driving on is bumpy and rutted and jars my frame. The trip becomes a not-so-serene tour of the foothills of Scotland. I'm about as far from civilisation as you can get in the U.K. I understand why he's here—getting away from the media, the Beatles, me—but I always find it hard to picture him in the country. For so many years Paul was a Beatle: a city man, sharply dressed, surrounded by guitars, soundboards and microphones.

Now, as I drive George and Ravi the final mile to the house, I find it even more foreign. Paul is near the barn, dressed in dungarees and baling hay with a pitchfork. He looks markedly different from when he wore Nehru jackets at Shea Stadium in 1966. And you know what? I think he likes it. I wonder if we are facing an uphill battle: when given the choice of a carefree career on the farm versus tension and arguing with John and George, will he even think twice?

Paul greets us warmly. Even though he is sweating profusely, he looks well rested and relaxed. He yells toward the house, asking Linda to bring out some tea for us as we head to the front porch. It's stiff but cordial; we discuss his television special, his kids, anything but the Beatles. At one point, I even ask how many goats he has on the farm (43, at his last count).

Paul finally breaks the ice. "What brings you to Scotland? I know this isn't a social call."

Ravi answers, explaining the situation in Bangladesh while George gazes out at the Scottish countryside.

"Paul, George has been organizing a concert to help my countrymen. So far, Eric Clapton has agreed to play, but finding enough famous artists to perform is difficult. To be honest, the only way we can get a large number of people to attend and make a real difference is to get the four of you to perform together. I know you have had your differences with your friends—" He glances at George, who is still intensely interested in the hills. "But would you at least be open to a one-time reunion to help my friends back home?"

Paul looks amused and stares at George as if waiting for him to make the request, and I wince, waiting for a biting response. But something amazing happens.

"Of course, Ravi, you can count me in. Just let me know where to be and what to do, and I'll be there."

Wide eyed, George speaks for the first time in half an hour. "You will?"

Paul winks at me. "Sure George, anything for you. I've been impressed by your leadership during the last album, and this is a great cause. Of course, let's not get excited yet. I'll bet you 50 quid you won't get Mr. Lennon there. But we'll still have fun."

Then I see what Paul is doing. Agreeing to the concert helps him mend fences with George. But he has also accepted because he knows that there's no way John will agree to appear in the same building with him. By accepting first, he has put the onus on John. He will be the man who won't make a Beatles reunion possible, and Paul will be the humanitarian, the peacemaker, putting aside his differences to help his fellow man. It's brilliant and shrewd.

But I don't care. We are one step closer to putting things back into balance.

* * *

11 June 1973
New York City

It's only my second time back in the States since the Beatles' last tour, the Candlestick Park concert in 1966, but it's the second time in three months. I'm a little nervous; John has been here with Yoko for a few months, and I catch bits and pieces of what he has been up to. His activism has continued to grow, but it's fuelled more by his continued use of drugs and alcohol than any anger or political leanings.

I think England has become too boring and too limited for him. U.S. President Richard Nixon was re-elected, but John has told the press that Nixon is the main obstacle to world peace. He has made Nixon's impeachment one of his chief causes. Earlier in the year, he and Yoko went to New York and took up with fellow activists Abbie Hoffman and Jerry Rubin.

So what am I doing here? A few days ago I found out that while we were on one side of the Atlantic planning a benefit concert, Hoffman and Rubin were doing the same thing. Having been at Woodstock and seen the power of thousands of people coming together for music, they planned to stage a concert, with the proceeds going to help free several political prisoners in America. John had recruited a backing band called Elephant's Memory, and after rehearsing with them for a couple of weeks, his confidence returned, and he agreed to play for the benefit. That's where I come in. I'm here to act as roadie again, back to my job at the failed Toronto concert that started this roller coaster ride.

The Great Lawn at Central Park is not packed, but I estimate that about 25,000 people are there—an astonishing number for a hastily formed concert. It's *déjà vu*: I'm behind the stage, watching John throw up again. But the members of Elephant's Memory are relaxed, joking and looking forward to the performance. Their demeanour is a calming influence, and when John takes the stage, he seems more at ease than he usually does before a concert. The opening number, a new song called "New York City," sounds good and tight, and my concern about his performance fades.

The concert's program resembles a church service, with speeches and testimonials interspersed with hymns from John, Yoko, and the band. New songs from John such as the feminist "Woman Is the Nigger of the World," "Attica State," which decried the conditions at Attica State Prison, and "Angela," a song protesting the arrest of activist Angela Davis, help pound the messages home. I'm just offstage, excited but nervous. I don't know what he's going to say or what he's going to do. But that's John.

As the concert progresses, spurred on by adrenaline and alcohol, John grows bolder and more daring, his language more dangerous. After he and the band finish playing his song "Power to the People," he urges the crowd to be quiet.

"Now you know you have a crook down there in Washington, don't you?" The crowd roars their affirmation. "He loves power; he'll do anything for power. He has the power to end the war in Vietnam, to free these political prisoners, to create peace. But he's doin' nothing." Another roar. "What did the French do when they didn't like what King Louie was doing?"

Someone in the crowd yells, "They had a revolution!"

"That's right! Revolution! And what did your founding fathers do when they didn't like what my king was doing?"

More people cry, "Revolution!"

"That's right! Revolution! So why are you taking this shite? Get rid of the bastards in Washington! What are you going to do about it?"

A mass of voices yell, "Revolution!"

"That's right! What are you waiting for? Revolution, now!" He repeats the last phrase over and over until the crowd joins in the chant, and he launches into the Beatles classic "Revolution."

He appears just out of the corner of my eye—a man in a dark suit standing near the stage, looking very much out of place and talking into a radio. Within seconds, I begin to see more dark suits—maybe a dozen—spaced along the wings of the stage. Others plant themselves on the front rows. After John finishes the number, Abbie Hoffman comes onstage, whispers to John, and he and Yoko move off, waving as the crowd continues to chant.

I watch John and Yoko talk to the men in suits, who handcuff them and lead them away, along with Elephant's Memory, Hoffman, Rubin and the other concert organisers. I am utterly helpless; I can't protect John from this.

Because I look like a bouncer and unimportant roadie, I am spared. Three different times agents try to detain me for questioning, but I tell them that I don't know him, that I don't know anything, that I was just hired for this show, that somebody's going to have to get this gear off the stage before the crowd take it themselves. Each time, the agents move on, and I continue to pack up the equipment. I don't know what else to do.

The crowd, meanwhile, chants for an encore that will never come.

Returning to my hotel room, I begin to panic. I call Neil Aspinall—who is not happy at the news—and even call Allen Klein to see if he had any sway with the American authorities. Three hours later I finally get a phone call from an agent in a federal building in Manhattan, asking me to come get John and Yoko.

When I arrive at the federal office, an agent with the Federal Bureau of Investigation pulls me aside and leads me into a warm, wood-panelled conference room.

"Are you the attorney for Mr. Lennon and Mrs. Ono?" he asks.

"Um, I am representing them, yes." I fear that if I say no they will be detained even longer.

"Mr. Evans, we have a situation here. I want you to know that we are releasing Mr. Lennon and Mrs. Ono. But you must get in the car with the two of them, go straight to the airport and leave the United States immediately."

"Wh—What? Why?"

"I can't tell you a lot. But Mr. Lennon and Mrs. Ono have been the subject of a federal investigation into subversive activities. They have been meeting with extremists regularly, and we have been monitoring their activity for a few weeks now. The FBI deployed agents at the concert just in case something might happen, and we had authorization to arrest anyone spouting dangerous political rhetoric. We determined that Mr. Lennon crossed that line, and we acted accordingly."

I stammer my apologies. He's harmless, totally out of character, I'm sure he regrets his actions. Lie after lie—or, talking out of my arse.

The agent ignores me. "We've searched his apartment, we've talked with everyone else involved, and we are now of the opinion that there was no organised plot to undermine the U.S. government. But we did find some controlled substances in his apartment, and he seemed to be under the influence of drugs or alcohol when we brought him in. He's sobering up now and is recanting some of the statements he made at the concert."

The agent rises from the table. "But you need to get them out of here. Understood?"

I nod my assent and look up, just in time to see a dishevelled, tired John and Yoko emerging from the questioning room.

I drive the car to the back of the building, hoping for a low-key exit, but reporters are already parked at every door, waiting. After a few minutes, federal agents escort John and Yoko out of the building, and the melee begins. I go out to meet them, trying to push back the reporters who are yelling, "Mr. Lennon, why do you hate America?" and "John, are you a Communist?" John is annoyed and follows me to the car, but at the last minute, he turns around. I motion him into the car, but he waves me off.

"I just want to say . . . I want to say that I'm sorry for what I said, and I didn't mean anything by it." The reporters launch a host of follow-up questions, and John ducks into the car. I start the engine and roar off toward the airport, with three unmarked cars following us.

I knew he should have kept his mouth shut; Derek would have wanted to control all media responses from Apple. But John will be John. The car is silent, save for John muttering to himself. I turn on the radio to mask the silence, but realise my mistake too late.

"...Federal agents released former Beatle John Lennon and his wife Yoko Ono a few moments ago after seven hours of questioning—"

I turn it off, but John yells at me, "Turn it back on, Mal!"

Click. ". . . Most of those involved have quickly distanced themselves from the musician and his comments. Activist Abbie Hoffman:" Hoffman's voice crackles through the speaker. "While we applaud John's activism and fervour, we are advocating a more subtle revolution, urging other forms of nonviolent protest such as civil disobedience, letters and town hall meetings, voter turnout at elections . . ."

"And they call themselves extremists," John spits.

But then he enters damage control mode. "Christ, I was just mouthing off," he says to no one, complaining and confessing at the same time. "Mal, if you know me as well as you say you do, you'll know that I keep sticking me foot in me mouth. Remember what I said about Jesus?"

My mind searches back to 1966, when John told a reporter that the Beatles were more popular than Jesus. No one in the U.K. batted an eye, but it caused a major controversy in the

States, and John had to issue an apology. I wonder if this latest spectacle will top that one, and if John will ever be able to come back to the United States again.

12

13 August 1973

"Ravi, this really isn't a good idea . . ."

My statement is more for the record than it is a plea for him to stop. He is about to ring John's doorbell and ask him to play at another benefit concert, this one with his former bandmates, most of whom have some grudge against him. I haven't seen John since the awkward plane trip back from New York. But Ravi has sensed an opportunity, thinking that John has been humbled by his failure in America and will be open to a reunion concert. George, still fuming from John's public comment and practical joke about "My Sweet Lord," wants nothing to do with John.

Ravi, of course, ignores me and rings the bell. I brace myself for anything—a blender flying through the window, a string of epithets—but instead, after being escorted in by the housekeeper, we find an even-tempered John lounging in the living room.

"Well, if it isn't the Indian welcoming crew and his pet, Mr. Evans," John exclaims. I am annoyed by the put-down but say nothing.

Ravi bows. "It is good to see you, John. I am sorry about what happened overseas, but I am impressed with your passion for change. You wanted things to happen, and you did something about it. My countrymen would applaud you for your work."

John is caught off-guard by Ravi's compliments and tries to joke with him as a defence. "Aw shucks, Gandhi, it was nuthin'. A few more hundred thousand angry fans and we would have had enough of an army, right, Mal?" he winks.

"I want to tell you a little more about what's going on in my neighbouring country, John. May I have a seat?" John nods, watching him carefully, and Ravi begins his now-well-rehearsed speech about Bangladesh. John seems to be losing interest; he is playing with a yo-yo, performing various tricks with it and occasionally grunting an acknowledgement. Ravi senses it too, so he gets straight to the point. "We're forming a concert to raise money for Bangladesh, and we'd like you to perform. Will you join us?"

John perks up but narrows his eyes. "Who else is playing?"

Ravi looks at me. Oh great. I get to tell him. "Well, er, so far we've got Ringo, Eric, Billy Preston..." I fidget. "Of course, George is playing. Paul even mentioned that he might join us—"

I hold my breath, hoping for an affirmation that I know will not come and bracing for an explosion. But John smiles. "Ah, there's a *Beatle* reunion in the works." He rises and pats Ravi on the shoulder. "No thanks, mates. I've had enough of benefit concerts for a while. And I don't need to be raising any old spirits, either." And that is that. John exchanges a few pleasantries with us while he walks us to the door.

On the way back to George's house at Friar Park, Ravi is quiet but upbeat, humming and smiling while I drive. But when we tell George what happened, George cannot contain his anger. "He didn't even think about it! We were so close, and he's ruining it."

Ravi says nothing, but he still has a mysterious smile on his face.

"What is it, Ravi?" George asks.

"There is an old Indian saying: 'Even a stone gets rounded by constant rubbing.' Are you going to give up this easily, George?"

George says nothing.

"I believe that the way to John is not to ask him, but to show him."

* * *

15 August 1973

I'm standing at John's front door again. This time I'm alone, and I have no idea what's in the envelope under my arm. George rang me up earlier and asked me to take it over to John's house.

I find John watching television in the living room.

"What brings you here again, Malcolm X? George send you over to give it the old college try again?"

"Nope. I'm just the delivery boy today." I hand him the envelope, and he studies it with mild amusement. I am afraid he'll toss it, but curiosity gets the best of him, and he tears it open with the zeal of a two-year-old on Christmas.

Inside the envelope are two tickets to Dhaka, Bangladesh, along with photos of some of the malnourished children suffering under the squalid conditions. The photos are labelled with the children's names and ages; in some cases, the date the child died is noted. Ravi has included a short note that reads:

These children are orphans; their parents have either died or are missing. They have nothing. Some have already died, and others may be dead by the time you read this.

Pictures do not adequately show the grief and despair that these people are experiencing. If you believe in changing the world, focus not on politics, but on helping your fellow man. Please, go and see for yourself what has happened to this country and its people.

Namaste,

Ravi Shankar

John drops the photos on the table in front of him but holds onto the note, scrutinising every word, apparently unnerved by the abrupt nature of the tactic. John grew up without a mother and a father in his life; he knew what being an orphan was all about.

John chews on his lower lip, saying nothing, then drops the note on the table. "What the hell," he says. "A trip halfway around the world sounds daft, exactly like something I'd do." He turns to Yoko, who has been standing in the doorway watching. "Whaddaya say, Mother? Holiday in Bangladesh?"

Yoko shakes her head. "The stars are not right for a trip east. We cannot go now. It's too dangerous."

He snorts. "Did you even check your horoscope, or are you just makin' that up? C'mon, it'll be fun." I bristle at the idea of having fun in the middle of a refugee camp but remain silent.

"No John. We're *not going*. That's final."

In the past, John would have meekly agreed with Yoko and dropped the subject. But at that moment, years of pent-up anger at Yoko and her controlling behaviour are released—anger at the failed Toronto concert, at her sub-par contributions to the double album, at the disastrous visit to America. Like a child, he screams at Yoko, "You can't tell me what to do! If I want to go to Bangladesh, I'll bloody well get on a plane to Bangladesh!"

"John, calm down."

"I'm tired of you, I'm tired of your stars and zodiac mumbo jumbo, and I'm tired of you being in charge. If you're not going, I'm goin' without you."

"Go, then. Go, knowing the stars are not looking out for you, that I'm not looking out for you. We'll see how far you get. And don't bother coming back."

"Well, you won't have to worry about that, love." John snatches the tickets and walks out the door. "Mal, come."

I stand there awkwardly as Yoko stares at the door, then stares at me. My gaze falls to the floor. "I'd best be on my way," I mutter, and run after John.

He is waiting in the car. How funny, I think, that he is running away from his wife but is dependent on me for whisking him away. It reminds me of my mum helping me pack when I decided to run away at the age of nine. For once, whether he knows it or not, I hold the keys to what he does and where he goes—literally. Sure, he can drive himself, but he's a terrible driver, and it will be awkward for him to go back inside to get his own keys.

John is quiet for a minute, then says, "The tickets are for today. You wanna go?"

I shrug. "Sure." I have nothing else to do.

I drive him to Heathrow Airport, stopping at a few stores on the way to get some toiletries, a change of clothes and some cash. It's another adventure for Mal Evans, Esquire; I hope I can stave off the demons for another week or so.

At the last minute before getting on the plane, I remember Mimi. I find the nearest pay phone and ring her.

"Hey luv, it's me." I don't wait for an answer. "Listen, John's asked me to go to Bangladesh with him."

No need to wait for an answer. Besides, I hear only silence on the other end. "It's—er, a humanitarian trip to visit the refugees there. He needs protection."

Still silence.

"Look, I'll be back in a few days. Give my love to the kids, will you?"

Click.

* * *

"Can you believe we're doin' this, Mal? Fantastic," John raves as he looks out the window of the aeroplane. "It's just like the old days, jumpin' on a plane whenever we want, nothing to tie us down."

The John Lennon I am sitting next to is a complete change from the one I met at Tittenhurst a few hours earlier; his anger has subsided, and what is left is the old John from 1963—personable, relaxed and joking. He has been talking almost nonstop, and I am drinking it in. He hasn't mentioned Yoko at all.

"I remember this time—I think we were in France—when we just off and decided to fly to Greece. Were you with us, Mal?"

"I was. I had to go track down Brian because he had your passports."

John laughs. "That's right! And he wouldn't give 'em to yeh!"

"I even tried to pay off the pilot so he could fly you there without a passport."

"We were off our rockers, weren't we?"

We remain silent for a bit.

"How have you been without your mummies and daddies around all the time?" he asks.

"It's hard, John. Really hard." I struggle with what to say, afraid that I will somehow mess it up and ruin any chance of a reunion. "I just wish things with the band were the way they used to be."

"Well, it wasn't always fun and games, now, was it?"

"But you were so good together. You still can be."

John laughed. "Mummy and Daddy don't like each other anymore, Mal. It doesn't mean we love you any less."

I'm losing him. "Just one concert, though, John. Can't you put your differences aside for just one night, for the kids? I mean, you can do more good with this one show than . . ."

"Than a bed-in for peace?"

I don't say anything, but that's what I'm thinking. John and Yoko invited reporters to their hotel room during their honeymoon, sitting in bed in their pyjamas and promoting world peace. John doesn't say anything else, but I take that as a good sign. And then, from out of the blue, I ask it. I guess I'm feeling a bit of camaraderie with John.

"John, do you believe you can experience part of your life over again?"

John is taken aback by the question—he physically jumps—and he looks at me oddly. At first I am embarrassed, realising that it sounds odd and out of the blue. He stares at me for what seems like an eternity, as if he is seeing me for the first time. But he also looks surprised, as if he recognises something in my question. After a while, he says slowly, "Yeah. Yeah, I do."

"What if I told you I think I'm living my life over right now, only things are different this time? That the first time around, the Toronto concert turned out okay, and you four broke up in 1970 and never reunited? That there was no *Everest*, only solo albums?"

Again he stares at me, but it's as if he's seen a ghost. He then says slowly, "I'd say you're daft, Mal." He turns away and is silent for the next half hour. I don't know who is more spooked, him or me.

17 August 1973
Dhaka, Bangladesh

We get off the plane and board a bus to the refugee camps. Our guide, provided by Ravi, introduces himself as Shyam. "It takes about three hours to get to the main camp, but you'll see a great deal of destruction along the way," he says.

He does not exaggerate; from what I can tell, the road to the Indian border is one giant refugee camp. There are no buildings anywhere, save for the shells of a few concrete structures. But there are people. Everywhere. People lining the roads in rows that stretch for miles beyond. People huddled in fetid pools of rainwater, staring aimlessly into space. People in hastily built shelters, a few boards nailed or tied together. People in shock, wandering aimlessly through the massive destruction. People wailing to us as we pass, in a language I can't understand. People reaching out and touching the bus, as if it has some magical healing power to lift them out of their hell. People traveling to the border, carrying their paltry belongings on their heads or backs. The looks on their faces are ones of resignation – blank and soulless, with not a hint of life or fight.

Shyam tells stories of murder, rape, looting and burning. We see bodies piled up, ready to be cremated, and the stench of decaying flesh overpowers the smell of raw sewage. I hear a lot of noises, but very little that represents normalcy. Aside from the people talking to us from the side of the road, I hear the occasional wail of a baby, probably hungry or sick or both. Goats are bleating periodically. Flies are buzzing around everyone's heads, entering the bus and encroaching on our space.

Ravi's good. This tour is a powerful way to send the message, I think.

"How can people live like this?" John whispers to no one.

"They don't," admits Shyam, overhearing him. "Thousands are dying every day. Cholera, mostly. There is no drinkable water and no sewage system, so once cholera appears, it flourishes. We try to inoculate them, but there are too many." He lets that sink in. "Others die from malnutrition. We simply don't have enough food to go around. The Indian government estimates that it costs about 60 million rupees a day—that's about £600,000—to take care of everyone. As you can tell, it's not enough."

"How long have they been here?"

"About two years. Well, they've been crossing into India for two years. About one out of every three succeeds in arriving."

John stares out the window, saying nothing. Outside the bus, a woman carrying her child gives in to exhaustion and collapses, her baby crying underneath her. People walk over her, sometimes stepping on her, not realizing or not caring what is beneath their feet. I say nothing, amazed and horrified at what I see. But John jumps up and goes into action.

"Stop the bus! Stop the bus!"

The driver slams on the brakes. John leaps from the vehicle, just out of Shyam's frantic reach, and into the sea of people, trying to fight his way back to where the mother and child lie. He is quickly enveloped by the sea of people trying to reach him, attempting to touch him as if he carried the magic healing power. To them he is not an adored Beatle; he is hope and salvation. Shyam and a few others run after John, grab him and half-carry him back into safety.

"You do that again, you might not make it back on the bus alive," Shyam says.

"Did you see that?" John asks, pulling his dishevelled hair back behind his ears. "I couldn't do anything. Not a damn thing. That mother and child are gonna die. And you didn't help them."

"A lot of them are dying, Mr. Lennon. And more are going to die. You're right, there's not a lot we can do. If we tried to save her, we might have died as well."

John stews in his seat, gazing outside. He then gets up again and walks back to the front of the bus. "I've seen enough," he tells the bus driver. "Turn the bus around and take us back to the airport."

Shyam starts to panic. "But, but, Mr. Lennon, we have more to show you. We haven't even gotten to the main refugee camp. And I have set up interviews with some of the relief workers and some refugees."

John turns to me and asks, "How much money do you have?"

I open my wallet and count the currency. "About 500 pounds."

"Give it to me."

I hand it over to him. He gives the stack of bills to Shyam. "Buy what you can with this now. I'll send more, but now I have to get back home. We have a concert to get ready for." He begins to walk back to his seat, and then turns back around. "And don't *ever* tell me that there's nothing I can do."

On the way to the airport, we stop by a Western Union office. My voice trembles as I dictate a telegram to Neil Aspinall in England:

JOHN IS IN. GET THE REST OF THE LADS TOGETHER FOR REHEARSALS. WE'RE ON OUR WAY BACK. –MAL

* * *

And just like that, we're on the plane back to London. The reality of what John just agreed to do is starting to sink in.

"I know George is pissed off at me," John says, tapping his foot nervously. "But what about Paul?"

I shrug. "He's hurt more than anything. He wrote that song 'Dear Friend' about you after you wrote 'How Do You Sleep'. I think he's up for a reconciliation."

"Yeah. What a load of fluff." But he is smiling. "I just don't know about this. I've burned a lot of bridges. I'm always burning bridges. Hell, I don't even know if I can go back to the States now."

"After a few minutes together, you'll forget all about your disagreements." I don't believe this, but it sounds reassuring. "Just think of the money you'll raise when we announce that the Beatles are getting back together."

John sighs. "Yeah."

13

28 August 1973

We have reserved the Playhouse Theatre in London under pseudonyms and have placed strict security all around the building. The press has been all over this; Derek Taylor has been on the phone all day and most of the evening issuing non-denial denials, refusing to confirm the rumours that the Beatles are performing at the concert. Of course, he knows full well that such denials will only fuel speculation.

We have sneaked Paul, George and Ringo into the building using a delivery truck backed up to the loading dock. John is coming later. For now, I am readying the sound system while warily watching the events onstage.

The atmosphere is tense. Paul is pretending as if nothing has occurred over the past two years, playing some cocktail music on a grand piano. George is trying to act civil, preferring to let the cause override any ill feelings he may have for Paul. He spends most of his time talking to concert organisers, making sure things are flowing smoothly. I'm sure he wants Paul to see him working hard on the show and being in charge. Ringo is smoking a cigarette, sitting in a chair just offstage. No one is speaking to anyone. I go back to work, testing microphones and running wires to the monitors on the stage, and wondering how this will ever work.

Paul stops playing in mid phrase, and the other two look up.

John is walking into the auditorium with a guitar case in hand, and by his side is May Pang, Yoko's assistant. Yoko is nowhere in sight. It usually wouldn't be abnormal for them to be together, except this time they are holding hands. John gets to the stage, turns to May and kisses her on the lips. He walks slowly up the stairs to the stage and says, "Okay mates, let's do this." Everyone stands there, mouths agape, except me. I remember that in my other life, John ran off with May in the early 1970s – his "Lost Weekend" away from Yoko that actually lasted 18 months.

No one asks what May is doing here, or where Yoko is. No one mentions "My Sweet Lord," or "How Do You Sleep?" or "Too Many People." Talking is limited to discussions about microphone levels, chord changes and song arrangements. And everyone waits for the argument that surprisingly never comes.

As he had with their previous album, George remains in control; he has worked on a set list, which consists mostly of early Beatles hits—things they could probably play in their sleep. Paul does what he is told; when he offers a suggestion here and there, George does not flinch, but instead acquiesces and listens to him. John cracks a joke, and the giggling begins. And then I see the old Beatles emerge—no power plays, no paranoia. They grow bolder and start to practise songs they have never played live, such as "Lady Madonna" and "Come Together." George teaches them a new song that he wrote with Eric Clapton called "Bangla Desh"—at least, that is what he tells the other Beatles. He had written the words but could only manage a snippet of the melody. Eric had stepped in and written the rest.

The rehearsal ends at 2 a.m., with the banter now flowing freely among the four. They agree to come back again tomorrow.

* * *

The Globe

29 August 1973

BEATLES REUNITE FOR BANGLADESH

Apple officials today confirmed that the Beatles will reunite for a benefit concert for the people of Bangladesh.

The Concert for Bangladesh will take place at the Isle of Wight on September 1. Joining the Beatles at the all-day festival will be Eric Clapton, Bob Dylan, Billy Preston and Leon Russell.

Besides marking a reunion of rock n' roll's greatest group, which disbanded a year ago, the concert is the first time the Beatles will play a scheduled show since 1966. Apple spokesman Derek Taylor would not confirm a set list, nor would he confirm that the reunion would last past the performance. "They have agreed to perform at this concert, and that's all, nothing more," he said.

Proceeds from the concert will go to refugees in Bangladesh, who have suffered through war and natural disasters over the past few years. Tickets cost £10 and will go on sale tomorrow at 8 a.m.

1 September 1973

The atmosphere is electric around the Isle of Wight, an island in the English Channel about four miles off the coast of England. A stunning island with breathtaking cliffs and sea ledges, it first became a venue for a festival in 1970, when Jimi Hendrix headlined the Isle of Wight festival. It attracted about 700,000 people.

Organizers have sold about 800,000 tickets for the event; they could easily have sold more, but the infrastructure—transportation, rubbish, and sewage—won't support any more people. Once people had secured their tickets, they began camping out in the fields near Godshill, squatting for a place in line so they could run near the stage when the gates opened; others who were not so lucky to get a ticket still hope to buy one, or are hanging around just to be close to the experience. Some security officials are estimating the overall crowd at close to one million.

The concert begins at about one o'clock in the afternoon. Ravi Shankar opens with a short set of sitar music that establishes the mood for all that follows. Few are paying attention, but their patience is not tried for too long. Following Shankar are Delaney & Bonnie, Leon Russell, Billy Preston, Eric Clapton, and then Bob Dylan, who, despite his previous objections, overcomes his stage fright and wows the audience with an hour-long set that includes "A Hard Rain's A-Gonna Fall" and "Blowin' In the Wind."

George has put me in charge of the transition between acts—making sure the artists get offstage, securing their equipment and setting up the stage for the next act. It's what I usually do, but I'm in charge this time, and it's empowering. It keeps me occupied throughout the day. Once in a while, I check with the boys to see if they need anything, but they are surprisingly relaxed.

Darkness finally sets in about eight thirty, and screams and shrieks erupt as I bring out Paul's familiar Höfner bass – the electric guitar shaped somewhat like a violin. Exiting the stage, I see the four waiting impatiently to begin. They actually want to go out there, ready to perform again. George nods to the other three, and they walk out on stage and pick up their instruments. As the spotlights turn up, the deafening roar of the crowd goes up another few decibels, and George begins the opening riff of "Dizzy Miss Lizzie" as the Beatles begin their first concert in seven years.

I'm just offstage with the set list in front of me; I have to bring out different guitars for John, Paul and George throughout their performance. I'm tuning the guitars as they play, but I'm listening more to them than I am to the tunings. The set resembles a Beatles greatest hits album: "Drive My Car," "It Don't Come Easy," "Lady Madonna," "Something," "Maybe I'm Amazed," "Come Together," "While My Guitar Gently Weeps," "Blackbird," "Yesterday," "Here Comes the Sun," and "Hey Jude." Since the Beatles quit touring in 1966, most of these songs had never been performed in public before; some critics had questioned whether some of their songs could be duplicated on stage, since they had been using multi-track machines and unusual techniques to record their songs. But it sounds amazing. The band looks relaxed, occasionally smiling at each other. John walks over to George and yells something in his ear;

George laughs and nods his head. Later, John goes over to Paul's microphone and sings harmony with him.

I can't believe it. Not only are my mates back, but they are *performing*—something I had never thought I'd witness again. My mind goes back to their days at the Cavern Club, to the Invasion of America, the concert on top of the Apple Records building during the *Get Back* sessions. Watching them live was my first exposure to them, and seeing it happen again is a treasure.

After "Hey Jude," the band exit the stage with the crowd still singing the never-ending chorus, and, of course, they are demanding an encore. The band is going over the chord changes for "Bangla Desh," but John interrupts them.

"Wait, mates. I've got a little tune I'd like to debut before 'Bangla Desh.'"

Paul, George and Ringo look at each other. I wonder what John might unleash on the crowd. The night has gone perfectly; no one wants a repeat of the New York incident to spoil the entire concert and bring notoriety to an otherwise magical event.

"I dunno, John," says Paul. "I mean—is it, uh, you know . . ."

Ringo interrupts. "Are you gonna act like an arse?"

John smiles. "Ah, Richie, yer gonna love it," he says to Ringo, winking, and he picks up an acoustic guitar and ambles onstage. We are all panicking, knowing full well we can't stop it.

"Mal, did you know anything about this?" Paul asks. "What's he gonna play?"

"I have no idea." I search my brain for another protest song that John wrote in my other life. Nothing comes to mind. George tells me to get ready to pull the plug on the whole sound system in case he gets out of line.

The crowd roars when John comes out, looking surprisingly confident. We wait in the wings, both curious and horrified. John looks offstage and says, "The others think I'm going to go off me rocker again," he says, eliciting another roar from the audience, and another panicked look from all of us. "But I want to play a new song for you. It's a way that we all can view the world if we all help each other. It's called 'Imagine.' "

The goose bumps on my skin appear at the sound of the word, and they last throughout the song. I didn't think John's piano ballad could be bettered, but with John armed with just an acoustic guitar, the song sounds like an idea still circulating in his head that he wanted to share with everyone that night—an idea about peace and vision that didn't include war or religion or hell.

I look over at the others, and they are mesmerised. I never got to see any of the other three's first reactions to "Imagine" in my previous life, but I can tell their respect for John has reached a new high. He plays the last chord of the song, and the crowd screams its approval.

They have no idea what they've just heard. I think back to when Paul debuted "Yesterday" to an unknowing crowd at the ABC Theatre in Blackpool in 1965. The crowd there were among the first people in the world to hear that song, but they had no idea what a smash hit it would become. That's what is happening at this concert with "Imagine." Millions will have heard this song decades from now for the ten thousandth time, but this is the first for everyone.

The rest of the band goes out to close the festival with "Bangla Desh." It's well-received simply because the crowd is on a Beatle high. They hadn't performed for the past seven years, but they could still turn an audience into a frenzy.

All in all, a good day's work. The demons are gone, and I am whole again.

Rolling Stone
January 5, 1974

Concert for Bangladesh Raises Millions in Relief

The Concert for Bangladesh has raised about $40 million for charity, according to Apple officials.

Even when accounting for the $1 million production costs, the concert and its successful album and movie will be able to feed, house and treat millions of refugees affected by war and monsoons in the beleaguered country. The concert itself grossed $8 million; the subsequent double album of the concert, fueled by the new hit song "Imagine," has sold 11 million copies, raising another $30 million. Plans are in the works for a movie featuring highlights of the concert.

Apple press officer Derek Taylor said that the first funds totaling $20 million have been transferred to UNICEF, a relief organization working in Bangladesh. Other checks will follow.

The September concert, attended by an estimated 800,000 people, featured the first live appearance by the Beatles since 1966. Other performers included Bob Dylan and Eric Clapton.

14

1 September 1973

We're at a local pub in Newport, not far from the festival grounds. We've reserved the entire pub to give the band some privacy and hired security at all the entrances to keep the fans out. That doesn't keep them from peering into the windows as if they're visiting a zoo, but the four are oblivious.

The band haven't done this since Beatlemania—going out on the town and getting blasted together. We're acting as if we were twenty-two years old instead of thirty-two. All of the tension, animosity and arguing has melted away.

"Another round, sir pub man!" Ringo announces, his words already slurring.

"Another pub, sir round man!" says John, eliciting giggles from everyone.

"Another man, sir round pub!"

Paul combs a hand through his hair. "God, did you *feel* the excitement in that crowd? Shea Stadium was nothing like that."

"Which one were you most excited about, Macca?" John asks, raising his eyebrows. George giggles.

"I don't do that anymore, John. I'm happily married," Paul says grandly, then pauses. "The blonde in the tight red blouse, second row, left side." All four burst into laughter, Ringo spewing ale across the table, and make catcalls at Paul.

"So what's up with the new gal, John?" Ringo asks.

John looks at me, then grins. "I fired Yoko. I'm, um, borrowing May for a while to keep me company."

"I like her better than Yoko," Ringo says. I giggle, and John glares me into silence. I can't help it. Yoko had not been mean to me; she just tolerated me. But the tension she brought to the rest of the band had sometimes been destructive. And John was very different with May, more like the laid-back, funny man we'd known most of our good years together. May was star-struck. She was fully supportive of John, letting him do whatever he wanted. And since the band preferred being by themselves again, we hadn't seen a lot of her since that first rehearsal.

Paul slaps John on the back and says, "Ah, women. Can't live with 'em . . ."

"Can't get rid of 'em, either," Ringo adds. The howling begins again.

Paul changes the subject. "You know, we shoulda played 'I Want to Hold Your Hand.' "

"Or 'Revolution,' " John adds. Another round of laughs.

"'Revolution #9.' " I wince. John's nine-minute sound collage was the worst part of the *White Album*.

"'How Do You Sleep?' " No one laughs, and John quickly goes into damage control. "Oh c'mon, Paul, bygones."

"You really hurt me with that stuff. The only good song I did was 'Yesterday?' "

John looks bewildered. "Jesus, Paul, you're still worked up over that? I hadn't given it a second thought. You know me—I get something off me chest and that's it. Like I said, bygones."

Paul still looks bothered.

"Macca, look, you gotta admit that some of your tunes are just rubbish. 'Bip, bop, boppity bop,' " he sings mockingly, throwing a peanut at him. "Face it, mate, you need me around."

"You need me just as badly," Paul grunts.

John stops and leans back in his chair, gazing out the window at the fans screaming at them. "*Touché*, Paul, *touché*." It is as close as Paul will get to an apology, but he looks pleased. And I know now that the two have finally grown up.

* * *

28 September 1973

I'm late coming into Abbey Road this morning, hung over and beat from an all-night recording session with John and Paul. I nod to the receptionist and enter Studio Two, ready to begin cleaning up the mess from the night before.

John and Paul are still there.

They're no longer recording; when I left at four a.m., I assumed that they were wrapping things up. But Geoff Emerick looks exhausted as he replays another track for the two, who are listening intently. Geoff looks up, almost pleading to me with his eyes, and I know he's been here all night. But what I hear is nothing short of masterful; it's the opening strains of John's "Whatever Gets You Thru the Night," his duet with Elton John, but it's now a Beatles song, with Paul doing Elton's part. Even though I love Elton, Paul's voice gives a new jolt to the song. Elton's version was carefree and soulful, but this somehow seems more musical—more serious and perfect. I always thought it should have been Paul singing it; now he is. Things are as they should be.

"Okay, I want a sax solo here at the beginning, George. And I need a raw, bluesy player—not one of them 'Sentimental Journey' types," John says.

I wonder which George he is talking about; George Martin, the Beatles' old producer, is in the back of the room, smoking a cigarette. His hair has greyed a little, but he is still the same dapper, dignified gentleman he was when I first met him in these studios almost ten years ago. He has probably been there all night as well, but not a hair is out of place, and his tie is still straight and tight against his neck. He has not been present in the same control room with the Beatles since *Abbey Road*. It's a good sign.

The two look up. "Hey Mal, you're missin' history here," John says. "Your mummy and daddy have kissed and made up, and they're making beautiful music together!" Paul gives John little air kisses. "Okay, Mal, you're here just in time to go get us some kazoos. We're accompanying Ringo on a song."

Of course I am.

Billboard

October 12, 1973

BEATLES RETURN TO TOP OF CHARTS WITH 'NIGHT'

Fresh from their command performance at the Concert for Bangladesh, the Beatles' latest single, "Whatever Gets You Thru the Night," rose to Number 1 this week, giving the band its 33rd chart-topper.

The up-tempo jazz tune marks new territory for the group, which has stuck mostly in the past to its pop-rock roots. Even the flip side, a cover of the Sherman Brothers' "You're Sixteen," is a departure from the group, with Ringo Starr manning the vocals and featuring Lennon and McCartney performing kazoo solos.

The songs were recorded mostly by John Lennon and Paul McCartney. George Harrison did not contribute to either song, according to the credits on the record.

Apple Records spokesman Derek Taylor also confirmed that all four Beatles would be working together on a new album. "They're very excited to be writing and recording again. I have no idea what to expect, but I'm sure it will be magical."

* * *

8 October 1973

I'm in the control room with Geoff Emerick. We're recording a demo of George playing a song called "Give Me Love (Give Me Peace on Earth)." I recognise it as a single from one of his solo albums, and I'm glad he has found it in his head and put it down on tape. After the recent lawsuit, he needs this.

The song is wistful yet beautiful, if somewhat preachy. It was George's last gasp in my previous life—the last of his songs that sounded like a Beatles song, and the last Top 10 hit that I knew of. I look around the control room and see smiles as the others notice that the old magic has returned.

George finishes the demo and bounds up the stairs to the control room, flashing a toothy grin. "What did you think?" he asks us. I nod my approval, and Geoff Emerick says, "That's a hit, George. Melodic, beautiful chord changes. I also like the little instrumental—throwing in a little Dylan there, I see."

George, who is looking through some acetates from yesterday's session, stops and looks at Geoff. "What do you mean?"

"Well, you know 'I Want You'? From *Blonde on Blonde?*" Geoff realises his faux pas and tries to backpedal. "It's just a little reminiscent, you know. It's good, magnificent, actually. Not much resemblance at all now that I think about it . . ."

George turns to me. "Go get the album. Now. I wanna hear it."

Unfortunately, I find a copy of *Blonde on Blonde* in the library, take it back into the control room, and place the disc on the turntable. The guitar chord sequence is somewhat similar, as well as a little instrumental melody, but it's not the same, not even close to being lawsuit material.

George hears it, though. He sits down and puts his head in his hands, whispering, "No, no, no," and then rises and leaves the studio. I glance at Geoff, who looks as if he's just broken his mother's priceless vase again. "Oops," he utters. "I should keep my bloody mouth shut."

Later that day, Geoff tells me George called in and ordered him to erase the only copy of "Give Me Love (Give Me Peace on Earth)."

* * *

4 November 1973

There is no way I'm going to miss this day. It's the auditions for the new album. And I have no idea what I'm going to hear.

As usual, John and Paul have been here before everyone else. John looks hung over and unshaven, not his usual peppy self. Ringo is having a drink with Neil, but George is not there yet. I begin to worry, and just as I am about to go look for him, he walks in.

I haven't seen George for a few weeks; he looks gaunt but rested, his hair and beard even longer. He is dressed in a saffron coloured robe, and he bows to me modestly as I approach him. I want to pat him on the back, even hug him, but he seems unapproachable now, almost sacred.

"Er, what's new, George?"

"Never felt better, Mal," he says. He looks at me as if expecting a follow-up question. I bite.

"Why is that?"

"I've found peace. Finally. I've given up everything—Pattie included—and joined the Krishnas. They've moved into Friar Park with me."

We are all stunned. George and Pattie? The inspiration for George's smash hit "Something"? I remember that they had broken up the first go 'round in 1974, but in this universe, I was hoping for happier times. And Krishnas at George's beautiful estate?

We have always looked to Ringo for some levity, and he comes through as always. "But what's up with the hair, George?" Ringo asked. "I thought you were supposed to shave it. You've gone and done it backwards."

"Yeah, you look like the Maharishi," John says, referring to the guru whom the four had visited in India in 1968. The trip to India has always been a touchy subject for George; Ringo left India early because he didn't like the food, but Paul and John became disillusioned with the Maharishi and left soon after Ringo. John's song from the White Album, "Sexy Sadie," was about the Maharishi.

George ignores the comments. "Things have been hard for me ever since the lawsuit," he says slowly, almost hesitantly. "And for the first time in my life, I have stability. I have a solid foundation."

His confession, his overall speech, is met with an awkward silence. John pipes up. "That's good, Georgie Krishna, but do you have any *songs*? And don't play me any sitar music."

George's serene expression falls. I suspect he is reciting some internal mantra to achieve balance again. But before he can respond, Paul jumps in. "Well then, let's get to work, shall we?"

It's happening again. I get to hear solo songs now being introduced as Beatles demos—"Band on the Run," "Jet," and "Mind Games"— and the chills return. I begin to form the future

Beatles album in my head. John takes a turn on the piano, and with a mischievous grin, plays a simple song that he wrote for Ringo, called "I'm the Greatest."

"I can't sing this one, Ringo. People will think I'm stuck on meself. Only you can pull this off without sounding cheeky." John had previously written that one for Ringo's self-titled album, the one in which Ringo got all the Beatles to play on one album, even if they never performed on the same song together.

"Seeing as I have nothing, sir, I'll take it and make it my own," Ringo says. I add that to my mental list, trying to figure out where I would place the song on the album.

The auditions continue. Paul debuts a song called "Let Me Roll It," which was the opening song on one of his most critically acclaimed albums, *Band on the Run*. John recycles a tune from the *Get Back* sessions that I recognize as his solo song "Gimme Some Truth." George is conspicuously quiet.

John notices. "Okay, George, your turn."

The colour drains from George's face. He looks as if he hasn't studied for a pop quiz. "I, er . . . Well, I'm working on a few things, but they're not fleshed out. Give me a few more days." He stands up and puts his guitar in its case, not having played a note. "I think we have a lot to go on. Let's start working on these and see what happens."

John shrugs. "Sounds good to me. Let's make a record, lads!"

* * *

12 November 1973

I enter Studio Two at four p.m. with a tray filled with tea and some sandwiches I just prepared in the canteen. All is as it was ten years ago; the guys are huddled around each other with their guitars, trying to stitch together several motifs in "Band on the Run." George Martin is back in the control room with Geoff Emerick, probably discussing where to place the microphones for the next take. It's been orderly, with little horseplay or time wasted, and except for an absent or tardy John, the band has kept to their schedule. Each member knows what songs he is going to practice each day, and groupies—assistants, friends and other Apple employees—have been ordered out during rehearsals. There's no Yoko, no Linda, not even May Pang. It's just the boys.

Seeing the food, the four break and descend on me. Within thirty seconds, my tray is empty.

Paul licks his fingers, savouring the last taste of his sandwich. "So I'm thinking a nice, smooth start, then make the second movement edgier, minor key."

"Bring in George there with a mean little riff," John says.

"Yeah, I like that. And then somehow transition to some 12-string guitars for the main part."

"Maybe some horns."

Suddenly George pipes up.

"I've got nothin' to give. I'm out. Sorry."

No one speaks for a minute. "Well, we were wondering why you were so quiet," Paul says.

"I'm snake bitten. Any song I write, I worry about whether I'm copying someone else. Nothing sounds original anymore."

"Nothing *is* original, George," John says. "Good artists borrow. Great artists steal. You think my stuff is original? Hell, I've been sued too. I ripped off Chuck Berry in 'Come Together', fer chrissakes. Doesn't bother me any."

Silence again. Paul looks up. "Look George, I know you have some songs that you've never released. What about 'Not Guilty?' We almost put that on the *White Album*. Went through about a hundred takes of it, from what I remember."

George grunts. I'm sure he doesn't want to think about all the time wasted on a song that was never released.

Ringo perks up. "Yeah, and what about the one about death and stuff?"

George looks puzzled. "You mean 'Art of Dying?' "

Ringo nods. "Yeah, that's the one."

"None of you liked that one, did you?" he laughs. "That's from eight years ago. You said it was too religious. I even left it off my album because I wasn't sure about it meself."

John shrugs. "So you're religious. That's who you are. I think we're old enough now to sing about what we want to sing about without offending everybody." He smiles. "Can't wait 'til Dick Nixon hears 'Gimme Some Truth.' " He punctuates it with a riff of "Hail to the Chief" on his guitar.

* * *

15 December 1973

It's three o'clock in the afternoon, and we've been waiting at the studio for John for three hours. We were supposed to start recording "Mind Games" today, but we can't find him anywhere.

George Martin stabs another butt of a cigarette into a full ashtray, exhaling loudly. "Did you try calling May?" he asks me. George hates being off schedule.

"Yeah. He didn't come home at all last night."

"Third time this week," Neil Aspinall whispers.

"Does anybody know what he's doing? Where he's going?" George Martin asks.

Neil shrugs. "Maybe he's stealing back to Yoko's."

"No, he wouldn't do that," I say. I've made doubly sure of that, watching him when I can. "He's just on all night benders from what I can tell. Just letting off some steam."

The door opens. John stumbles in, singing "Maggie Mae," an old folk song from Liverpool about a prostitute who robs a sailor. His words are slurred, and the look in his eyes resembles that of a caged animal.

"Oh, dirty Maggie Mae, they are taking me away!" John sings, half giggling and half butchering the verses. "Maggie Mae Pang!" Maggie Mae Pang!" He tries to sit down but misses the chair, landing on his ass. His giggle turns into cackles as he switches Maggie songs, now butchering the Rod Stewart classic. "Come here, Maggie Pang, I think I've sumpin', sumpin' to do to you . . ."

No one says a word, and he finally notices. He looks around with his wild eyes, and they land on me.

"Wha the fuck you starin' at, Mal?" I go over to help him up, but he kicks me instead.

"Don't *touch* me, Mal!" He struggles to his feet, walks over to George Martin, and salutes. "Sergeant Pepper reporting for recording, Sir George Martin-in-the-Fields." And he collapses in a heap at Martin's feet.

Martin looks at me in disgust. "Get him out of here, and don't bring him back until he's been sober for six hours. If that's possible."

Neil and I carry John to my car, laying him in the back seat. "Jesus, when he gets away from Yoko, he can really get on the rampage, can't he?" Neil says.

"I'm surprised he even showed up."

John raises his head. "Mal. Drink. Scotch and soda." He lowers his head and passes out again.

"Well, it's good that he's free to do what he wants, but this isn't what I was hoping for," Neil says. "Yoko's strict, but maybe that's what he needs."

I don't want to agree with him. *He needs us.* I don't need him back with Yoko, but his behaviour is worrying me more and more.

I start the car and ease out onto Abbey Road. "How long do you think he can keep this up before he goes completely daft?" I ask Neil.

"Let's hope it's after the album is finished."

The Globe

17 December 1973

Beatle Tossed from Nightclub for Midnight Antics

Musician John Lennon was thrown out of a pub late last night and continued his romp through Leicester Square in the wee hours of the morning.

According to sources, Lennon was taunting patrons at the bar and refused requests to cease his antics. The owner of the pub confirmed that he was forcefully removed from the establishment.

Later, Lennon was seen walking through Leicester Square singing Beatles songs loudly, waking residents who live near the square. Police were called to the scene, but Lennon had already left.

Lennon had no comment. Apple spokesperson Derek Taylor did not return phone calls about the incidents.

20 December 1973

George Martin has called the four into the studio for a special meeting separate from the regular rehearsal schedule—something that he rarely does. Even John has showed up, somewhat irritable but sober. His antics from the past few nights have caused him to slow down, more by Derek Taylor's request than his own motivation. Still, he is here; perhaps the called meeting has piqued his interest. *This must be something big*, I think, as I fetch the lads some drinks.

George Martin arrives with a grin on his face. "Gentlemen, I've been approached by the producers of the new James Bond movie. They have asked me to compose the score for the film, but I was hoping I could entice you to contribute something— perhaps the theme song."

John groans. "My God, it's come to this. We're pitchin' a bloody movie theme. What's next, George? An ad for laxatives?"

George Martin ignores him. "The movie will be called 'Live and Let Die.' I thought it might be something fun to work on. We all love movies, especially spy flicks. And, Mr. Lennon—" he turns in deference to John, "—I believe you have written songs for and starred in a few films. You're already part of that establishment. George, Paul, you've composed scores for movies as well."

George Harrison scowls. "We don't need that anymore."

Martin challenges him. "What? You're too good for writing on demand? What happened to the days when you would challenge each other to write a new hit that would pay for a new house or a new car?"

Paul has walked over the piano and is doing his usual tinkering, playing little ditties. I then hear the soon-to-be-famous chords blast their way from the depths of the piano. "Y'know, I've been fooling around with something that may fit with some sort of spy theme." The bass stays the same while the chords change ever so slightly. He begins singing softly, "Live and let die . . . Ooh, live and let live . . ." He nods, pleased at what he has come up with. "Yeah, George, let me play with it for a few days and see what I can do." John rolls his eyes but keeps quiet.

The next day, as the other three are rehearsing, Paul bursts breathless into the studio yelling, "I've got it! I've got it!"

As I hear the band put together the pieces of "Live and Let Die"—my God, is it even more powerful, more bombastic, than the original?—I know that the Beatles are venturing into something new as a group. Just as George Martin predicted, the song has challenged them to stretch themselves. They're thinking in new ways, challenging Geoff again to create innovative techniques to record them. They're having fun with it, too: John comes to rehearsal dressed in a tuxedo *a la* Agent 007, and Paul wears a trench coat. George Martin hires an orchestra to accompany the group on "Live and Let Die," and the group makes plans to use it in "The Art of Dying," "Mind Games," "Band on the Run" and even "Jet." The album is turning into a movie soundtrack on its own, and the Beatles' sound is more grandiose than ever.

15

26 December 1973

"Merry Christmas, Mal!" May Pang walks into Apple Records with her hands full of books, food and bags. She forces a smile, her eyes twinkling but tired.

"Happy Christmas, May!" I like May.

I help her with her load, taking it into an internal office. John walks in behind her, empty-handed save for a lone cigarette between his fingers. He mutters something to May, brushing up against her, pouring a drink and moving into the next room.

"Thanks, Mal. You're a real gentleman." I search her face, wondering if she were somehow comparing me to John. All I see is fatigue.

"Rough night?"

"Yeah, you could say that." She brushes her hair out of her face. "John didn't come in until about four thirty this morning. He was sick as a dog. I had to sober him up for today's meeting."

Again? I lift another bag onto the table. "Er, is John okay?"

"I don't know. Most of the time he's so sweet, but when he gets moody . . ." She hesitates. "I try to stay away from him. And it's getting harder to control him. It's like . . . I just can't get through to him anymore."

"He hasn't hurt you, has he?" I knew John's temper could get out of control.

"Oh no, no, nothing like that. He does scare me, though."

I wonder what is possessing John. And I try to think of ways to purge it, or at least delay it for a few months. This new album is keeping me alive, but is it slowly destroying John? I shake my head to rid myself of the thought. *It's just John being John.*

11 January 1974

We're still waiting for John. It's the third day in a row he's stood us up, and we're wasting valuable, expensive studio time playing cards instead of putting the finishing touches on this album. May says he's not feeling well, but the tabloids tell us otherwise. Still more antics, brushes with the law, drinking and carousing until daybreak. Everyone's patience is running thin.

12 January 1974

"'Imagine,' take 37."

I used to like this song.

John is about as bad as I've seen him—as white as the suit he wore at the Toronto concert. For the first fifteen takes, he couldn't play the correct chords on the piano because his hands were shaking so much. Paul volunteered to play it for him. Jesus, by this time I think I could pick it out, I am so familiar with the accompaniment. Now in the last twenty-two takes John has been stumbling through the song. His voice cracks in one place, and he forgets the words in another part. It's painful to watch, and painful to hear.

Things are looking good for the first minute of this take until John just stops, staring off into space. Geoff stops the tape and speaks over the intercom. "John, everything okay?"

No answer.

"John?"

After about five minutes, he snaps into reality. "Again!"

Take 38 only lasts about 20 seconds before John's voice starts quivering. He buries his face in his trembling hands, sobbing uncontrollably. I look over at May, who has stayed after bringing him in, at our request. But she is already out the door of the control room and down the stairs to see to John, who by this time is a tiny, solitary figure down on the floor of the massive studio.

May reaches out and embraces John's shoulders. As if by reflex, his grief turns into rage as he shoves her away, jumps off his stool and tosses it across the studio. May backs away as he grabs everything in sight – guitars, amplifiers, microphone stands – and slings them around, narrowly missing several people on the floor of the studio.

I run down the stairs to the studio floor and lunge at John, who is hitting and kicking the piano repeatedly. He tries to fight me, but I'm much bigger and stronger; I quickly restrain him. I drag him up the stairs to the control booth, not caring at this point whether I'm hurting him or not. He's screaming threats toward me, still reaching out and grabbing some invisible demon that has continued to taunt him for the past few months. I don't stop at the control room. I go out into the hall and take the stairs to the roof, pulling John by the collar. John's screams of rage turn to yelps of pain as his lower back hits each step.

We finally arrive at the roof. The cold air hits both of us like a knife, and it releases John from his spell. I sit down, out of breath but confident that he's had enough. And I wait. No one says a word for about half an hour, but I don't dare leave him by himself for fear of what he might do. John finally gets up, lights a cigarette, and goes to the edge of the roof. I move toward him, apprehensive, ready to pull him back, but he stops and calmly looks out over the London skyline. The lights are burning dimly through the fog that has settled in the late evening.

"Er, John, can I get ya anything? A coffee?" No answer. "You cooled off enough? Wanna go back down?" I knew the answer to that before I even asked it. *Stupid question, Mal.*

I move off to one side, letting him have his space, but close enough so that I can catch him if he tries to do something crazy.

Another twenty minutes pass in complete silence. I am freezing. The door to the roof opens, and Paul ambles over toward us. I've never been so relieved to see anyone. He walks over to John, who is still smoking and staring over the edge of the building. I don't think he's moved in the last fifteen minutes.

"You're not gonna jump, are you?" Paul asks.

"Now that would top off the night, wouldn't it?" he answers. I haven't taken a decent breath since I had been up here, and I exhale a sigh of relief. "How's everybody?"

"Well, you destroyed a couple thousand quid of equipment. But we can buy that back. Everybody's worried about you."

John shakes his head as if disapproving of someone else's antics. Paul asks for a cigarette. It's just as quiet as it was before Paul got there, but it's not as awkward somehow. They both welcome the silence; I wonder if they're communicating telepathically, these two marvellous songwriters. Paul lights the cigarette and takes a long drag. "Do you remember the last time we were up on a roof together?"

John smiles. The Beatles' famous rooftop concert atop 3 Savile Row at the end of the *Get Back* recording sessions, which attracted dozens of onlookers on the streets below until the police stopped it. It was freezing that day, too. "God, you were such a bastard then. I thought you were going to kill Yoko."

"Well, I did want her out of the studio. Dead? Never. I actually like her. Most of the time."

No one speaks for a while.

"She called today. She wants me back."

It's Paul's turn to be silent. He forces a smile.

"I'm goin' back to her, Paul." John sighs, throwing his lit cigarette into the cold air and watching it fall like a meteor to the ground. "I can't explain it. Even though I'm having the most fun in years, I'm outta control. I don't know who I am. I don't know who that was that threw all those instruments around." He exhales, smoke dissipating into the night air. "The thing is, I *need*

Yoko. She takes care of me. She keeps me in line, calms whatever demon is inside of me. I just can't live without her. At least, I know I can't go on like this."

I finally speak up. "Even if she controls you too much? Even if it could mean the end of all this?"

John refuses to look at us. "Yeah."

* * *

13 January 1974

I've just arrived at the car park at Abbey Road Studios. Paul is in the back seat of my car, humming a yet-to-be-named tune. As we pull in, we see John wheeling out of the lot, and I have to swerve to miss him. I stop and roll down my window to say hello, but he drives on by without stopping to check for traffic, seeming not to notice us. That's odd; usually John is up for a quip or two; hell, he's been known to back up traffic while talking to people from his car, and when the horns start blowing, flip them off while continuing to talk.

We walk into the studio, and Geoff is labelling another set of tapes. "You just missed John," he says. "He finally did a decent take of 'Imagine.' Took him two tries." He shakes his head. "When he's on, he's on."

"When is he coming back in?" Paul asks. "I had a few things I wanted to suggest for the song."

Geoff shifts nervously. "Um, he said he wasn't coming back. Had his luggage with him and a ticket to Japan. Said something about Yoko being on holiday there."

Paul stares at Geoff for a few seconds, trying to comprehend the meaning of those words. I wonder if Paul is going to get upset, if everything will come crashing down. But instead, Paul smiles and sighs. "Okay, then."

He gets up to walk into the studio. "Let's put one more track down, Geoff."

It's an acoustic ballad called "Venus and Mars." I never liked this song – the title track to one of his albums with his second group Wings, released while I was on a downward spiral in my first life. But again, as has happened before, I am hearing this song differently. Though Paul is smiling, there is sadness in his already drooping eyes. The lyrics refer to a good friend who loves astrology, and it dawns on me that it's another personal note to John, sent this time not in anger but friendship. In line with the mystical and fantastical theme for the album, he adds overdubs, including a synthesiser that lends a cosmic touch to the track. Three hours later, he pronounces it done. "I hope this time John will like my final addition."

* * *

22 February 1974

"Hello—Yoko?" I can't believe she has finally answered. The phone has been ringing for about five minutes.

"Yes, Mal. How are you?" she says in a cool voice.

"Fine, thanks." I hate small talk. I decide to cut to the chase. "Listen, the album's being released Tuesday, and we're holding a press briefing at the office the day it's released. John needs to be there around two o'clock, if that's okay." I hope it is. We have been trying to reach them for two days to check his schedule.

"I'm sorry, Mal, but John's taking some time off from the band so we can spend more time together. I'm sure the others will do a great job without him."

Her response stuns me; not sure what to say, I try another tactic. "Well, is John around? Can I speak to him for a second?"

"He's asleep right now."

Her brusque tone is irritating, and for once I grow impatient with her. "Well, wake him. This is important."

"I'm sorry, Mal. I'll tell him you called. Thank you for letting us know, and goodbye." She hangs up before I have a chance to respond.

He doesn't call back.

For immediate release

Contact: Derek Taylor

26 February 1974

BEATLES RELEASE NEW MAGIC WITH ABRACADABRA

Mystical and mysterious, bold and magical, the Beatles' fourteenth studio album, Abracadabra, takes fans to a new level, with twelve perfect songs that find the band at their creative peak.

Acclaimed producer George Martin is back at the helm, and the Beatles are operating at a supernatural level. With songs imagining utopian worlds, other planets and philosophical themes such as death, truth and the self, their songwriting has managed to dig deeper into their psyches while still capturing the public's fancy with memorable tunes.

"I believe in magic words. Words are powerful. People have always used them to summon spirits and gods," says guitarist George Harrison of the dark themes surrounding Abracadabra. "The supernatural has always held a certain mystique, and we're dabbling in that type of mystique with this album."

"I think we've said all that needs to be said about love, and some of us have tried political statements," says bassist Paul McCartney. "We're exploring new worlds here, but we also felt that our music needed a lift as well."

Martin has employed full orchestras to accompany the four on many of the tracks, lending to the larger-than-life sound on the album. At times maddeningly quick, at times soothing and affirming, Abracadabra has something for everyone wanting a magical musical experience.

ABRACADABRA TRACK LIST

Side 1:

1. "Imagine" (Lennon)—The band have transformed John Lennon's acoustic performance at the legendary Concert for Bangladesh into a warm piano piece with strings.

2. "Band on the Run" (McCartney)—a rocker that is classic McCartney—gorgeous melodies in a mini-suite, with numerous key changes and tempos.

3. "I'm the Greatest" (Starr/Lennon)—Drummer Ringo Starr tries to be egotistical in this lazy, rolling farce, and he fails marvellously.

4. "Jet" (McCartney)—The first hint of things to come. McCartney flirts with glam rock with this energetic number accented with horns.

5. "Mind Games" (Lennon)—A soaring, beautiful statement from Lennon, this song was originally demoed in 1969.

6. "The Art of Dying" (Harrison)—The last song on Side 1 is a sneak preview to the maddening pace of Side 2. Harrison unearthed this track after leaving it behind seven years ago.

Side 2

1. "Let Me Roll It" (McCartney)—McCartney trades licks with Lennon's guitar accompaniment in this throwback number.

2. "Let It Down" (Harrison)—The Beatles' second medley on an album (*Abbey Road* showcased the first), starts with this manic-depressive song, punctuated with horns, crashing cymbals and a choral accompaniment.

3. "Live and Let Die" (McCartney)—The pace quickens with the first contribution by the Beatles to a movie soundtrack.

4. "Nobody Loves You (When You're Down and Out)" (Lennon)—The last chords of "Live and Let Die" fades away as Lennon laments a time when all of us will be dead and forgotten. Horns return to affirm the melancholy mood.

5. "Venus and Mars" (McCartney)—McCartney takes the album to another dimension—literally—with a space-age ballad. Synthesizers—rarely used in a Beatles song—fade away with the music.

6. "Gimme Some Truth" (Lennon)—Lennon echoes his anger and frustration at the fake people and concepts in society, including U.S. President Richard Nixon. George plays a classic guitar solo that will go down as one of the best in Beatles history.

* * *

185

The New York Times

February 27, 1974

Abracadabra: Simply Magical

Thank God the Beatles have reunited. They have saved us from what has been turning out to be the worst year in the history of modern music.

In the midst of such mediocrity as "Seasons in the Sun," "Billy, Don't Be a Hero," and a rebirth of Paul Anka's career, the four legends from Liverpool have delivered *Abracadabra*, an album that makes their last masterpiece, *Everest*, seem like, well, a Paul Anka album.

The band never utters the magical incantation on the record, but its influence is felt throughout. Mystical themes are the common thread; John Lennon references karmic wheels and Druids in "Mind Games," while in their previous single "Imagine," Mr. Lennon tells us to pretend there is no religion. Paul McCartney references astrology in "Venus and Mars."

The Beatles want us to be concerned with the end of the world (or the end of life) and what happens after that. George Harrison's "The Art of Dying" searches for the meaning of life, admitting that there is a time when we all must go. Their contribution to the upcoming James Bond movie, "Live and Let Die," brings up death again. It becomes dire and just plain depressing when Mr. Lennon admits on "Nobody Loves You (When You're Down and Out) that everybody loves you when you're dead and buried.

Phil Spector is no longer behind the controls, with George Martin returning as producer. But from the sound, one could never tell. Mr. Martin has padded almost every song with orchestration, at times dictating a maddening, apocalyptic quality. Even when the Beatles aren't talking about death and the supernatural, it sounds like it. "Let it Down" is George Martin at his most Spector-like, with the song exhibiting two personalities: a soothing, almost hypnotic mood for the verses, and then exploding into a loud, brash chorus.

Leave it to Ringo Starr to throw a bit of levity into such a serious album. His Lennon-penned track, "I'm the Greatest," is a boorish, egotistical song that revisits Ringo's fictional character Billy Shears from "Sergeant Pepper's Lonely Hearts Club." The fact that the most humble, affable Beatle is at the vocals makes the message even more ironic. Mr. McCartney's mini suite of the album is "Band on the Run," an acoustic-based number that is instantly catchy.

The album's finale, "Gimme Some Truth," has Mr. Lennon singing with a biting sarcasm, his voice possessing an echo that sounds as if he's from beyond the grave. He puts all religion, psychotherapy and other panaceas aside, stating that he just wants the truth. After listening to *Abracadabra*, one could make the argument that the Beatles *are* the truth.

16

8 April 1974

I leave my house for the Apple offices early; I hope that I can get there as fast as I usually do.

But traffic is backed up for several blocks, and it is going nowhere fast. I slip off a side street and try to go around it, but everyone else seems to have the same idea. Frustrated, I finally pull into a car park about five blocks from the office and leave my car there, opting to walk ahead and see what the problem is.

I hear the crowd before I see them, and my pace quickens. As I turn the corner, I notice that police have barricaded the street on Savile Row, and hundreds of people have gathered in the road in front of the office building. They are holding signs, lots of signs that read "BEATLES = OCCULT" and "BURN THE BEATLES AT THE STAKE!" Savile Row is usually quiet but busy, and this scene is foreign and out of place. It's unnerving. Alarmed, I make my way through the crowd and enter the office.

The third floor, where the press office is located, is like a bunker during a war zone. Dozens of coffee cups have been orphaned on all the desks, phones are ringing off the hook, and people are everywhere, all talking at once. Neil Aspinall and Paul are standing at the door of Derek Taylor's office; I head that way.

"What's going on, Derek?" I ask.

He stares at me, dumbfounded. "What planet have you been on? Have you not read the papers?" He thrusts his copy into my hands.

The Daily Mail

8 April 1974

CONTROVERSY SURROUNDS NEW BEATLES ALBUM
Groups Claim Occult Connections in Songs

Religious groups are calling for a boycott of the Beatles' new album *Abracadabra*, citing its numerous references to what they say is the occult and Satan worship.

"Several years ago, John Lennon told us that he was more popular than Jesus, and now his band is trying to kill Christianity," said American fundamentalist leader F. James Prescott. "Satan is among us and living in the songs of the Beatles."

Besides the title, the new album, released Feb. 27, contains some references to magic and death. Guitarist George Harrison seemed to confirm this when, in a press release issued by Apple Records, he said, "I believe in magic words. Words are powerful. People have always used them to summon spirits and gods. The supernatural has always held a certain mystique, and we're dabbling in that mystique with this album."

Harrison's track "The Art of Dying" refers to reincarnation, and a John Lennon-penned tune, "Mind

Games," refers to the Druids, an ancient order of Celtic priests and magicians. The penultimate track, "Venus and Mars," includes references to astrology.

Prescott, however, claimed that backward messages in "The Art of Dying" contain medieval incantations. The cover, which features the four members' heads floating on a black background, is a reference to black magic, he said.

Controversy has always trailed the Beatles—from Lennon's proclamation that the Beatles were bigger than Jesus Christ to the claim that their song "Helter Skelter" was the basis of Charles Manson's murderous rampage. With *Abracadabra*, the controversy appears to have continued.

The controversy spread quickly in America following the death of a 15-year-old American teen. The young man committed suicide Friday, and the new Beatles album was playing on his turntable when a friend found his body.

Religious groups across America, who had burned Beatles records after Lennon's comment about the Beatles and Jesus, are building bonfires again this week, claiming that the album is an affirmation of the occult.

Apple spokesmen could not be reached for comment.

* * *

"Holy shit," I say mostly to myself. I had no idea that this would happen. "What is wrong with these people? It's a fucking album."

"There will be no more talk like that around here," says Derek. "We're living for Jesus now." He turns to Paul. "Okay, how's this?" He reads from a sheet of paper just given to him. " 'There are no hidden messages on *Abracadabra*. We have summoned no spirits, ghouls, or demons, no ghosts of Jim Morrison or Paul McCartney, nor any otherworldly entities. There are no backward messages and very few forward messages. We are sorry to disappoint all of you with vivid imaginations. All we do is play music.' "

"Great," Paul says. "Start calling the media. Let's hope we can nip this thing in the bud."

"And if it gets out of control, you may sell even more records," Derek adds.

* * *

12 November 1974

I am sitting up in bed, feet on the floor and head in my hands, covered in sweat. Beside me, Mimi lightly snores away, oblivious to my exasperation. The house is quiet, but I can hear my own heart beating in my chest and my head. My chest is heaving up and down, and I gasp for air as if I had just run for my life.

The dreams have started again—the third time this month. Sometimes the setting is different—my boyhood home in Liverpool, the Apple offices—but the ending is always the same: G Taylor staring down the barrel of a gun, smiling and saying, "Time's up, Mal." The gun goes off, echoing in my ears, and I lie awake for the rest of the night, wondering what is going on.

The dreams last occurred when the Beatles broke up after

Everest. Now that John has left the Beatles again, the dreams have returned and, I'm wondering if there's a connection, if I'm headed down that path of destruction once again, if my survival is indeed dependent on the Beatles' survival.

Mimi stirs and awakens. "Another bad dream?"

"Yeah. Must be what I'm eating before bed."

She sits up and massages my shoulders. "You're stressed, love. You need to go out and find some work. The money's not coming in anymore, you know." She sniffs a few times. "What's that smell? Mal, is something on fire?"

I haven't noticed, but as I breathe the air in, the smell is unmistakable.

Gunpowder.

I promise Mimi to search the house for any signs of fire, but my legs are shaking. The dreams are becoming more real, and short from staying up all night, I don't know what to do about them. I return to bed, proclaim the house fire-free, but my heart is still pounding. I try telling myself to take it one day at a time. But one day without the Beatles is tough. I don't know how I will survive a year or even a month at this rate.

* * *

18 January 1975

I have no idea what I'm doing.

I'm poised at a control board, pushing buttons and sliding levers, listening to how they change the music I hear in the headphones. The sound is uneven; at times, the drums are overpowering the entire song; at other times the instruments and voices are at the same level, creating a cacophony that bears no resemblance to music. No matter what control I manipulate, no matter what dial I turn, it doesn't get any better. Surely, like a monkey with a typewriter eventually typing a Shakespearean play, I can hit upon the correct combination of reverb, compression, equalization and delay to come up with something listenable.

It's the second stab I've taken at the solo album by the Who's drummer Keith Moon—I also tried in my other life—but it sounds just as bad as it did before. This time, when Ringo asked me if I could produce the album, I first said no, afraid of repeating the same mistakes again. The mixes I created for Keith in my first life were so bad that the record company declared them to be unlistenable; I was removed from the project and the songs were re-recorded with another producer, who basically had to start from scratch. That was the beginning of the end for me, and the downward spiral that sent me to that flat in Los Angeles.

However, I had learned a lot over the past few years, and when it came to the Beatles at least, things could be changed from the first go 'round, and my life seemed to be better. Surely over the last few years, with *Everest* and *Abracadabra,* something new had leaked into my head. Some of Geoff Emerick's master production techniques must have made an impression on me.

I also had nothing better to do. No Beatles meant a lot of spare time for me. I needed the work to help pay the bills and fill the hours during the day. I had more time to spend with Mimi and the kids now, and that was new to me. I was finding that I was not a very good father. The days with them would creep by; I just didn't know what to do with the kids. Producing seemed much easier than parenting.

"Hey Mal, that sounds a little—well, I dunno what's wrong here," Keith says. "Can you try taking my drumming back a notch or maybe five?"

I move the lever that I think is the percussion, but all the Hammond organ disappears. I mumble a few oaths under my breath, bring the organ back up, and finally find the percussion. It sounds better.

Despite the new techniques that I have learned—and despite new, improved equipment—there is no difference in the result. It still sounds awful. I look over helplessly at Keith, who smiles almost out of pity. I remember being fired from the project after record executives heard the first initial mixes. I don't want that humiliation again. Leaving the tape playing, I quietly take the headphones off and place them on the soundboard.

"Look Keith, why don't we get one of EMI's engineers to take a listen? I think they may have some ideas." Keith nods his head in affirmation, and I quit before I'm fired again.

I walk outside to the fire escape – the place where we usually go to cool off and be alone. But as I open the door, I see that someone has beaten me to it. Paul is there, leaning over the railing with a cigarette in his hand. He turns to look at me.

"Bugger off Mal!" he says instinctively. But I see it; his eyes are red and swollen, and inside the anger is pure sorrow. I shut the door not so much out of duty but embarrassment. *What happened?*

As I go back into Abbey Road Studios, I hear some murmurs coming from a break room down the hall. Walking by, I peer into the room; it's George Martin and Linda. I stop on the other side of the entrance.

". . . should have known that it's not up to his standards, and that's why the critics killed it. That's what I told him, Linda, but it's up to you to help us with those judgments. You can't keep being his cheerleader," Martin says.

"I'm always amazed at what he does, George," Linda replies. "Everything he writes isn't "Hey Jude," but I understand what he's trying to say in these songs. They connect with me."

"That's fine if he gives them to you as a Christmas present, but some of these songs just don't belong on a record. None of these would have made it on a Beatles record."

"You have no right to say that."

"Oh, I do, Linda. I've been there for almost every album. Paul is getting lazy, and I never thought I'd say this—because I really think he's a genius—but his laziness has made him normal."

"You've crushed him, George."

"No, I think the critics crushed him. I just validated it."

I walk away and find the latest edition of *Melody Maker.* The review of his latest record, called *London Town,* is one of the harshest, meanest pieces I've ever read.

I feel pity for Paul. And that's a first.

* * *

17 June 1975

Neil Aspinall downs another pint of beer and slams the glass down on the table.

"That's five, Mal, you're one behind now," he says, motioning the waitress over for a refill. "You're gettin' soft. Hell, I remember you putting away a good baker's dozen in the old days and not even battin' an eye." He looks over my large frame and grunts. "Course, it's got a lot of places to travel in that body."

I smile at Neil, who is already tipsy and heading straight for stiff drunk. It's the first time he and I have gotten together for a drink in about a year. Given all the attention that we both gave the four, I often forgot my relationship with Neil, but he and I have been through it all since the early days. We were together all the time, once even rooming together when Mimi didn't want to move to London.

"So how is Apple?" I ask, hoping to hear some word of the band members. Neil is still entrenched in the record company as CEO, keeping the ghosts of the Beatles alive despite the hiatus. Licensing, solo Beatle albums—there is still a lot to do.

"Blah!" He makes a face. "I mean, it's okay. Mostly corporate stuff, meetings, contracts. But I do miss being on the road, spending late nights setting up things for the mates."

"Do you see them much?"

"Oh yeah. But never all together. Paul mostly. He comes in to do a lot of recording, and he's more interested in the business side of things. I see a lot of Yoko, but John not so much."

The waitress returns with pint number six, and Neil begins to dispose of it. "How about you?" he says in between gulps.

"No, I haven't seen any of 'em. I used to go out with Ringo every so often, but he's in the States quite a bit now. There's just not a lot for me to do."

"You should ring them up. They get so wrapped up in themselves, they forget about everyone else. Spend a few days with George. Go fly out to L.A. with Ringo. Have some fun!"

"What you forget, Neil, is that they only want me around when they need something. If they're wrapped up in themselves, I'm the last person they want to see."

"Nah, they just need to be reminded of you."

I grunt. "Great. I need to remind the Beatles that I exist," I say, half to myself. Neil doesn't hear me and instead looks around at some of the ladies who are congregating at the bar.

Thinking of not having the four around dampens my mood, and an evening of small talk grows into an awkward silence. I think Neil senses this; maybe he regrets having said anything about the Four, or maybe he feels sorry for me. He guzzles down number six and brings the evening to an end. "Pussy," he growls, laying some bills down on the table. "I beat you six to four. Winners pay." He gets up and sways slightly, his eyes starting to roll back into his head. "Whoa, let's go, Mal, I think you're gonna have to make sure I get home."

As we head out into the late evening, I sense some uneasiness. We're in a dangerous section of town—vagrants, prostitutes, drug deals taking place in the open. It's times like these when I miss the limo waiting outside. I wait for a cab as Neil leans on me, his lips becoming looser and his sentences becoming more incoherent.

"Look at ya, Mal," Neil says, his eyes trying to focus on me. "Helping another drunk out. You've done this for the Fab Four so many times. Now yer doin' it for the Fifth Beatle! Ha ha!" He frowns. "Or are *you* the Fifth one? Or was Brian? Do you mind, Mal, if I'm the Fifth Beatle?"

I smile. "Not at all, Neil."

Neil slaps my back. "Good ol' Mal. Always there. Don't know why, but you're always there."

The streets of this part of London resemble some post-apocalyptic war zone or a third-world country. Newspapers and beer bottles litter the streets; the stench of urine and beer hangs in the air. Nearby a wino lies in a semi-conscious state, his head lolling from side to side. I imagine that he is one of the casualties of whatever war hit this neighbourhood. How did he get there? How close am I to joining him? Hell, if I didn't like Neil so much I would have parked him right alongside the man.

Beyond the wino is a man who looks even worse. Tall, gangly, with pustules all over his face, he looks like the walking dead. A placard hanging over his body reads "REV 2:10." He is spewing vitriolic speech with such fervour that sweat beads on his brow. He looks familiar, but I can't place him.

"Jesus will separate the wheat from the chaff. On Judgment Day, he will welcome the saved with open arms, and to the unbelievers, he will cast into the fires of an eternal hell!" Spittle collects in the corners of his mouth as he looks around for reactions.

"Shut up," says a college-aged young man, hitting the street preacher on the arm as he walks by with a group of friends.

The street preacher begins following the student. "They that hate you shall be clothed with shame, and the dwelling place of the wicked shall come to naught!" The student continues walking away, throwing his middle finger up in the air, and the preacher turns on a dime and continues his rant to no one in particular. I try to ignore him—*no eye contact!*—but he's zeroed in on me.

Inches away from me, he stops. I haven't met too many people taller than I, but he is almost a head taller. I pretend not to notice him, but I can feel his eyes piercing my head. I've always been spooked by unbalanced people—never predictable, potentially dangerous. Do I run? Walk away? Like a fool, I stand there and do nothing.

"You. You're running out of time," he whispers, his face bending over and almost touching mine.

I now remember. The street preacher. He was walking down the sidewalk and yelling at me after John and Yoko's protest, when I was sweeping shite off the streets.

His breath is stale, almost toxic, and I struggle to look away, holding my breath. "I know who you are," he continues. "You think this is real? You think you're going to just live your life like this, changing things, without any consequences? Forget it, mate."

What is he talking about? I begin to sweat as well.

A taxi finally appears, and I run it down, dragging Neil along with me. The voice follows me. "'But as for the cowardly, the faithless, the detestable, as for murderers, the sexually immoral, sorcerers, idolaters, and all liars, their portion will be in the lake that burns with fire and sulphur, which is the second death.' A *second death!* It will find you!"

I shove Neil into the taxi, dive in and slam the door. My heart pounds as the preacher's words echo in my head. *A second death. It will find me.*

* * *

1 November 1975

"Welcome, Mal!" John says as he opens the door to his Tittenhurst mansion. He is much thinner, the thinnest I've seen him since his days on heroin. His hair is pulled back into a ponytail, and while I've seen him with long hair before, the ponytail somehow emasculates him. It doesn't help that he is wearing a kimono—*a kimono!* He resembles a geisha more than a rock star.

On his shoulder is his son, Sean Ono Lennon, wailing his tiny lungs out. Just last month, after Yoko gave birth to Sean, John announced his departure from the Beatles for a second time. They had unofficially split up when John flew to Japan to reunite with Yoko, but to the public it was only a hiatus from recording. At least this split was amicable and somewhat necessary. When Sean was born, Neil and I assembled a basket of presents from the other members of the Apple staff, and the other three telephoned their congratulations to John.

John invites me into his home, which looks quite different now; baby cots, mobiles, toys and diapers are strewn everywhere. The foyer looks like a nursery. John, however, is oblivious to all this and is excited to show off his son. "Being a dad is fantastic,

Mal. I wasn't around when Julian was born, so I want to spend every second I can with Sean. I want to see him grow, laugh, speak and poop. There just isn't any room for music," he says.

Sean's crying goes up a few decibels. John turns around and yells to no one in particular. "Yoko? Mal's here. Can you take Sean?"

Yoko yells back. "I'm on the phone, John."

John's face darkens, then fades into embarrassment. He smiles. "Oops . . . Anyway. I might pick the guitar up again someday, but right now, I'm content staying at home, baking bread, heating baby bottles, and changing nappies."

This is weird. "What does Yoko do while you're playing house daddy?"

"Oh, she's in charge of the finances, making our millions." He goes over to the stove, where a bottle of milk is heating in some water. He takes it and shakes a few drops on his wrist. "Ow! Christ! Too hot." Sean continues to scream, but John is oblivious and just talks over the shrieks. "You know, Mal, we did a piss-poor job of dealing with money. Yoko is building our wealth back up. She's great at it."

Oriental music is playing on the stereo. Several albums of Eastern origin lie around the turntable; there is not a Rolling Stones album or Beatles recording to be found.

"It's called *Warabe uta*. Children's music. Most Western people find it tuneless and maddening."

No kidding.

He chuckles as if reading my mind. "It's far out—like some wild acid trip. Even more bizarre than George's Indian cackling, if you ask me. But if you open your mind and embrace the sentiment—not so much the notes but the mood—it opens your mind even more. Sean likes it, don't you, Sean?" Sean pays no attention and continues to scream, his face turning red.

I ask him if he's seen anyone from the band lately, and he shakes his head. "Just a few phone calls, but I think everyone knows to stay away. Present company excepted, of course, Mal," he winks. I blush, feeling as if I've committed some faux pas. But John is oblivious, running back over to the kitchen to take some bread out of the oven. There are at least a dozen other loaves on the counter, and the rubbish can is loaded with discarded loaves and empty boxes of flour. "You gotta try this loaf, Mal. I made it with Parmesan cheese and a little bit of rosemary." He beams with pride as I sample a steaming slice, and it is good. Christ! I'm eating Parmesan bread baked by John Lennon.

John is chatty, about as cordial as I've ever seen him, but it's like talking to a stranger. After a few more minutes, I say my goodbyes, relaying all the congratulatory messages from the gang at the office. I leave with the taste of rosemary on my tongue, wondering what just happened. Who was that man in the kimono? And where is John Lennon?

* * *

5 January 1976

At first, I didn't think about it. Or, perhaps I tried not to think about it.

But as January 5, 1976 approached, I remembered its significance. I wondered if my life had an expiration date no matter how I managed to play it out. Granted, I had no divorce papers from Mimi yet, and I was not living in Los Angeles. But things have not gone well for me. Since 1963, I have never gone more than 18 months without being around all four Beatles together. And it's now been about 18 months.

I have managed to keep an unsteady trickle of income between EMI and Apple. I think both companies feel an obligation to keep me on as a "special assistant," but my work is limited to odd jobs and errands. I truly thought I was having a second chance, but as that awful day approaches, I wonder what has really changed for me. Will life end for me again? Can I get over that hump, and if I do, will I ever have to worry about that old life again?

Midnight comes. I kiss my kids, who are sound asleep, tell Mimi I am going to be at a recording session, and check into a cheap inn. I have nothing with me except for a few sandwiches and drinks. I put a "Do Not Disturb" sign on the door and lock it. I get in bed, turn on the telly, and wait for the Second Death to arrive.

I watch an old Thomas Cooper flick. I have no idea what it's about. At around three a.m. I fall asleep. I awaken around eight as the couple next door begin their day with showers, telly, and idle chatter about what they have planned to do. They are tourists, and I envy their ability to leave their room and walk about London unafraid. But maybe Death is also waiting for them around the corner, coming in an IRA terrorist attack, in front of a streetcar or in a mugging. At least they don't have to wait knowingly for Him.

I turn on the small clock radio on the nightstand, tuning it to a local rock station, and begin to play games with each song that comes on. Had I met the artist before? When did I hear the song for the first time? It occupies my time for about an hour, but I keep turning back to the task at hand: waiting for Death.

My mind goes through possible scenarios as to how I might perish in this room: heart attack, hotel fire, food poisoning from my sandwich. A bite from a flea that carried bubonic plague. A meteor. I think about taking a sleeping pill, but I am afraid that I might overdose, or vomit in my sleep like Jimi Hendrix and die. Even as I nod off, I jump, afraid that my eyes are closing for the last time and I won't awaken.

The stereo plays a song that's a little too familiar, a song from Paul's recent solo album *London Town*, and judging from the reviews, one of the better songs. It's a syrupy love ballad, but one that pulls at my heartstrings. The music is ingenious, and I am reminded of how talented those four blokes are. How *does* Paul find these melodies that no one else finds? Why do they affect us so? I'm not very good at musical terms, but sometimes I hear a particular chord change or a melody, and part of me just aches. It's a feeling I never want to stop, a feeling of such deep emotion and profound depth, it's as if I have already died and am hearing the music of the spheres. What else does Paul have up his sleeve that I will never hear?

This song is my requiem.

I turn off the stereo and lie back on the bed. The alarm clock ticks, sounding slower than it usually does, each second lingering as long as possible before giving way to the next one. *How do people sleep with that clock ticking away?*

Who makes clocks? Why do we have to wind them? There was an alarm clock in "A Day in the Life." I rang it. I made that alarm clock ring. But does anyone outside of me and Geoff know that? Where is that alarm clock now? I could sell it at Sotheby's and bring a few hundred quid, I bet.

I check the time again. 6:37 p.m.

Why is Death coming so slowly? I am convinced that it's coming, but it remains so far away. I want to scream. I kick off the covers, drenched in sweat, turn my pillow over, and wait some more. I hear a siren in the distance, and I wonder if it's G Taylor coming for me again, guns blazing. The siren passes, and I breathe a little easier. Maybe it's going for the couple who was next door.

The shadows begin to fall dimly against the dark walls. One of them is Death, and I wait for him to slink across the wall and swallow me. I have always heard that Death comes quickly, that it will be like sleeping, and I so want to sleep. I think about John's old song, "I'm So Tired."

I might soon cease to exist.

This isn't fair! There is so much that I wanted to do: walk on the piers in Liverpool again, have a chocolate ice cream cone, watch a spider spin a web, smoke a nice cigar, experience a storm rolling in on a spring evening, its cold wind making me shiver down to the bone. A cold wind. What was that poem I learned in grade school? Mrs. Firth's class. I sat behind Sally Robbins, blonde hair, pigtails . . .

Ah yes. "The north wind doth blow, and we shall have snow, and what will poor robin do then? . . .

"Poor thing. Poor, poor thing. Poor . . ."

I bolt upright, confused. Death feels so peaceful. I look at the clock.

2:35 a.m. The sixth of January, 1976.

I made it.

I escaped. I am now living longer than I ever have before. And I will never think about that day in Los Angeles again.

17

27 April 1977
Liverpool

The scene is idyllic: a perfect Saturday morning, a slight nip in the air as winter tries to hang on to the oncoming rush of spring. The sun is attempting to burn through the last bit of fog, but the air isn't heavy, just mild enough to cool the sweat from my son's brow as he runs down the football field. His hair is long—circa John in 1966, a little more than moptop—and it flies wildly as he tries to catch up with the ball before it rolls out of bounds.

I am on the sidelines cheering him on, Mimi by my side. It's as close as I have come to that perfect family moment; hell, I can't even remember ever doing something like this. I've never noticed the way Thomas takes a stutter skip before launching into a run, or how he runs his fingers over the top of his head.

I shudder to think how much I've missed, but in spite of the picturesque setting, something's wrong.

I know what it is, and try to erase it from my mind by cheering as Thomas dives to save the ball from going out of bounds. But my mind fades from the field. Is Paul working on another album? I recently read that Ringo was headed to America to star in his own talk show. I haven't heard a thing from John or George.

Life is now regular and predictable. I have quietly retired from the music business and moved back to Liverpool with Mimi and the kids, taking back my old job at the Post Office. This is the way life should have been if I hadn't gone to the Cavern Club that day.

I wonder if the Four have even noticed that I'm gone. They never called anymore. Here, I'm just going through the motions, cheering instinctively at a good move on the field, feigning interest in dinner conversation, kissing my wife hello and goodbye every day without any emotion.

"Mal. Mal!"

I snap out of my daze. Mimi is calling me.

"I'm sorry, luv, did you want something?"

"Susan wants you."

I turn my head, and my daughter Susan is pulling impatiently on my jacket.

"Dad, Can I have some money for a cool drink?"

"Sure, luv," I say absently, pulling a coin from my pocket. I look over at Mimi after I hand Susan the money, and she is looking at me disapprovingly.

"Wha? What'd I do?"

"That's the second drink she's had today, and the third time you've given her money."

Really? I shrug. "She's a crafty one, that Susan."

"Mal, you can't just hand out money like that. This isn't the Beatles. This is real life. We have a budget, and you need to help us stick to that."

"Er, sorry, Mimi. I'll remember." We've had this discussion a few times. The Beatles never worried about money, even when they were broke. I never worried, either, and I never had any. It was good to feel as if you did, though. Being reminded of it is disheartening, even annoying.

Thomas wins the ball from a member of the opposing team and starts dribbling. I applaud my son for his great tackle and his convenient distraction.

* * *

13 January 1978

There it is. Abbey Road Studios.

I volunteered to courier some forms down to the Central Post Office in London just so I could go by the studio and Apple Office. It was a four-hour drive, but now that I'm here, it all seems worthwhile. This is the second time this month I've driven down; the first time I actually called in sick, told Mimi I was going in to work, and drove down without anyone's knowledge. I'm glad I'm on the clock this time.

My head is filled with possibilities—seeing Geoff or George Martin, hoping my presence will remind them of some small production job they need to be done. I wonder whether Paul will be here by chance, recording a new album. If he is, I can run a few errands for him. This could turn into a multi-day engagement.

I enter the lobby, and the receptionist is new; she looks up at me, doesn't recognize me, and instantly puts on her bored expression. "Yes, may I help you." Just like that. Not even a question.

"Ah, yes, you see, er, I'm Mal Evans and um, I used to work here—well, I didn't work here, but I worked for the Beatles . . ." She's filing her nails, she's heard this line dozens of times. ". . . and I was wondering if George Martin or Geoff Emerick or Paul—"

"I'm sorry, they're in a meeting. I'll tell them you dropped by." The phone rings, and she moves on to other business.

I wait out the phone call; it turns out to be a friend or boyfriend, and her demeanour turns from bored to playful. She laughs, half whispering into the phone while half glaring at me as if I were disturbing her. She finally hangs up, and her expression turns back to the stone face that greeted me.

"Is there anything else I can help you with. If not, good day."

I try to counter with some quick retort or some bit of trivia that only an insider would know, but I am aware that her dismissal is a rehearsed line, and there is nothing I can do. I slump and turn toward the door.

* * *

17 May 1978

"Ringo! How's life in America?"

I have spent several hours trying to get through to him; his American handlers had never heard of me, and I left message after message, complete with lengthy explanations about my relationship with Ringo. I do not look forward to the time when Mimi gets the telephone bill.

"Always a blast, Mal. The country that never sleeps, you know? Peace and love, peace and love."

Ringo is finally finding some level of success. His variety show is quietly picking up steam in the ratings, and the critics are likening him to a cross between Dick Cavett and Sonny Bono.

"Yeah, Ringo. I try to catch your show on repeats over here. You're doing great!"

I hear a commotion in the background as Ringo talks with someone else. "Yeah, yeah, in a minute, baby. . . What's that Mal? Say, did I ask for something? What's the phone call for?"

I seize the moment. "Well, I was gettin' worried about you being over there by yourself with all those Yanks trying to meet your needs."

Ringo shouts away from the phone. "Now cut that out! I'm on an important business matter of—er—enormous importance." *He's drunk.* "Who is this, anyway?" I realise he's now talking to me.

"It's Mal, Ringo."

"Mal! Howareyoumate don'teverchange!"

I am getting impatient and exasperated. "Ringo. Do you need me out there?"

"Nah, Mal. Doing great. I know you're busy. You keep doin' what yer doin'. Great job. Peace and love, don't ever change."

Click.

That leaves John. I've already tried George and Paul and gotten nothing from them. George needs nothing now—he is deep into the Hare Krishnas, having sold off most of his possessions except for Friar Park, which is Krishna Central, and I am no help there. Paul has developed an army of assistants, seeing to everything from equipment to babysitting, and while he is kind, he doesn't need me either.

I ring up John, determined to hang up if Yoko answers. But to my surprise, he answers. I go through the same charade, small talk, awkward transition, trying not to sound too eager—you see, I'm more concerned about *their* well-being, you know—only trying to help them out. Once again, I brace for the same answer.

"Well, I'm about to go to Greece on holiday—need a little time to meself. I get that way, you know, and Yoko's sending me away before I blow my top again." Great. But then it happens. "But what the hell. It'll be nice to have some company and talk with someone who doesn't piss in their pants. Meet me at the airport Monday morning at eight o'clock sharp."

* * *

22 September 1978
Patmos, Greece

It should be a pleasant holiday—perfect weather, a posh rental on a private beach. I had told Mimi that John "needed me," asked the Post Office for a week's holiday, and boarded the plane with John. Now, only twenty-four hours into the holiday, I am counting down the hours until we leave. John spends his day watching the telly, and occasionally reads a book or the morning paper. I try to make my way into town, running errands and sightseeing to pass the time. It's not what I expected, but it's life with a Beatle. I guess in that sense, I am happier.

This morning is more of the same. I make breakfast—hash browns and fruit—and fetch the *Athens News*, the leading English language newspaper in Greece. Usually John recounts the most amusing news over breakfast, but this morning he is fully engrossed with the entertainment section.

"What is it, John? Boring news day?" I ask.

John grunts. I leave him be.

I wash a few dishes, then hear him mutter under his breath.

"What's wrong?"

John continues to stare at the newspaper. "It's Paul. He has a new album. There's a review here in the paper."

Paul? A new album? I used to know these things. "Oh, wonderful . . . Er, did they like it?"

He stares at the paper a bit longer, his brow furrowing. "Yeah, you could say that."

"Good for him . . . Does that bother you?"

"Yeah. Yeah, it does." He puts down the paper. "I never minded it before, but . . ." He jumps up, looks at me and says, "C'mon Mal, let's go record shopping."

McCartney Finally Delivers with *'Silly Love Songs'*

Athens News

21 September 1978

In what has been up until now an extremely ordinary and almost mediocre solo career, Paul McCartney feels some pressure to live up to the ghosts of music past. Most songs have been tuneful if anything, but they also lack any substance or forethought.

About three years have passed since McCartney's last solo record, the vapid *London Town*. His recordings seemed to be his attempt to get little jingles out of his head as quickly as possible; as a result, they sounded half-finished and half-planned.

Not so with *Silly Love Songs*. The title of the album might suggest that it's more of the same McCartney modus operandi, but it's much more. Although the songs are still as maddeningly catchy as ever, McCartney has taken some time to let the ideas incubate, and the result is a more sophisticated, deeper effort.

The title cut is his response to the criticism that his music is shallow, and while it is fluff, it's good fluff, and the single should go straight to the top of the charts.

There are other future hits waiting to emerge. McCartney finally embraces disco with "Goodnight Tonight," with such an infectious chorus set to an intricate bass line. "Comin' Up" is an energetic, horn-filled track that finds McCartney at his funkiest. Who says the cute Beatle has no soul?

While McCartney still focuses more on the music than the lyrics, it's his forte. But what is welcoming is that he seems to have come to terms with this ability to create memorable melodies.

If you do something well, why not showcase it? John Lennon gave us things to think about, but Paul McCartney gives us things to sing about. And considering that the other three Beatles are silent these days, it's all we have, and we welcome it.

* * *

The trip into Skala, the capital, takes only about 10 minutes. I've done it many times over the past week, but this is the first time with John. He doesn't say much on the ride, occasionally pointing out interesting landmarks or oddities.

The Beatles have a history with Greek islands. Back in 1967 they flirted with the idea of buying a set of islands so they could create their own utopia, isolated from most of the Western world. We even went so far as touring a few islands, but the boys were too stoned to pay much attention. After a few days, we went back to England without an island, and the subject never came up again. John chose this island for his holiday not because of its beauty, but because it was in the middle of nowhere.

Patmos is no doubt idyllic – a tiny island located in the Aegean Sea. Bright blue water is always in sight, and the drive is lined with olive trees. The city itself is composed of small, faceless stone buildings that all look identical. I have no idea where a record store is, so I ask the first person I see. He points me around the corner to an establishment that looks like a pawn shop, selling everything from antiques to food and bicycles.

The manager of the store looks up and sees tourists, and goes back to sorting new merchandise. Delighted by the apparent anonymity, John asks him where the records are, and the manager points to his left without saying anything. I wasn't expecting much, but the record section consists of a stack of about 40 discs. John doesn't care, though, and starts thumbing through them, pulling out every other one for his own collection.

John stops. "Aha! Who is this?"

I see a copy of *Rubber Soul* in his hands. He shrugs, and adds it to the collection. "I see this as paying meself." He goes to a second stack, and there are a few new LPs here – the *Grease* soundtrack ("Look! *Grease* in Greece!" John laughs), albums by Pere Ubu and Elvis Costello, and some by the Greek equivalent of Cliff Richard. But then, against astronomical odds, there it is: *Silly Love Songs.*

"Yes! We have succeeded in our mission, Mal! My nemesis, Mr. McCartney!" He carries his load of albums over to the sales counter, goes back and adds a beat-up acoustic guitar, a few dime store novels, a fisherman's hat and some sunglasses to the pile. The clerk rings up the purchases, which total 16,000 drachmas—about £38 in British money, and he's shocked by the total.

"Well, sir, I do believe this is your lucky day," John says to the clerk as I pull out some cash for the albums. Something about his voice makes the sales clerk look a little harder at John's face, and then the recognition hits him. "You're . . . You're . . ."

"Yes, it's me, Englebert Humperdinck." He pulls out the *Rubber Soul* album, takes a pen and signs it. "Here's a little thank-you for your trouble," he says, handing the LP to the manager, and takes his purchases out the door. I turn to the sales clerk and put my finger to my lips as he looks out the door, dumbfounded.

* * *

"Listen to that bass line, Mal! Fuckin' genius!"

John is almost raving mad at this point. He is on his third listen through *Silly Love Songs*, and each time he's found something new about it. A few songs he smirks at, but even those are growing on him. I sense some jealousy going on, but his comments change from critical to laudatory.

Hearing the record is a treat for me as well; until now, most of what I have heard from the four has been retreads—things that I had heard the first time around. But these songs—"Silly Love Songs," "Goodnight Tonight," "Coming Up"—are all new to me, and I hear Paul as I have never heard him before. This is what I've been waiting for.

"See how he goes from a low note immediately to a high note? That's a whole octave," John says as Paul sings "Agaaaiin" in "Silly Love Songs." "Only he can get away with that! I always stay on the same note. I don't know how he finds that melody." I find it fascinating; he's 1,000 miles away, but Paul is getting to him. I can see the competitiveness emerging again.

He plays the record all afternoon. Around four o'clock, he summons me. "Go into town again, Mal. Paul's winning, and I don't like that. I need me some recording equipment." I can tell he's not angry; instead, the friendly rivalry between them that they used to spur each other toward greatness is back.

I ride into Skala again and go back to the general store. The manager is thrilled to see me this time, and helps me find a beat-up reel-to-reel recorder, an amplifier and microphone, and some threadbare cables. I pay for the items, put them in the boot of my car, and travel back to the villa, wondering what songs have been hibernating in John Winston Ono Lennon's head.

* * *

30 September 1978

John has been playing guitar all week, trying out new melodies, jotting down words on paper. It's as if he has turned on a faucet, and his brain is releasing pent-up songs that are almost finished products when they emerge.

While I'm fixing the screen door, John calls me into one of the bedrooms. He is moving the furniture to one side of the room, and all the sound equipment is strewn across the bed along with a tangled pile of cords.

"I need your help, Mal. You gotta play Geoff Emerick for me. Can you help me make this room into a studio?"

He doesn't need to ask me twice. We begin to work, and I'm pulling out all the tricks I've learned from Geoff Emerick and Phil Spector: sealing the windows and doors with tape and towels, hanging quilts on the walls to dampen sounds, taping the mike to a broom and leaning it against the bed, close to where John's guitar will be. After a while, John pronounces it good enough, and we begin recording.

I notice a change in his music, a certain maturity that I haven't encountered from him—none of the raw, naked truth from his solo album, none of the sweet, sappy tunes from *Everest,* and no political statements. It's all about love, life, and contentment. There is a lullaby to his son called "Beautiful Boy," a love song to Yoko called "Woman," and a simple ballad about time called "Watching the Wheels." He ends with another beautiful song, "Grow Old with Me," that brings a lump to my throat. Within two hours he has six demos recorded. "There are a few more that I still need to flesh out, but those are the good ones," he says.

"Wow—you wrote all those in the last few days?"

John grins. "Nah, these have been floating around in me head for the last few years. I even messed around with a portable tape player once back home but didn't finish them. But these are good. Very good."

* * *

Later that evening, I overhear John making a phone call in the kitchen. I know whom he's calling, but I eavesdrop anyway.

"Hello, Paul. I see you're doin' all right without me," he says. ". . .Yeah, I'm good. I'm on some Greek island, still searching for some real estate, haha . . . Well, you got me blood boilin' again. I've been writing . . . Yeah, read a review of your album in the paper. You know, people have heard of you in Athens. Quite shocking." Silence. "You do? Well, I can be back in London by, say, Thursday." More silence. "Oh, Los Angeles? Hmm . . . Sure, why not? I'll prolly need to get me papers in order, but I can be there by Monday."

He hangs up the phone and I scurry back to the sofa, my heart pounding with excitement. He doesn't emerge, though, and within a few minutes, I hear him talking again. *What, is he trying to get the whole band back together?* I go back over to the door to listen.

It's not George or Ringo.

"It's no big deal, Mother. I already have my clothes here, and the EMI studios will have equipment . . . It's only gonna be a few weeks . . . No, I think it'd be best if it were just me and Paul at first." John is quiet for a while, but when he speaks again, his voice is louder and growing in frustration. "I don't give a shit about what the stars say. I need this . . . Mother, please listen to . . . I'm sorry you feel that way, but I'm goin'." I hear him hang the phone up, and I run back to the sofa again.

He emerges from the kitchen, shaken but smiling sheepishly, like a kid who was disobeying his parents. "Pack yer bags, Mal! We're going to Los Angeleez. Paul's gonna be performing on Ringo's show. Let's meet him there."

* * *

7 December 1978

I am one of only six people in the world who knows that John Lennon and Paul McCartney are playing together today: me, John, Paul, Ringo, Yoko and Linda. Earlier, the two ex-Beatles sneaked into the EMI building in Los Angeles after reserving a studio under the name George O'Winston. Paul called Neil Aspinall to pull a few strings at the top to allow us exclusive use of the studio—no engineers or producers around. Surely the staff know something is up, but so far we haven't run into any curious bystanders or snoops.

I haven't encountered a Beatles session so laid back since the days when they were recording *Rubber Soul*—about 1965. Paul and John are goofing off, playing piano, exchanging instruments and making verbal plays on words. The improvisation turns to real songs, starting off with some old Buddy Holly tunes, and then the 50s tribute morphs into John demoing one of his new songs, a doo-wop number he is tentatively calling "Starting Over." He pounds out the chords in triplets on the piano, with Paul looking over his shoulder at the lyrics. After a few run-throughs, Paul takes the words and starts finding harmonies; when he suggests a few modulations between verses, John works them into the song. Paul begins to experiment with a bass line on his guitar.

I am in the control room, and tape is running. I may not be a world-class producer, but I can press "Record" when I need to.

To see another song evolving from these two, and to know that I'm the only one witnessing it, is difficult to explain. But I want to experience the collaboration between the two most famous (and arguably most talented) Beatles, without any filters or outside influence. The magic is back. It's as if the two are reading each other's mind, anticipating chord changes and adding flourishes that improve the songs.

After about an hour, John debuts another demo called "Nobody Told Me," and the process begins anew, this time with Paul on drums and John on guitar. Paul continues the fifties vibe with a new song called "Call Me Back Again." Both songs are campy and formulaic—an obvious throwback—but it's done well, with a perfect homage to the genre. The songs just ooze from them, and with only a few overdubs, they are basically done. And that's the way it was back at the birth of rock 'n' roll; with high studio rates, record companies couldn't afford hours of rehearsals and takes, and technology had not advanced enough to lay down individual tracks. Bands were recorded while performing live.

Paul introduces another song called "Take It Away," but John begins looking around the studio and fumbles through the first half. Paul senses it, and he backs off. "Why don't we give it a rest for a bit, John?"

"Yeah, yeah. Sounds good. Say, when are you visiting Ringo's show?" John asks.

"Tomorrow around one o'clock. I'm supposed to play something from the new album with my band."

"At least you won't get any questions about us getting back together."

"When people find out we're here, they're gonna start talking."

"You know, we should surprise them all and show up together."

Paul laughs. "That's utterly daft."

John looks up. "Let's do it, then."

* * *

8 December 1978

I call Ringo. It's one a.m., and he's in bed. He answers the phone, slightly irritated and somewhat comatose.

"Whaddayawant?"

"Ringo, it's Mal."

"Who?"

I'm in no mood to remind him of who I am after almost fifteen years together. "Look, Ringo, I'm here in Los Angeles with John. We're at EMI. Paul and John are thinking of playing tonight on your show. Can you come over and practice with them?"

Ringo comes to his senses. "Whaa? Now? Today? Here?" I hear him drop the phone and curse. "Uh, sorry about that. You gonna be there for a while?"

"Of course."

"I'll be there in half an hour."

* * *

I am spending my time before the show alternating between roadie and security guard: making sure no one gets to John and Paul, and getting their instruments tuned and ready to go. Running back and forth, I am working up a sweat; I must be a sight to behold—a six-foot, four-inch man lumbering back and forth, bumping into people every other second.

Although the producers and public relations people for Ringo's talk show didn't announce the planned reunion, the rumours were soon circulating that a Beatles reunion was in the works, even making it onto the evening newscasts. ABC officials were expecting a long line of people to get into the show since Paul was going to be performing, but the crowd has dwarfed their biggest estimates; tens of thousands have been turned away.

As showtime draws nearer, I see none of the trademark nervousness that John used to display. He is playing gin with Paul and drinking a soda. Linda and the kids are in the studio audience; right now it's as if John and Paul are the only people on the planet. They are cracking jokes and conversing in high-pitched, aristocratic voices whenever they discard or draw a card.

The knock on the door comes to announce the five-minute warning.

"I do say, Master Paul, someone knocked, and they aren't even participating in the game," John says.

"Not fair, ol' chum, just as I was about to announce gin."

"Thank you darling, I'd love one."

They put their cards down, knock on the table anyway, walk outside and take their places behind the curtain as if it were just another rehearsal. As the show comes back from commercial, I hear Ringo speak.

"My next guest is a dear old friend of mine; we used to play together in a little band back in England." The audience laughs.

"His new album is called *Silly Love Songs*, but apparently he doesn't want to play anything from that tonight. He has an old friend with him and wants me to play too." The crowd's laughter turns to screams. "So if you'll please excuse me, I'm gonna go back up Mr. Paul McCartney and Mr. John Lennon."

The lights come up on the other side of the stage; there are only about 200 people in the audience, but from the roar, it sounds like 2,000. John is playing the guitar; a member of Paul's backing band, recruited at the last minute, is on bass; and Paul is on the piano, waiting for the screams to die down before he begins the introduction.

The four are loose and carefree, and the sound is surprisingly tight for a group that has had only one rehearsal. John performs admirably in a backup role as Paul assumes lead vocals on "Call Me Back Again." They are still my old friends, but transformed: a middle-aged John, gaunt and weathered and without spectacles; Paul, impossibly and forever young, as confident as I've seen him in a while; Ringo, sweating away in his talk-show-host suit as he pounds away on the drums. My thoughts turn to George, wondering how his life is without music, and whether he will even notice that the three are playing without him.

The band play their final chord; I've spent the second coming of "The Ed Sullivan Show" daydreaming. The crowd is ecstatic, and the three are arm in arm as Ringo thanks the rest of his guests for coming. I doubt anyone remembers John Ritter from "Three's Company" having been on the show earlier.

* * *

"It's time to go celebrate!" John exclaims as we get ready to leave the dressing room. It's about five o'clock in the afternoon, and I sense a bender coming on. "Ringo, where's a good place to go? The town is yours."

"Does it matter if it's good? We just need some alcohol."

"Good point. Paul, you in?"

"Yeah, but I gotta go back to the hotel and get Linda and the kids situated. How about an hour?"

Ringo gives us the address of a bar east of the studio, and John and I walk out to a white Mustang convertible waiting in the rear of the studio. Uncharacteristically John jumps over to the driver side. "I'm driving today, Mal."

I hesitate; I've never considered John to be a good driver. "You sure? You know, they drive on the right side in America."

"Of course. They do everything backwards here. Race their ponies counterclockwise instead of clockwise. Call football 'soccer.' I got it."

I shrug and get on the passenger side. For sixteen years, I have been doing whatever the Beatles tell me to do. Why stop now?

The car has a manual transmission, and John jerks down the street, trying to understand the workings of the clutch. Stopping is a problem; he stalls at each intersection, cursing every time it happens.

"Wasn't that amazing, Mal? It was like we were back on Ed Sullivan there for a minute. What a rush!"

I smile. "Yeah, I was thinking about that."

John isn't bothering to stop anymore as he discovers that he would only have to change gears yet again. "I'm real excited about this, Mal. You know, for once it can be just me and Paul working on something. Sure, Ringo can fill in on drums every once in a while, but no George to worry about, no George Martin making suggestions. We can make it sound the way we want it to. We're listening to each other for the first time in years."

I remember my thoughts about George. "You know, you're probably gonna have to talk to George about what happened tonight. He's gonna be miffed that you did this without checking with him."

John laughs. "He's probably holed up in some Hindu monastery chanting Hare Krishna. I bet he doesn't even know we were on the telly!"

I had called the front desk of our hotel earlier and received five messages from Neil. I bet George knows.

"Yoko's gonna kill me. Me and Paul, back together again!"

"I think it's good, John. I mean, your stuff sounds amazing. I think you're really on to something." I was never much for constructive feedback or conversation, but that's not why they kept me around.

"It's just like 1962! We're churnin' 'em out! It's so easy! Paul has been impossible in the past, but nothin' gets me writing like he does. Of course, I do the same for him. I mean—"

I see the police car coming through the intersection too late to say anything; John doesn't see it at all. In fact, he's already raced through the stop sign.

The Mustang hits the squad car right in the centre, pushing it about a hundred feet before the cars come to a stop. My collarbone slams against the restraints of my seatbelt, and I gasp in pain as my right shoulder snaps. Out of the corner of my eye, I see John's body hurtling against the windscreen, and I wonder with horror why I didn't tell him to put on a seatbelt. I hear the sickening sound of metal screeching on the pavement, of breaking glass and chaos.

The car finally grinds to a stop, and I think, *Death has found me.* But a sharp pain in my shoulder alerts me to the fact that I am alive and breathing.

I can tell that John is dead. His body is splayed across the hood, arms outstretched, his neck in an awkward position. Blood is pooling from his head and his waist.

No, no, no!

I yell for help. The officers in the other car are already out and coming over to assess the situation.

"Please help," I yell frantically. "That's John Lennon. Do something, fer chrissakes, do something!"

I manage to unbuckle my seatbelt and kick the door open; one of the officers pulls me aside as the other policeman checks John's vital signs and begins CPR.

"Are you hurt?" the officer asks me.

I am dizzy from the pain. "I think my shoulder's broken, but who cares about me? It's John, it's John," I mumble. All I can do is look at the other officer's futile attempts to revive John. I look for some miracle, some sign of life from John, but I see nothing.

A crowd of people begins to gather along the residential street, assessing the damage. Traffic is at a gridlock, and I can hear horns blaring. For a crazy moment, I am embarrassed to be the cause of a traffic jam. But then I hear the sound of a far-off ambulance siren, and the thought passes.

"How long until the ambulance—"

I look up at the officer and freeze.

I have only seen his face for a few seconds before, and I thought it was forever wiped from my memory.

His LAPD-issued badge. It reads "G TAYLOR."

I look away and shake my head, not believing what I am seeing. I look up again and stare at his face; his eyes lock onto mine and he tilts his head, gazing more intently.

"Have we met before?" he asks.

I look away, down the street. The area is so familiar; I recognise houses and trees on either side. I see a sign at the intersection: *W Fourth Street.*

My old apartment, the apartment where I went crazy and aimed an air rifle at G Taylor in some other lifetime, is about one block away.

My eyes begin to roll back in my head. I look toward the crowd for some validation that it's not happening; instead I see a tall man on the side of the road, laughing and pointing at me. He's wearing a placard that reads "REV 2:10."

I black out before my head hits the sidewalk.

18

9 December 1978

I open my eyes, blinking a few times, and things begin to come into focus. The white sterile environment and the smell of antiseptic—I must have been hurt worse than I thought. I feel an IV poking into my hand; my right shoulder is aching, and the back of my head is pounding.

Looking over beside the bed, I see the face of Neil Aspinall, who leans forward and smiles, his tired face showing some relief.

"Hey Mal, you feelin' okay?"

I don't answer at first. "What am I doing here?"

"You were in a car accident. Doctor said you broke your collarbone in the crash, but you're here because you bumped your head on the sidewalk afterwards. Quite a nasty bump— knocked you out cold."

The images of the wreck come flooding back—John's body lying on the car, the badge reading G TAYLOR, the street preacher laughing. I have no idea what reality I am in anymore. Have my two experiences somehow come together? Am I still alive? Was I saved from the floor of my flat? Maybe I'm in the hospital from the gunshot wounds, and I've awakened. Maybe there are two Mal Evanses walking around now. The idea causes my head to spin and pound even more.

I collect my thoughts. "John's dead, isn't he?"

Neil breathes a sigh of relief and relaxes, probably glad that he didn't have to tell me. "Yeah. The police said he died instantly. I was already on my way over after hearing about what you were doing on Ringo's show."

Tears well up in the corner of my eyes as reality sets in. John. Dead. I think of all the times he had skirted death—massive amounts of drugs and alcohol, crazed fans trying to break into his home, the near stampede in Bangladesh—he seemed immortal. But at the same time, John's life may have been too tragic to end any other way. I recall the Who's "My Generation," with lead singer Roger Daltrey wishing that he would die young. It had happened to me once; now it has happened to John.

"John . . ." I try to sit up, but the pain causes bright lights in my head.

"There, there, Mal. No need to worry about that. You just get better."

"No, there are things to do. There's Paul, and the album, and Yoko . . ."

"We have it taken care of, Mal."

I lie back, defeated. I am powerless. My thoughts turn to the accident, and then to G Taylor.

"The police—did . . . did any of them say anything about me?"

Neil looks puzzled. "No, why would they? . . . It wasn't your fault, Mal."

"Yes it was, Neil. They were coming for me."

* * *

Los Angeles Times

December 9, 1978

LENNON DEAD IN CAR ACCIDENT

Former Beatle John Lennon was killed yesterday in an automobile accident in downtown Los Angeles, moments after a successful reunion with his longtime songwriting partner Paul McCartney.

According to a Los Angeles Police Department spokesman, Lennon, who was driving a white 1979 Mustang, drove through a stop sign on 3rd Street and collided with a police car driven by Officer George Taylor. Lennon was thrown through the windshield and died instantly, police said.

Mal Evans, a longtime assistant of the Beatles, was also in the car and suffered minor injuries. He was taken to Saint John's Hospital for observation. Both policemen in the other vehicle reported no serious injuries.

Lennon was traveling from ABC Studios, where he had performed with McCartney and Ringo Starr on "The Ringo Show." The performance was already fueling rumors of a Beatles reunion. Instead, Starr taped a short message to viewers, saying "This was supposed to be a happy time for us, but instead, I am mourning the loss of one of my closest friends."

A makeshift memorial has sprung up at the scene of the accident as visitors pay their respects to Lennon. Candlelight vigils have also formed at the Beatles' recording studio and offices in London, as well as in Liverpool, Los Angeles and several other cities around the world.

Beatles spokesperson Derek Taylor released a statement from the three remaining Beatles that read, "We all had a great amount of love and respect for John. The four of us went through a lot together, and we made some beautiful music. We are shocked and stunned by his death. He was an incredible musician, an advocate for peace, a loving father and husband, and an honorable man."

Lennon's wife, Yoko Ono, was not available for comment.

* * *

13 December 1978

I'm sitting in the sanctuary of St. Peter's Parish Church in Liverpool. I'm not sure why; I haven't attended a church service since my kids' christenings. Perhaps it's because there was no formal funeral for John. Yoko had chosen to have a silent vigil for him instead. But I need to say goodbye to him and mourn his loss—privately. Even though John was not that religious, I feel like his spirit is still among us. I wonder if he is looking at me in judgment, knowing now what only I knew before. I beg him for forgiveness and plead with him to absolve me of my sin.

I am also trying to make sense of that evening, thinking about all the things that had to happen in order for the accident to occur. We should have ridden with Ringo or Paul. I could have insisted on driving, told him to put on his seatbelt. If there had been one more stoplight. Officer G Taylor could have stopped at a doughnut shop, or made a detour to respond to a robbery. But instead, we met at that same intersection, only a block from where I had stood with a pellet gun, threatening the same officer a lifetime away. There must be thousands of police officers in the Los Angeles Police Department. The odds that Officer Taylor would be on a collision course with our car were beyond astronomical, nearly impossible. This was no coincidence.

I have been living on borrowed time.

Ever since the night in that hotel room, when I outlived my former self, I have been stealing time. Each second I survived, I was snatching it from someone else. But Death had been looking for me all this time. I had cheated Death, and He had exacted His revenge upon me in a cruel way, taking one of the four dearest people from me. Even the street preacher, who had warned me that my time was running out, was there to gloat in my punishment.

I fall to my knees in anguish, hands held to heaven as I wail, beseeching God to take me instead as a sacrifice instead of John. Jesus looks down from the cross, quiet and still, his eyes looking down at me with pity.

* * *

14 December 1978

No one needed to tell us to show up at the Savile Row offices. We have come here by instinct, hoping to find some solace in the familiar faces. The Apple staff are working diligently, sending out bios via telegram and Telex—as if people needed information on John's life. They are finding their work here to be some kind of therapy for their grief.

Paul, Ringo and George are here, along with Neil, Geoff, and Derek. George greets me with a hug and puts on a good face, saying that death is only a small stop on John's continuing journey, but I see he is tired and haggard; I think he must be in shock.

Neil is sitting by himself in the corner, looking over a press statement. I head over and have a seat next to him.

"This is a good turnout," I say, not knowing how to start the conversation. I'm not really even sure if I'm in the mood to talk.

"Well, with one notable exception." I think he's talking about John, which startles me, but he clarifies his statement. "Yoko."

"Oh, I see."

"She gave Derek an earful when he called her," Neil continues "Seems she blames us for his death. He shouldn't have gone over there to play with Paul, the planets weren't aligned, lots of that. She talked for ten minutes straight and then hung up on him before he could say anything. And she hasn't spoken to any of the other three."

Yoko. In all the self-serving pity we as a group—the Beatle elite—are going through, I have not thought about her. I wonder how she is dealing with John's loss, and my pity turns to her. *She hates us all.* I was with him when he died, so I'm sure she blames me most. I'm sure she wished she had been there with him instead of some hulking former Postal employee.

I make a note to go check on her and see how she's doing.

* * *

3 January 1979

Friar Park is an otherworldly experience; driving through its wrought iron gates is like entering the gates of heaven. Isolated on a high hill, George's Victorian estate is full of lush gardens, an underground grotto, and a replica of the Matterhorn. It's like nothing I've ever seen. Even in the dead of winter, it's full of life. Gnome statues litter the estate, and I half expect them to come jumping up to my car. It's part of the fantasy that Sir Frank Crisp created at the turn of the century, and George is painstakingly restoring it to its former glory, plant by plant and stone by stone. As I travel up the long drive to the mansion, I know I am hoping for some comfort here.

I haven't been to Friar Park for several years, but I am amazed by the progress George has made. When he bought the estate back in 1970, it was a mess. But since his self-imposed retirement from music, he has been busy, as he and the other Krishnas have cleared away the weeds, added new gardens, and planted new flowers and bushes.

I find George meditating among the gnome statues in one of his gardens; set against the pristine grass and ornamental plants, he is a picture of peace. I am not sure he is aware of me, so I clear my throat. He says nothing for a while but finally opens his eyes and smiles.

"*Namo namah*, Mal Evans," he said, bowing slightly. "For what do I have this honour?" He is a different person from the George I have known for the past fifteen years.

"Oh, I dunno, just in the area, thought I'd drop by and see how you were."

He smiles again. "Please, have a seat. I think we both know there is a reason you are here."

I sit, unsure of what to say, but the silence is welcoming. I listen to the birds, feel the cool breeze on my face. It is comforting. And it comes out, the entire story: the showdown at the apartment, getting shot, going back in time to the Toronto concert, the new Beatles albums that weren't possible. I talk about the homeless preacher, the dreams, G Taylor, the accident. It takes me forty-five minutes, but George listens closely, never asking any questions or expressing any surprise.

At the end of my monologue I freeze, afraid of what my story might sound like to someone else once said out loud. "I know you must think I'm off my rocker, but I feel if anybody understood, it would be you, George."

Again, there is silence—this time more awkward. Finally, he speaks.

"Well Mal, you've had quite a journey." He picks up a piece of grass and gazes at it in wonder, as if viewing it for the first time. "Krishna tells us, 'As a person puts on new garments, giving up old ones, similarly, the soul accepts new material bodies, giving up the old and useless ones.' It seems as if you passed on in that apartment and became reincarnated as the person you are today."

"Yeah, but I'm the same person, experiencing the same period over. You were in my other life, George. And you were a Beatle, and it was the 60s, and you broke up in 1970. You recorded a triple album in 1970 called *All Things Must Pass*. Do you remember that?"

"No, I don't. But that doesn't mean it didn't happen."

"You do think I'm daft, don't you? You don't believe me."

"It's not important whether I believe you, Mal. I have no opinion on it. I do not judge you. But this situation is obviously affecting you, and you must deal with it." He rises. "Live your life and live it well. I believe that you will be rewarded in your next life."

"But John's death, George. I really think that was meant for me."

"Well, you can look at it one of two ways. One, this may be fate. There may have been nothing you could do to prevent this, that John was destined to die and it had nothing to do with you. The second explanation is karma. This happened for a reason, Mal. There's something you still need to do in spite of John's death. One suffers or enjoys his life according to one's particular karma. Correct it, Mal, fix what is broken, and you'll enjoy life again."

Correct it, Mal, fix what is broken. My mind clears, and the burden of my guilt lifts away from me. I know what he means.

* * *

I waste no time, driving ten hours to Campbeltown, Scotland. Paul always retreated to his farm during stressful times, and a quick phone call to Neil confirmed that he was there.

I pull into the McCartney farm at about ten o'clock p.m. and see the porch light come on in response to my headlights. Paul sticks his head out the screen door, squinting. He looks five years older than when I saw him only two weeks ago; his famous droopy eyes are sagging even more from the weight of the past events.

"Mal, what the bloody . . . Come in, you look exhausted."

I realise that I have driven ten hours with no change of clothes or toiletries, stopping only twice for petrol and toilet stops. "Sorry for the late intrusion, Paul. I should have called first, I know."

Paul's house is charming but dignified, with a homey feel. I greet Linda with a peck on the cheek, and she goes to the kitchen to fetch some drinks and snacks. I see no children; I can only guess that they are already in bed.

Paul sits in his easy chair. "What're you doing here that can't wait?" he asks. "Do I need to sign something?"

"No, Paul. I'm here to get the Beatles back together."

Paul flinches. "That's not funny, Mal."

"I'm serious, Paul. There's somethin' we need to finish."

Paul says nothing, stewing. He knows what I am talking about.

"Look, you two already had some songs in the can. It was the start of something big. He recorded a few others while we were on holiday. I know it'll be hard. But I think you need some closure on this."

"*Closure?*" Paul laughs. "How can you have closure with a dead man?"

"Well, how about a proper tribute?"

Again, he says nothing. He rises from his chair and rearranges some papers on a small desk. But my question has hit home.

"Those songs are just sitting there at Abbey Road, Paul. Don't you think the public needs to hear what you did? Maybe you don't remember it, but I do. It was beautiful music, Paul."

He turns around, and his face looks even sadder. "I don't think I could do his work justice. I mean—I'm nothing without him. And he's gone."

I get up and walk over to him, looking him straight in the eyes—as an equal—something I had never done before. "He's there. On those tapes. Just finish what he started."

A flash of life flickers in Paul's eyes.

* * *

4 January 1979

I drive into the Abbey Road car park. Finally. Even though we saved some time by driving three hours to Glasgow and catching a charter plane to London, it feels as if we've been traveling all day. At the insistence of Paul and Linda, I stayed at their house last night, but I had first called Ringo. Without hesitating, he said he would announce a hiatus from his show to join us in the studio. He is due to fly in tomorrow. Earlier this morning, I rang up George; he was a little harder to convince, but agreed to lend some guitar work to the project. I felt as if he were doing it more out of pity for me than for John.

Walking into the studio as a Beatle once more, with me trailing him, Paul receives a hero's welcome. Geoff gives us all a warm embrace, and we trade pleasantries. But Paul wants to start.

"Geoff, we have some work to do. I sent over the tapes of me and John a few days after the accident. Can you get them? I'd like for us to go through them, and you can tell me what kind of shape they're in."

Geoff looks panicked, his face pale. "Er, I thought you knew . . ."

Paul loses his patience. "What? They never got here? What the hell, I sent them by special courier."

"No, they arrived three weeks ago. But two days ago, um, well, Yoko said that she wanted them—"

Turning on a dime, Paul bolts through the door, making sure to slam it behind him.

19

The Times

10 January 1979

McCartney, Ono battle for Lennon Demo Tapes

Beatle Paul McCartney has asked his former songwriting partner's wife, Yoko Ono, to return a slate of recordings the two had created just before John Lennon's death.

The request asks for the return of seven tracks that he and Lennon had recorded at Capitol Records in Los Angeles. McCartney has claimed a vested interest in the tracks as a performer and as a business partner. "These songs were forming the basis of a new album by the Beatles, of which I am a member," he told *The Times*. "I also played bass guitar on all songs and had contributed drums and vocals as well." In addition to the Lennon tapes, there exist several McCartney-penned tracks that are his outright, he says.

Ono, speaking through a spokesperson, defended her possession of the tapes, saying, "Mrs. Lennon now owns 25 percent of Apple Records, and she represents John's musical and business interests. Many of these tracks were for a double album that Mrs. Ono and Mr. Lennon had planned to record together."

The tracks in question include six songs written by Lennon: "Woman," "Starting Over," "Watching the Wheels," "Borrowed Time," "Grow Old with Me," and "Nobody Told Me."

Two are by McCartney: "Call Me Back Again" and "Take It Away."

* * *

15 February 1979

Neil has sent me home. I think my pacing and numerous ideas on how to settle the disagreement were driving him crazy. But being at home has not helped me at all.

I pick up the phone for the third time in three days and dial the office. Judy, the receptionist, answers and puts me through to Neil.

"Jesus, Mal, go back to work. Go play with the kids. You can't do anything about this."

"So no news?"

"No. Just like the day before and the day before that. I'll ring you when something happens, but you need to pace yourself. Something like this will take months to settle."

"It could be so easy. Surely there's a way to compromise."

"That's not up to us, Mal. It's up to Paul and Yoko."

1 March 1979

It always comes down to a disagreement.

The first time around, Paul sang about legal squabbles on "You Never Give Me Your Money." Then the band broke up in a flurry of lawsuits and accusations in the media. Now, in one last try to get my Beatles back together, I have hit a roadblock.

And as I pace outside the front gate of Tittenhurst, trying to gather enough nerve to ring the house, I wonder if I am fighting fate, like the time I waited for Death. This last Beatles album may be too much even for the gods to deal with. But it's my only hope.

I haven't talked to Yoko since the accident. I had made a point to reach out to her, to tell her how sorry I was, but I was afraid— afraid that she might blame me, afraid that she would only say what I am thinking: *It should have been me.* I should die for my own sins, to meet my maker instead of running from him.

But if I am to meet my maker—if, indeed, there is a maker up there, dictating events—then I am powerless to hide from him. If he wanted me, he could have taken me in the accident. I am here; John isn't. And until I breathe my last, I am going to do everything I can to bring the remaining Beatles back together, even if I have to bring John's voice back from beyond the grave.

I reach my hand out and ring the bell.

* * *

"How are you, Mal?" Yoko asks as she invites me into her home. She has aged twenty years since I saw her six months ago. Her long hair is now shorn, and there are bags under her eyes. I hear Sean playing in another room; he sounds happy. One Lennon is oblivious to John's loss, but the other is still suffering.

"I have thought about you a lot during the last few months," she says. "I know it is hard being caught in the middle like this."

I smile, taken aback by her friendly tone. She has invited me inside and she is talking to me. If there is any residual ill will, she is not showing it.

We head into the kitchen, where not so long before John had been baking bread. The house is unkempt, and signs of John are everywhere—record albums and singles, newspapers, boxes of Corn Flakes. Yoko is keeping John in the house for as long as she can.

She has already heated some water for some tea, as if she were expecting me. "You know, John had the utmost respect for you," she says. "I never heard him say a negative thing about you, and he never let anyone say anything bad about you." For a moment I wonder who tried to say something bad about me and what it would have been, but I regain my focus.

"I'm sorry I haven't visited before. It was just . . . Well, er . . ." My voice trembles, and Yoko reaches a hand out.

"Mal, you weren't driving."

"Yeah, but I should have been. He'd still be here."

"Nonsense. I know John. You couldn't convince him to let you drive if he really wanted to."

I smile. This was true. "Thank you, Yoko. Your kind words mean more to me than I can express."

I take the cup of tea from her, nodding my gratitude. "So how have you been, Yoko?"

"I am dealing with it. People have been very gracious."

"How's Sean?"

"He has adjusted pretty well. He asks where John is from time to time. And he cries a little when he wants to see him. But he is doing okay."

We spend a few minutes recounting our favourite John moments, and I laugh for the first time in weeks. I bring up an anecdote with Paul, and Yoko stops me. "No stories about Paul."

I decide to dive in. "Yoko, we need to end this."

Her demeanour changes, and her eyes flash with anger. "Go tell that to Paul. Why are you here? Did he send you?"

Dammit. She's getting defensive. Time for another tactic. "Look, from a sentimental viewpoint, every one of those songs is yours. I agree. But the ones that Paul worked on—they have sentimental value for him, too. I mean, can't you both share those last songs of John's? You both loved him. And you both want to honour him."

"No!" she screams. She pauses to calm herself. "Mal, you just don't understand. Paul doesn't understand. So many of these songs mean a great deal to me and Sean. I hear so much of John's love in each song. Giving them away . . . It's like taking a piece of him from me."

A tear falls down her face, followed by another one, and before I know it, she is sobbing as if in pain, falling to the sofa. I have never seen Yoko like this, so exposed and vulnerable. But I take a seat beside her anyway, and she buries her head in my chest, wailing and hitting me. The Yoko that everyone sees in the media is gone, and I feel nothing but love and pity for her. I hold her for what seems like hours, and we both mourn our beloved John.

Finally the sobs subside, and she lifts her head. "Okay, where do we start?" she asks, wiping her eyes.

Two hours later, we have divided the songs in a way that is satisfactory to Yoko; she would still have ownership of a few more songs than Paul, and I hope and pray that Paul will accept the compromise. But just as I am leaving, Yoko tells me to wait. After a few minutes, she returns with two cassettes.

"These are some demos that John recorded a few years ago after Sean was born. They don't sound very good, but maybe you can do something with them." I remember John mentioning the demos when we were on Patmos; I guess these are the ones.

She goes over to a cassette player and plays them for me. She's right—they sound awful, with pops and cracks and background noise. But they are vintage John, and they sound like lost Beatles songs.

I love them already.

* * *

Billboard

March 12, 1979

PAUL, YOKO STRIKE DEAL

Settlement makes way for possible Beatles album

Representatives from Paul McCartney and Yoko Ono, John Lennon's widow, announced a deal today that divides the late singer's final recordings between the two parties.

The settlement comes months after McCartney discovered that Ono had secured some recordings that Lennon and McCartney made in Los Angeles shortly before Lennon died in a car accident. The deal, brokered by long-time Beatles assistant Mal Evans, consists of the following conditions:

McCartney will retain possession of three tracks that he and Lennon recorded days before Lennon's death—"Call Me Back Again," "Nobody Told Me" and "Starting Over."

Ono will keep four demos that Lennon recorded while on holiday in Bermuda about a week before his death—"Watching the Wheels," "Borrowed Time," "Grow Old With Me" and "Beautiful Boy."

"Woman," the track that features McCartney on vocals, will be shared between the two.

Ono will give the Beatles access to two demos that Lennon recorded several years ago—"Free as a Bird" and "Real Love."

Apple officials would not confirm or deny any plans for the three surviving Beatles to start recording together, but it has been widely rumored that McCartney was securing these demos to organize a final tribute to Lennon. Ono has already announced plans for an album featuring songs from her and her husband.

* * *

17 March 1979

The sounds of John Winston Ono Lennon emanate from the studio monitors, sounds we already associate with sadness and loss. It is the voice of a man we loved who is now gone, and it's hard to hear. I don't know if I will ever hear another Beatles song of his without feeling grief.

The survivors are all here—Paul, George and Ringo. George Martin is with us, as is Geoff Emerick. Yoko politely declined; I think it was easier for everyone that way, and although Paul grimaced at the news, I knew it was because she couldn't bear it.

George Martin tapes a piece of poster paper on the wall and begins writing the tracks on the paper. "Nobody Told Me," "Starting Over," "Woman," "Free as a Bird" and "Real Love."

"Here is the core—it's what we have to work with—one side of an album. What else do we have?"

I think we are all shocked when George pipes up. "I'd like to play a few things for you."

You could have heard a pin drop. "A few things? We haven't heard a peep from you in years, and now you have 'a few things?' " Ringo asks.

"Yeah. John's death awakened something in me. This first song was the easiest thing I ever wrote." He picks up a guitar and begins playing an up-tempo song that sounds joyous, but the lyrics seem to speak straight to John, telling him things that he had meant to say all these years. In fact, he calls the song "All Those Years Ago." George looks over at me as if to say, "See? I'm helping you out."

Paul is beaming like a proud father. "George, that may be one of the best things you've written. You've kept your light hidden for a long time. I'm glad you let it out."

"And that, Paul, may be one of the nicest things you've ever said to me," George replies. "Thank you."

He continues, this time playing a song that he says he wrote for Ringo. It's a quirky, upbeat song called "Wrack My Brain"— simple and easy to sing, and Ringo loves it.

Paul then plays "Free as a Bird" on the cassette player, the first of John's two demos. This is even harder to hear; John's thin voice sounds otherworldly, as if he were a ghost in the room. Ringo shakes his head. "I don't think I can do this, lads."

Paul counters. "Look, let's just pretend that John's off on one of his benders, and we're here to lay down the finishing tracks. We've done it before, so let's just do it again. We know what he likes. We know he hates my syrupy music and lyrics." The other two Beatles laugh at Paul's self-deprecating comment.

The second song, "Real Love," begins. It has an annoying hum that plays throughout; the quality is even worse. Ringo grimaces. "C'mon, John, give us more to work with." George Martin shakes his head. "The tape is in bad condition. He's speeding up and slowing down, and there's a lot of hiss. But I'll see what I can do."

"I think we need a few verses for the bridge. And some of the chord progressions need help," Paul says. "George, why don't we go work on that in the other studio? Ringo, you want to work on laying down some drum tracks for them?"

And with that, the Beatles start to work piecing together their tribute to John.

* * *

2 May 1979

Having spent a few hours cleaning up in Studio Two, I am just about to leave for the night. I'm beat; it's almost two a.m. As I lock up the doors and begin to leave, I notice the red light on in Studio One. Since we had pretty much taken over Studio Two during the past few weeks, I'm curious as to what is going on at this hour. I crack open the door to the control room; Geoff and George Martin are leaning over the console, adjusting some controls. On the floor of the expansive studio is the dim outline of Paul McCartney sitting on a stool with an acoustic guitar.

"This is going to be hard to get through, George," Paul says. "Please bear with me." I sit down, wondering what I am about to hear. The tape begins to roll. At first Paul does nothing; he is gathering his courage to sing. Then he begins a sad ballad—just him and the guitar—called "Here Today," which, like "All Those Years Ago," addresses John personally. I hear the pain in Paul's voice as he recollects events in their lives that no one else knew about: their quarrels, times when they both cried, things that should have been said a long time ago.

It takes him several takes to get it just right, and once he has to regain his composure, his voice shaking. By the time he finishes it, the tears are running down my face. Geoff and George are wiping their eyes as well. Paul's head hangs in sombre respect for his friend; I hear sniffles coming through his microphone. Geoff nods at me. "He did another one earlier called 'Tug of War.' Almost as sad. I tell you, I don't know where he gets this stuff. It's as if God himself came down and whispered the song into his ears."

George Martin turns on the studio mic. "That's all we need on that track, Paul. This is your gift to John. George and Ringo don't need to be playing."

Paul isn't listening. He's putting his guitar away. I sneak away as quietly as I came, feeling blessed to have witnessed this moment.

* * *

NME

28 May 1979

Album Review: *Love, Yoko*

Yoko Says Goodbye with a Fitting Tribute

Like many an in-law, Yoko Ono has been tolerated, if not always loved. Her presence with the Beatles has at times been unnerving and distracting. The late John Lennon, always polarising, seemed even more offbeat and independent from the group while he was with her.

But we fail to recognise that Lennon needed Ono. She breathed new life into a man who had grown tired of the mainstream success of the Beatles. And while we sometimes ridiculed their collaborations in the past, we secretly envied their avant-garde approach to art and music—even if it wasn't "She Loves You."

With her album *Love, Yoko,* Ono enters the mainstream with a marvellous eulogy to her late husband. The first side, called, "From John to Yoko," consists solely of the tracks Ono obtained as part of the agreement between her and Paul McCartney over the last demos Lennon recorded. Listening to these songs, one realises why Ono prized them. They are extremely personal, from the Eastern-tinged lullaby to his son, Sean ("Beautiful Boy") to love songs ("Woman," "Dear Yoko"). But the highlight is the final song, the ironically titled "Grow Old with Me," in which Lennon paraphrases a Robert Browning poem, "The best is yet to be." One only wonders what could have been if Lennon were still alive.

The second side, "From Yoko to John," represents a departure for Ono. Her music has taken a decidedly pop slant, and some of her songs seem destined for the clubs and the top of the dance charts. It's by no means comparable to Lennon's work, but it's a huge improvement over her previous work. And if you don't like it, just keep it on Side One and thank Ono for sharing Lennon's last gifts with us.

256

For immediate release

Contact: Derek Taylor

BEATLES RELEASE THEIR FINAL MASTERPIECE

<u>Free as a Bird</u> Contains Previously Unreleased Lennon Demos

In a moving tribute to the late John Lennon, the surviving members of the Beatles, along with Lennon's widow, Yoko Ono, are proud and humbled to release <u>Free as a Bird</u>, the final album in a long and historic career.

The album, which began as a Lennon-McCartney collaboration, contains material from sessions that the two participated in just days before Lennon's tragic death in an automobile accident.

"We felt like we needed to say goodbye to John in our own way," says George Harrison. "We had these unfinished songs that needed to be completed. What a better way to pay our respects than to complete what he started?

Paul McCartney says it was difficult to record with Lennon's voice in their headphones. "At first, we didn't want to do it. But we agreed to pretend that John had already finished his part and we were there to lay down a few more tracks on top of it. That made it much easier."

"We felt like he was in the studio with us, and sometimes we forgot that he had passed on," says Ringo Starr. "And in some way, he still lives on in these songs."

The album consists of the following tracks:

Side 1:

1. "In Spite of All the Danger" (Harrison/ McCartney)—Unearthed from the Apple vault, this fragment of a song is the first known recording ever of McCartney, Lennon and Harrison, playing as the Quarrymen in 1958. McCartney had bought this from the Quarrymen's drummer and decided that it would set a proper tone for the Lennon tribute.

2. "(Just Like) Starting Over" (Lennon/ McCartney)—The 1950s feel of this song fits well with the Quarrymen's song. McCartney and Harrison lend background vocals to this Lennon original.

3. "Take It Away" (Lennon/McCartney)—Another song that Lennon and McCartney performed during the final session, it was actually recorded after Lennon's death. Producer George Martin has added horns to this up-tempo number.

4. "Nobody Told Me" (Lennon/McCartney)—A tongue-in-cheek number by Lennon that is stream-of-

consciousness, referencing UFOs, marbles, and idols.

5. "Call Me Back Again" (Lennon/McCartney)—McCartney continues the fifties feel, backed by another brass section that sounds like a big band orchestra.

6. "Wrack My Brain" (Harrison)—Starr takes the microphone on this George Harrison-penned song, adding a little humour to end Side 1.

Side 2

1. "Free as a Bird" (Lennon/McCartney/Harrison/Starr)—All four Beatles receive credit for this song, made from a cassette demo provided by Ono. The song ends with a backwards message from Lennon saying, "Turned out nice again."

2. "Woman" (Lennon/McCartney)—Lennon and McCartney are at their best, singing sweet harmonies together for the last time.

3. "Tug of War" (McCartney)—The opening number of the memorial medley for Lennon, this lament from McCartney is sweeping, majestic and sombre.

4. "All Those Years Ago" (Harrison)—Harrison's personal tribute is a stunning work, wistful and bittersweet. It will be the first single from the album.

5. "Here Today" (McCartney)—McCartney is front and centre, the last to pay his respects to Lennon as he recounts their most private moments.

6. "Real Love" (Lennon/ McCartney/ Harrison/ Starr)—The finale, culled from another cassette demo from Lennon, features another compilation from all four. Lennon spoke of love often in his songs, and this ending is the perfect curtain call for the four.

Melody Maker

1 June 1979

ONE FINAL ENCORE FOR THE FAB FOUR

John Lennon was snatched from us way too soon. In the song "Rust Never Sleeps," Neil Young preferred burning out to fading away, and too many of our gifted musicians have opted for that path. It leaves us mourning their legacy and wishing we could hear more.

Fortunately, Lennon left us with just a wee bit more to appreciate. Earlier this year, we heard his contributions to an album from Yoko Ono, and this week, we have a new nugget to hold; we can hear his music one last time. *Free as a Bird* is the last Beatles album. Period. And it is a fitting epitaph to one of history's greatest songwriters, from history's greatest rock group.

The first side, according to Paul McCartney, consists mainly of what was originally supposed to be an album of just him and Lennon. The opening track, "In Spite of All the Danger," is a McCartney/Harrison tune from 1958 and has never been heard before. It's the earliest recording ever found of the Beatles. And while the quality is poor, it sets the tone for the first half of the record, which consists of a jaunt through the 1950s.

Lennon does his best Elvis Presley impersonation on a doo-wop number called "(Just Like) Starting Over," and McCartney shines with what may be his best vocal performance on the bluesy "Call Me Back Again," which brings to mind "Oh, Darling" from *Abbey Road*. One only wonders what the complete Lennon/McCartney album would have sounded like.

But it's the second side that will move the listener to tears. It's a eulogy from the Threetles, with Harrison and McCartney penning three of the six songs as a personal tribute to Lennon. Perhaps the most poignant is

McCartney's "Here Today." He confesses that he finds it hard to keep from crying; the two songwriting partners' relationship was volatile, and we can only see the surface of that relationship in the song. Only McCartney knows what lies deeper.

The biggest surprise of the album is from George Harrison, who has shaken the Chiffons' monkey from his back. "All Those Years Ago" is his first new song in almost 10 years. It's fresh, catchy as hell, and bears no resemblance to anything— except the Beatles. Sadly, it has taken Lennon's death to get him out of his funk.

Two songs—the title cut and "Real Love"—were pieced together by the three surviving members based on rough demos left behind by Lennon. It's a little strange sounding—Lennon's scratchy, treble voice mixed with clean, modern 1970s technology. But the songs are pure Beatles, and it gives us two more pieces of John to remember him by.

It's hard saying goodbye to the Beatles for the last time, but with this gem they have given us a glimpse at their entire career, bowed, and said, 'Thank you.' John Lennon has died, and now the Beatles have followed. Long live the Beatles.

20

6 June 1979

Paul signs a copy of *Free as a Bird* for me. For each album the Beatles recorded, I have painstakingly gotten each member to autograph a copy. This will be the first without all four names on it. But in a way, John's signature is all over this album, from the hand-drawn sketch that serves as the cover to the intensely personal songs he had given us before his death.

It's finally happened—all the hope, shock, tears, recording, and mixing have finally yielded a masterpiece. We're holding a huge party at Apple Records, and the whole gang is here— George Martin, Derek Taylor, Geoff Emerick, Neil Aspinall, and current and former Apple employees. Even Yoko and May Pang are here. As the record plays, we stay up late talking about old times and about John. There is a lot of laughing and crying. The best part of my life—everything I have worked for, most of the past that meant anything to me—is here in this room. I love these people. Every damn one of them.

The door opens, and in walks Mimi, Thomas and Susan. I had hardly thought about them during the last few months, but I run over to them and hug them, not wanting to let go, and we all cry. Mimi kisses me on the cheek.

"Congratulations, luv. You did it."

"I'm so sorry Mimi. I'll come back—"

"Let's not talk about this right now. The kids wanted to see you. They're so proud."

"Yeah, Daddy, your name was in the newspaper! Finally!"

That's something I never thought I'd see. I received a lot of attention after the settlement was announced, and people around the office and Abbey Road studio looked at me a little differently. The three remaining Beatles stopped using me as an errand boy and included me on more important decisions regarding instrumentation, album credits and release dates. But I am happy with the finished product. I laugh and hug my kids again, and give them autographed copies of the albums as well.

Yoko seeks me out. "Mal," she smiles. "What can I say but thank you? If it weren't for you, this magnificent tribute wouldn't have happened."

I blush. "Yoko, you made it happen. And your album set the tone for all this."

"You have made me so happy and proud. And John is proud of you as well." And she gives me a tight, warm hug—the type of hug that only friends can share, friends who have cried together and worked together. And I feel—somehow—that John is indeed satisfied with the result.

Ringo practically bumps into me, looks up and shakes his head. "I don't know how you did it, Mal. I really don't." He looks as if he wants to say more, but instead he gives me a great bear hug and attempts to lift me off the ground. I return the hug and take him six inches off the floor as he laughs and howls.

It's as if I have taken the Fifth Beatle title back from Neil tonight; the congratulations continue. I see George from across the room and see him wink at me, mouthing "You did it" to me. *Yes, I did.*

The party finally ends about four a.m. Mimi took the kids home hours ago, and I am walking through the office, remembering all the times I had done so at the height of Beatledom. I see ghosts of John everywhere—sitting in Derek's white wicker chair, sitting cross-legged in the white room, listening to records in the conference rooms. I make my way to the front office; Paul is sitting alone, leaning back in a chair with a drink in his hand.

"Well, Mal, this is it," he says, smiling.

"Yeah, we did well, didn't we? I told you this was what we needed to do."

"You were right. And it turned out swell. But what I meant was, this is it for *you*. The end of the road."

My pulse quickens as I search for meaning in his words. "Are . . . are you firing me, Paul?"

Paul laughs. "After what you just engineered? No way, mate. But this dream, this fantasy of yours. It's run its course."

I say nothing. *What is he getting at?*

He leans forward in his chair and places his glass on the table. "This thing with the Beatles still together during the seventies.

You know you're still lying on the floor in Los Angeles. Full of bullet holes. You're dying."

The blood drains from my face. I had finally put death behind me, but Paul is now hitting me over the head with my mortality.

"Bloody hell. How . . . How did you know about this?"

"I have no idea. It's your dream. Someone—maybe you, maybe some supreme being—is making the decision to end this. They picked me to pull you into it, and for some reason they've picked me to send you back."

It was Paul's voice I heard coming from the ceiling after I was shot. It had been so long since I had heard his voice that it was unfamiliar to me, but now it all becomes clear: *"Not yet, Mal. Hang on. I want to show you another path."* This trip through the 70s was the other path.

I search myself for gunshot wounds, wait to feel pain in my body, but nothing happens. Feeling light-headed, I manage to find a chair and sit down.

"Are you here? Are you real?" I ask.

"Who's to say? I could get all experiential like George. Maybe this did happen. Maybe it's going on somewhere else, in an alternate universe. Maybe there's another one where the Vietnam War never happens, and we trade John Lennon for Mick Jagger." Paul laughs. "Tell me, Mal. Did it seem real to you?"

"Yeah. Very real. Some things were the same as the first time—John left Yoko for May, that was the same—all of those songs that you wrote, I had heard before, but Paul, the first time around, all of those songs—'Maybe I'm Amazed,' 'Imagine'— they were all solo songs. And many times, they were the only good things on your solo albums. This time, you put them all together, in one album, and it was so natural. It was as if this was the way it was supposed to be."

"Well, you've been privy to something special here. To everyone except you, the Beatles broke up in 1970, and they never got back together again. Bloody shame, too." He shakes his head. "But you've seen a different outcome, one that could have happened but didn't." He lights a cigarette. "Look, we all knew that we made each other better. Even I'll admit that my solo work wasn't as good as my work with the Beatles. Somehow, we all brought out the best in each other. It could have been the competition between me and John. Or, with George, he felt motivated or pushed to write better material. But once we lost that competition, we became stagnant. As much as we tried, we could never leave the shadow of the Beatles."

"Yeah." *Someone finally knows.* I try to explain everything that's happened—things that don't matter in the realm of what Paul knows. "You know, the cops that John ran into. He was the one who shot me. I—I thought somehow John had taken my place, that it should have been me instead of him. And that somehow he—"

"No, Mal. John's still alive in 1979, taking care of Sean. He'll die in 1980 for real, though. Some nutcase is gonna shoot him."

I shake my head in confusion. "No, no."

"In real life, John is going to die in 1980 without us getting back together. Ever. So there won't ever be a reunion. Sure, the three of us will work together on some things, but the Beatles will no longer be possible. In the real world, we'll always think about what could have been, what we lost. Here, you have created what could have been, what should have been, and in your own way, what *was*."

For the second time tonight, the tears come. This magnificent experience is drawing to an end.

"Paul . . ." I begin. ". . . I always wanted to keep you guys together. Did you—did you know what you and your music could do to people—to me?"

Paul smiles. "Yeah, I did. It freaked me out sometimes, the music we could come up with. I mean, 'Yesterday' came to me in a dream, can you believe that? John – 'Strawberry Fields Forever' seemed to come from another world. There's nothing else that sounds like it. And then, from out of the blue, George writes 'Something,' which still brings a tear to my eye when I hear it, it's so beautiful." He sighs, shaking his head. "I don't know how we did it, Mal, I truly don't. I know that sounds boastful, but I don't know how it all came to us. It really is as if God had sent the songs down to us to transcribe."

I remember Geoff saying the same things a few weeks ago.

"I think he did. Even though I hung around you every day, I still sensed some . . . some magic with you. I mean, I held you in *awe*. In fact, I don't think I ever got used to being around you. I would have done anything for you guys, but I never felt as if I were your equal. No offence, I hope."

Paul waves me off. "You did anything and everything for us, Mal. And you weren't our equal because we had our heads too far up our arses. We took you for granted. We chewed you up, spit you out, and went on. Jesus, we didn't even pay you a proper salary. You deserved better, actually."

I sniff, taking off my glasses to clear the tears. "It wasn't that bad."

Paul laughs. "We pretty much broke up your family! I remember John kicking you in the arse when you were bending down to pick up a broken martini glass that he had thrown on the floor. You fell on all fours and cut your hands and knees, and we laughed. I remember asking you to go buy some ale at the market and kept sending you back because I wanted a different kind. Just because I could." He puts down his glass. "It's daft. We were little boys who never grew up, and you were our toy."

The visions of those humiliating incidents come back at me like they were grade-school pranks. Paul walks over and puts his hand on my shoulder. "Mal, first I want to apologise for treating you the way we did. And second, I want to thank you for this dream. You helped create three new albums, and they're priceless. Especially this last one. That was all because of you. If you hadn't pulled it together, the *what if* would have haunted me the rest of this life—and probably my other life as well."

"But it didn't happen. It's all in my head."

"Again, who's to say? If it's in your head, then maybe it did happen. Your dream may have just created a reality somewhere, and at least in this alternate universe, people are enjoying three new Beatles albums—something your other world will never comprehend or have the pleasure of experiencing. Who knows? Maybe after you're gone, I'll wake up in the middle of one of my countless solo albums again, and I will have lost it all. Maybe you're going back to Los Angeles and will live another life where there will be even more unheard Beatles songs."

Paul snaps his fingers. "That reminds me. I meant to show this to you." He walks over to a wall and removes a painting. Behind it, there is a safe. I always knew it was there, but didn't know the combination or its contents. He turns the dial back and forth a few times and opens it. "This is my safe. Each of us has one, but no one knows the combination except the owner."

He takes a cassette from the safe and walks over to a tape player. "I think you've deserved to hear this. It's me and John a few weeks before we finished *Abracadabra*. He dropped by my apartment in London one day to pick up some things. We started talking, started playing some guitars, and began to play. I recorded it on a portable cassette player. We were just goofing off, but something clicked. We were still riding the high from our songwriting collaboration, and it just worked so well. I've never had the heart to do anything with it or play it for anyone."

It's poor quality, what you'd expect from a portable tape recorder. The song begins with Paul on the piano—simple chord progressions—and a few seconds later John joins him on acoustic guitar, playing what seems to be the same thing, but it's almost a countermelody at a different tempo. Both of them are singing together, John on lead and Paul harmonizing. It's similar to "If I Fell," a little faster than a ballad, but with more inventive chord changes, like "A Day in the Life." It's uplifting and poignant at the same time. Beautiful and melancholy, sweet but exciting. The words are only halfway there, John mostly singing gibberish while he finds the melody, but what I hear addresses a new heaven and a new earth, a place where true love exists. There is no death or sadness or pain. Lennon's last lyric, which talks about having a second chance at love, is undoubtedly his wishful thinking during his estrangement from Yoko, but it strikes something deep in my soul. And then he sings, "A second chance at life" and it hits me. *I have had my second chance.*

My voice trembles with emotion. "Wh—Why are you keeping this from people?" I ask. "You could have used this on *Free as a Bird.*"

"No. Somehow I couldn't bring myself to use it. I wanted one piece of John and me together—just for myself. Not even George, Ringo, or Linda know about it. It'll never see the light of day."

I feel as if I have heard the secret of life. The front door opens, and that well-described bright light shines through it. I smile at Paul.

"Thank you for sharing it with me. Thank you—for everything."

Paul shakes my hand, then grabs my arm and hugs me tightly. "Thank you, Mal. Godspeed. You are my friend and my companion. And you are a Beatle."

* * *

5 January 1976

I return to my apartment in Los Angeles a new man, a changed man. The past five years are still fresh in my mind, and my position on the floor now seems foreign and benign. I now have a new past and consequently, a new ending to my life. I look up at G TAYLOR and smile, whispering, "Thank you." He looks at me and lowers his gun, dumbfounded, wondering why he is receiving thanks from a man whom he has just shot. Maybe he even remembers me from that previous life.

I know I am leaving now. I can take my place in the ranks of the Beatles' faithful because I believed in them and kept them going through every trial and separation. I am joining the other unforgotten giants of Beatledom, where there is happiness and music, glorious music. I will join Stu Sutcliffe, the first bass player for the Beatles, who died so long ago. I will see their first manager, Brian Epstein, and will tell him all about their worldwide success and legacy. I will see John's mother, Julia, Paul's mother, Mary, and George's mother, Louise. I will tell stories of how I kept them together and urged them to create new masterpieces, and we will listen to every song and bask in its beauty and perfection. We'll be waiting for John and the others, where we will live for eternity as equals.

I have paid my penance. I have deserved this.

Author's Note

This book is a work of fiction – a dream within a work of fiction, if you will, like *The Wizard of Oz*. It's what some people call "fan fiction," stories written by fans that take the Beatles in a new direction—love affairs, chance encounters with the Fab Four, even time travel. There are websites dedicated just to Beatle fan fiction.

Like fan fiction, this book involves real people; Paul and Ringo are the only two surviving members of the Beatles, and Yoko Ono is alive and well, as are Geoff Emerick and George Martin. And some things in the book really happened to the individual Beatles (see "What Really Happened" in the next section), but the context in which these events have been placed has all been made up. Other events (for example, John's trip to Bangladesh) have been added to create more plot twists and tension in the story.

I have loved the Beatles ever since I first heard "Hey Jude" on my parents' stereo the Christmas after John was killed. After going through their full catalog, I wanted more. Their solo albums showed some promise, but I always wondered what would happen if you put together the best from each solo album on one Beatles album. And that's how this book started. I tweaked song lists, exchanged some, and then started researching when and why these solo songs were created. And I found that a lot of the songs still had ties to the Beatles in one way or another—a Beatle played on another Beatle's record, the song was written when the Beatles were still together—and the "What if?" started burning inside me.

Fate is a funny thing; I could have made Ringo an astronaut, George an accountant, or John and Paul a comedy team. But for them to create the music that they did—and the original intent of this book was to create those Beatle fantasy albums out of what was already there—I felt as if they needed to stay on their life's path, with everyone else on the ride with them. I could not create better fictional songs than the real ones they released.

So yes, almost all of the songs are real, but they are all songs recorded and released by the Beatles as solo artists; the only fictional song is the unnamed final number Mal hears before his dream is over. All of the newspaper articles and magazine reviews, as well as the press releases, are fictitious. None of the interaction between the four ever happened. That's because after the recording of *Abbey Road* in 1969, the four were never in the same room together, never recorded together in a studio, never performed at a concert together.

Would they have created different music had they stayed together? Of course. There's no guarantee "Band on the Run" would have ever been a song. But it's hard enough describing how "Isolation" sounds to a reader who's never heard it, much less creating another Beatlesque song that has never been made, and then trying to describe that (as I did in the last chapter). And where's the fun in a new Beatles album if you can't go buy the solo songs and put it together yourself?

Mal, Geoff Emerick, George Martin, Neil Aspinall, Derek Taylor – all played a crucial part in the Beatles' success during the 1960s. I tried to track down the names of some of the assistants and secretaries who worked at Apple; although they have minor parts in the book, they have their own part in Beatles history as well. The only names that have been changed are those of the police officer involved in the shooting, and Mal's wife, son and daughter, out of respect for their privacy. All others are real celebrities acting out Mal's—and Beatles fans'—wishes in his head.

I have tried to get into each character's head as much as I could and map out each person's personality and reactions based on how events in the book were playing out. As a result, all of the dialog comes from me; I am projecting what I think that person would have said at that particular moment. Biographies helped me gain some insight into their psyche; each Beatle had at least one biography written about him, and others, such as George Martin and Geoff Emerick, wrote their own memoirs. However, Mal, being the subject of so few words in Beatle literature, was even more of an enigma.

I wish we all knew more about Mal; from what I have read, he was indeed a "gentle giant." He played such a crucial role during Beatlemania; I hope that somehow this book helps solidify his status as a Fifth Beatle and helps to give him the credit he so richly deserves.

What Really Happened

"This is the funny thing, isn't it? If the Beatles had continued making records, all of the solo stuff that we'd done would have been on Beatle albums."

- George Harrison, UNDERCOVER magazine, 1995

Mal's "What if?" scenario in this book is something Beatle fans (myself included) have always wondered about. Why did the greatest rock group ever suddenly disband in the prime of its career? What would have happened had they stayed together? It's been the subject of numerous debates in bars, Beatle festivals and Internet discussion groups. Speculation is all we have, because on April 10, 1970, Paul McCartney released his first solo album, *McCartney*, and announced that he was quitting the Beatles.

The announcement sent shock waves across the globe. Paul, John Lennon, George Harrison, and Ringo Starr had released their finest album, *Abbey Road*, only six months before; a month before, the single "Let it Be" had been released, and the album and the film of the same name were slated for release in May (what was originally referred to as *Get Back*). Confused fans wondered whether they would ever hear the Beatles as a band again.

They wouldn't. While many groups part ways amicably, this divorce was bitter. Paul sued the other band members to dissolve the Beatles' partnership in 1970, and for all practical purposes, that was the end of any talk of a reunion. Granted, there were close calls:

- All the Beatles played on Ringo's self-titled album in 1973, but they never played together as a group on any one cut and were never in the studio all at one time.

- In 1974, John and Paul actually played together at a studio jam session in Los Angeles, along with Stevie Wonder, Harry Nilsson and several others. A few demo tapes exist, although the group produced nothing of any quality.

- In 1976, Lorne Michaels of "Saturday Night Live" offered the Beatles $3,000 to reunite on his show. The offer was obviously a gag, but in a freak coincidence, Paul and John were at John's New York City apartment that night watching the show and almost went down to the studio to perform.

In 1980 Lennon's death at the hands of a crazed gunman put to rest any possibility of an actual reunion. A decade of feuding ended with no resolution, no shaking of hands, no retrospective. But we came tantalizingly close fifteen years later with the release of "Free as a Bird" and "Real Love," two Lennon demos that were dressed up with contributions from the other three. It was a marvelous moment, and it gave us a glimpse of what we had missed over the last twenty-five years: John's haunting voice, a new bridge and harmonizing by Paul, George's signature slide guitar, and an amplified beat from Ringo.

So the Beatles broke up, and the members lived mostly separate lives. But were the parts as great as the sum? Hardly. There were glimpses of genius in each of the solo Beatles' careers: George's *All Things Must Pass*, John's "Imagine," Paul's *Band on the Run*, and Ringo's eponymous album. But one could argue that their careers after 1970 were for the most part disappointing.

So what happened to our heroes during that decade?

Mal

Mal Evans is an unknown outside of Beatle fandom, just as he is made out to be in the book. Mal's real life mirrored his "first life" in the book; after the Beatles broke up, he was lost. He produced a few albums, hung out with various celebrities, and watched his life spiral downhill. He was in the process of writing his memoirs, tentatively titled *Living with the Beatles Legend,* but on January 5, 1976, estranged from his wife and doped up on Valium in Los Angeles, he was shot by a police officer who thought Mal's air rifle was a dangerous weapon. Mal died instantly. (I have given some artistic license to that, giving him time to evaluate his life, experience his flashback and accept his fate.) His body was cremated and sent back to England, but in yet another cruel punctuation mark to his life, his ashes were lost in the mail.

John

The Plastic Ono Band indeed performed at the Toronto Rock n' Roll Revival Festival, but it was a telegram from John's personal assistant Terry Dolan, not Mal Evans, that got the attention of Eric Clapton's gardener, who woke up Eric and got him to the airport. After the successful concert, John told Allen Klein that he planned to leave the Beatles, setting the wheels in motion.

After Paul made the official announcement a few months later, John was released from the tight controls of being a member of a band and having to share studio time. He was free to express his (and Yoko's) political and emotional views. After some avant-garde albums with Yoko, he released the cathartic *John Lennon/ Plastic Ono Band* in 1970, recorded after his Primal Scream sessions with Dr. Arthur Janov. It featured the songs "Isolation," "Mother," "God" and "Working Class Hero." John's next album, 1971's *Imagine*, was the high point of his solo career. In addition to the title cut, it contained a few other songs featured on my fictional Beatles album ("Gimme Some Truth," "Jealous Guy"). Also on the album was "How Do You Sleep?", John's cutting attack against Paul after Paul released "Too Many People" from his second solo album, *Ram*. The song added fuel to the fiery relationship between the two during the 1970s.

John and Yoko moved to New York in 1971 and did become involved with the anti-war movement, attracting some attention from the FBI. There was a benefit concert in Ann Arbor, Michigan that became the basis for the album *Some Time in New York City*, but Lennon was not detained after the concert. The government did try to deport them at one time, but despite numerous attempts, they never succeeded; in fact, John never made it back to his home country, staying in the United States until his death.

John and Yoko separated in 1973 while he was recording the album *Mind Games,* and the ensuing eighteen months are usually referred to as his "Lost Weekend." He and May Pang moved to Los Angeles, and John made headlines over his drunken escapades with fellow singer-songwriter Harry Nilsson. They moved back to New York in 1974, and he released *Walls and Bridges* later that year, yielding his only Number One single in the United States, "Whatever Gets You Thru the Night" (with Elton John, not Paul McCartney). But he and Yoko reunited after John made an appearance with Elton John at a concert. Less than a year later, their son, Sean, was born, and John went into a self-imposed five-year exile.

After hearing McCartney's "Coming Up" while on vacation in Bermuda (not Patmos), John began writing songs again. His comeback LP with Yoko, *Double Fantasy,* was released in November 1980, just weeks before his murder.

John's legacy is one of a peace activist and lyricist, and his anthem "Imagine" is universally known. But his discography is spotty—varied chart success and inconsistent albums—and without Paul serving as his regulator, his raging mind ran wild. Melody often took a back seat to political statements and idealism.

John never went to Bangladesh, never threw feces on reviews of his album reviews (although they did participate in unique press events such as the bed-in for peace, sending acorns to all the world leaders, and "bagism," which involved covering up one's entire body in a bag to show that one could not judge others by what's on the outside), and never talked to a reporter about "My Sweet Lord" that forced a settlement—although he did tell *Playboy* magazine in an interview just before his death, "He must have known, you know. He's smarter than that . . . He could have changed a couple of bars in that song and nobody could ever have touched him, but he just let it go and paid the price. Maybe he thought God would just sort of let him off" (David Sheff, *Playboy,* January 1981). He didn't throw instruments in a rage during the recording of "Imagine," although author Albert Goldman has claimed Lennon was violent at times. And, of course, he didn't die in an automobile accident. But Lennon's murder in 1980 shook the foundations of rock 'n' roll and scarred the remaining Beatles, especially Paul.

Paul

Paul has had the most success—over forty albums both as a solo artist and with Wings, and twenty gold or platinum singles. He has also had the most criticism heaped upon him. Because of his enormous talent, he has disappointed many with albums that just couldn't compare with what the Beatles released. It was apparent from his debut album, *McCartney,* which shined at times ("Maybe I'm Amazed," "Every Night") but slipped into jam sessions or hastily written tunes. His second album, 1971's *Ram,* opened with his jab at John, "Too Many People," and also featured the hit "Uncle Albert/Admiral Halsey." Song for song, it was one of his better albums, and had he continued to focus his attention on solo efforts, he might have had better critical reception. But he was determined to have his own band to prove that he was the genius behind a group's success.

Paul never had a BBC special called "Heart of the Country," although "James Paul McCartney" was a variety special in 1973 in much the same mold—little vignettes of songs interspersed with live performances.

Paul released album after album with his new group, Wings, at a rate comparable to a dime-store novelist. The only one to achieve universal critical acclaim was 1973's *Band on the Run,* which featured the hit singles "Jet" and the title cut. He had several other hits throughout the decade, but few well-received albums.

Wings disbanded in 1981, and Paul's first solo album after the breakup, *Tug of War,* was a critical and chart success. It contained the two songs from *Free as a Bird* that were tributes to John: the title cut and "Here Today," as well as "Take It Away." But after that he slipped back into neutral, with critically panned solo albums and a movie during the decade following John's death. It took 1995's Beatles *Anthology* to get him on the right track; his next album, 1997's *Flaming Pie,* was heralded as a return to his Beatles roots. The albums that followed, while not achieving chart success, were finally met with the praise that had evaded him.

At times, Paul seemed content to put anything down on tape ("Bip Bop," "Temporary Secretary"). Without John's cutting criticism, those tunes survived. "The only person he's got to tell him if the song's good or bad is Linda," George once said. "In the Beatle days, if someone came in with a song that had a corny line and some of the others got a bit embarrassed by it, we'd say it!" (Keith Badman, *The Beatles: After the Break-Up 1970-2000*)

John's death made him a martyr, and Paul has been haunted by his partner's ghost ever since. John is still the visionary, the legend, while Paul still tries to prove to fans—and himself—that he is a master composer, trying to mold his own legacy. And his recent critical success has helped cement that legacy, if there was ever any doubt. He is now Sir Paul McCartney, having been knighted by Queen Elizabeth in 1997.

George

George started off with a bang: Since most of his material had been passed over by the Beatles, he had plenty of songs in the can, and he put every one of them on his triple album *All Things Must Pass*. All of his contributions to the first two fictitious albums come from this one album.

It was a smashing success, and critics lauded his effort. But as John told Paul, "[George is] a hip boy. Still, he's got to follow it up, hee hee" (Keith Badman, *The Beatles: The Dream Is Over*). "My Sweet Lord" was a worldwide hit, but George was sued by Bright Tunes for the song's similarity to "He's So Fine." George defended himself by saying it was taken from the gospel hymn "Oh Happy Day" (which is in the public domain). There's no record of him playing it for the Beatles, although it's interesting that Phil Spector, who produced the album, didn't hear the similarities. The case was tied up in courts for years. (As mentioned before, John had nothing to do with the outcome.)

George's follow-up, *Living in the Material World*, generated only one hit single ("Give Me Love, Give Me Peace on Earth," which George did not erase after being told it sounded somewhat like a Dylan tune). He did engineer the popular Concert for Bangladesh in Madison Square Garden, but Ringo

was the only Beatle to make an appearance. (George wrote
the song "Bangla Desh" by himself without any help from Eric
Clapton.) Mediocre albums followed throughout the 1970s, and
his next major hit didn't come until 1982's "All Those Years Ago,"
which was his tribute to John after John's murder.

George longed to get away from the Lennon/McCartney
spotlight, but the light shone too harshly; his songwriting soon
took a back seat to his religion, and the two were sometimes
too heavily mixed, as seen on tracks such as "It Is 'He' (Jai Sri
Krishna)" and "The Lord Loves The One (That Loves The Lord)."
And although he remained steadfast to the Krishna religion,
he never turned his Friar Park estate into a monastery for his
Krishna brethren.

Ringo

Ringo's career followed the pattern of George's: a stunning
debut album and then disappointment after disappointment. He
had two Number One hits from his self-titled album: "You're
Sixteen," which featured backup vocals and a kazoo solo by
Paul, and "Photograph," a song that he co-wrote with George.
The John Lennon-penned song "I'm the Greatest," which also
featured John on backing vocals, was also on the album, and
Paul contributed a song called "Six O'Clock" (which almost
made it on *Abracadabra,* but I opted for "I'm the Greatest"
instead).

Unlike George, however, Ringo had no expectations, and in
a way, the public embraced him more than George. Despite his
lack of chart success, he seemed to adjust best to life without
the Beatles, appearing in films and television shows, acting
as a session drummer by playing on various artists' albums,

and eventually touring the world with "All Starr" bands of famous musicians backing him. His self-deprecating humor has always been easy to digest. He never hosted his own American television show, although I'm sure it would have been fun to watch.

What's it like to be a solo artist after being in a band? Instead of pooling your best work with everyone onto one album, you're forced to write more than you ever had. The result? Disjointed, watered-down albums full of both promise and disappointment. As producer George Martin said in an interview, "I think the four of them are greater than the individuals and obviously each individual album that has been produced is good because they're all very talented people, but I still don't think they're as great as they were when they were Beatles together" (Badman).

The Beatles scoffed at this; in his 1980 interview with *Playboy*, John declared, "Why should the Beatles give more? Didn't they give everything on God's earth for ten years? Didn't they give themselves? You're like the typical sort of love-hate fan who says, 'Thank you for everything you did for us in the Sixties -- would you just give me another shot? Just one more miracle?' " (Sheff).

Yes, we do ask for a miracle. We wish for the songs that were never created. We yearn for the solo songs we know might have been richer when produced by the Four. We can always dream.

Make Your Own Beatles Fantasy Albums

The albums in *The Death and Life of Mal Evans* are my fantasy albums. A lot of care and thought went into getting the right songs on these albums, ones that would sound the most like the Beatles and not a disjointed "Various Artists" compilation. Most of the songs had one of five reasons to be included (in this order):

- It was written while the Beatles were still together, giving it some status as a "Beatle" song.

- It featured two or more Beatles playing on the song.

- Another Beatle praised the song (meaning it may have passed a Beatle audition).

- It fit with the way the album was coming together thematically.

- It *sounded* like the Beatles.

Everest

This title was originally slated for the Beatles' *Abbey Road* album in 1969, and was indeed based on Geoff Emerick's cigarette of choice. They were intent on flying to the Himalayas to take the photo; but either laziness or the growing tension in the band prevented them from making the trip. It was easier to step outside the recording studio and walk across the street; hence the iconic *Abbey Road* name and album cover were born.

1. "Too Many People" (McCartney, from the album *Ram*, 1971). Some may object to a song criticizing John on a Beatles' album, but the first time I heard the opening chords to this song, I immediately thought it sounded like the Beatles. And the sharp lyrics made a nice turning point in the plot (as did Linda's vocals).

2. "It Don't Come Easy" (Starr, *Ringo*, 1973)—Ringo's hit single featured George on acoustic guitar and Mal on tambourine.

3. "Every Night" (McCartney, *McCartney*, 1970)—Paul debuted it during the *Get Back* sessions in 1969, with John even playing a slide guitar during one take.

4. "Oh My Love" (Lennon, *Imagine*, 1971)—This ballad appears on demos from 1968's *White Album* sessions. George plays guitar.

5. "Apple Scruffs" (Harrison, *All Things Must Pass*, 1970)— The song mainly lends to the acoustic feel of *Everest*. Mal Evans played a wooden block on it, and with the full harmonies, it does sound like a lost Beatles track from *Abbey Road*.

6. "Isolation" (Lennon, *John Lennon/Plastic Ono Band*, 1970)—Beatlesque chromatic chord progressions abound here; Ringo plays drums.

7. "Isn't it a Pity" (Harrison, *All Things Must Pass*, 1970)— Dates all the way back to 1966. (A lot of George's offerings were rejected.) Ringo plays drums.

8. "Wah-Wah" (Harrison, *All Things Must Pass*, 1970)— George wrote this in 1969 after he temporarily quit the Beatles during the *Get Back* sessions. Ringo plays drums.

9. "Look at Me" (Lennon, *John Lennon/Plastic Ono Band*, 1970)—Written during the *White Album* sessions around 1968.

10. "Maybe I'm Amazed" (McCartney, *McCartney*, 1970)— Paul began to write this song in 1969, when the Beatles were starting to splinter.

11. "Jealous Guy" (Lennon, *Imagine*, 1971)—Originally titled "Child of Nature," this song was written by John while the Beatles were in India in 1968.

12. "The Back Seat of My Car" (McCartney, *McCartney*, 1970)—You can hear bits and pieces of this song during the Beatles' *Get Back* sessions in 1969.

13. "All Things Must Pass" (Harrison, *All Things Must Pass*, 1970)—Another reject from the Beatles *Get Back* sessions. Ringo plays drums.

The Concert for Bangladesh

The track listing for the Concert for Bangladesh was based on what I could find on live albums. For Paul, this was no problem; he's released eight live albums. For others, though, I was limited in what I could find; John and George released only two, and John's two albums contained precious few Beatles songs (or fantasy Beatles songs, for that matter).

1. "Dizzy Miss Lizzie" (Lennon, *Live Peace in Toronto 1969*)

2. "Drive My Car" (McCartney, *Paul is Live*)

3. "It Don't Come Easy" (Various Artists, *The Concert for Bangladesh*)

4. "Lady Madonna" (McCartney, *Wings Over America*)

5. "Something" (Various Artists, *The Concert for Bangladesh*)

6. "Maybe I'm Amazed" (McCartney, *Wings Over America*)

7. "Come Together" (Lennon, *Live in New York City*)

8. "While My Guitar Gently Weeps" (Various Artists, *The Concert for Bangladesh*)

9. "Blackbird" (McCartney, *Wings Over America*)

10. "Yesterday" (McCartney, *Wings Over America*)

11. "Here Comes the Sun" (Various Artists, *The Concert for Bangladesh*)

12. "Hey Jude" (McCartney, *Tripping the Live Fantastic*)

13. "Imagine" (Lennon, *John Lennon Anthology*)

14. "Bangla Desh" (Various Artists, *The Concert for Bangladesh*)

Abracadabra

Abracadabra was an early working title for the Beatles 1966 album *Revolver* until the group discovered that another group had recently used it. Finding songs that fit the criteria was a little more difficult, since several years had passed since the band broke up, and the members were starting to venture into new sonic territory.

1. "Imagine" (Lennon, *Imagine,* 1971)—Why wouldn't "Imagine" be a Beatles song? It's an instant classic that would have fit on any Beatles album.

2. "Band on the Run" (McCartney, *Band on the Run,* 1973)— This song ties in with the timeline nicely – 1973. John also liked the entire album, so I don't see him vetoing this song.

3. "I'm the Greatest" (Starr, *Ringo,* 1973)—John wrote it for Ringo for his self-titled album. John also plays piano and sings background vocals, and George plays electric and slide guitar.

4. "Jet" (McCartney, *Band on the Run,* 1973)—See "Band on the Run" above.

5. "Mind Games" (Lennon, *Mind Games,* 1973)—Was originally demoed when the Beatles were still together in 1969 (called "Make Love, Not War").

6. "Art of Dying" (Harrison, *All Things Must Pass,* 1970)— Dates back to 1966 and never made it onto a Beatles album, perhaps because of its religious theme.

7. "Let Me Roll It" (McCartney, *Band on the Run,* 1973)—
   It's been said that Paul tried to mimic John's echo-style
   production in the song.

8. "Let It Down" (Harrison, *All Things Must Pass,* 1970)—
   Written in 1968, it failed the *Get Back* auditions but fits
   nicely with the mystical motif of *Abracadabra.*

9. "Live and Let Die" (McCartney, "Live and Let Die" single,
   1973)—The reggae-flavored bridge would have never
   made it, but the verses sound Beatlesque.

10. "Nobody Loves You (When You're Down and Out)"
    (Lennon, *Walls and Bridges,* 1974)—Written in 1973, it
    serves as a perfect reminder of Lennon's anguish during
    his time apart from Yoko.

11. "Venus and Mars" (McCartney, *Venus and Mars,* 1975)—
    This is actually a reprise to the song "Venus and Mars"
    from the album of the same name. The song is not about
    John, but he and Yoko were interested in astrology, and
    during this time, John was supposed to visit Paul in New
    Orleans, where he was recording the album. Another near
    miss for a reunion.

12. "Gimme Some Truth" (Lennon, *Imagine,* 1971)—
    Originally demoed during the *Get Back* sessions. George
    plays guitar.

Free As a Bird

By this time the four had drifted away from each other so much, their output so inconsistent, that it was hard to piece together an album from the same era. This album comes together simply from songs during that time—trying to find songs that fit the Fifties vibe that John and Paul were trying to achieve in the book. It also featured any tributes the three wrote for John, plus the two demos that actually brought the three remaining members together in real life.

1. "In Spite of All the Danger" (Harrison/McCartney, *Anthology 1*, 1995)—The first known recording ever of John, Paul and George, playing as the Quarrymen in 1958.

2. "(Just Like) Starting Over" (Lennon, *Double Fantasy*, 1980)—I can hear a voice that sounds like Paul in the backing vocals.

3. "Take It Away" (McCartney, *Tug of War*, 1982)—Paul's hit single from the *Tug of War* album, released a few years after John's death. Ringo plays drums.

4. "Nobody Told Me" (Lennon, *Milk and Honey*, 1984)—A leftover from the *Double Fantasy* sessions, it was not released for another four years.

5. "Call Me Back Again" (McCartney, *Venus and Mars*, 1975)—This is definitely out of sequence. I pretended that Paul was holding this one back for a special occasion; it has the 1950s flavor I was looking for.

6. "Wrack My Brain" (Starr, *Stop and Smell the Roses*, 1981)—George wrote the song and played guitar on it.

7. "Free as a Bird" (Lennon/McCartney/Harrison/Starr, *Anthology 1*, 1995)—This scenario, of course, actually happened; Yoko gave Paul an old demo of John's, and the three surviving Beatles added to the demo to create the song. I simply pretended that she gave him the tapes sixteen years earlier.

8. "Woman" (Lennon, *Double Fantasy*, 1980)—The harmonies sound very Lennon/McCartney here.

9. "Tug of War" (McCartney, *Tug of War*, 1982)—Paul's description of his complex relationship with John has to go on this album.

10. "All Those Years Ago" (Harrison, *Somewhere in England*, 1981)—George's tribute has to be here as well, and it is arguably the best song he's ever written. Ringo played drums, and Paul provided backing vocals. Another near-miss reunion.

11. "Here Today" (McCartney, *Tug of War*, 1982)—Paul's personal message to John is more than fitting.

12. "Real Love" (Lennon/ McCartney/ Harrison/ Starr, *Anthology 2*, 1996)—Another project culled from a Lennon cassette tape and embellished by the three surviving Beatles.

Acknowledgements

This book has been some ten years in the making; a great deal of research has gone into finding the right songs for the albums, the proper context and the meaning behind each song. It began as a nonfiction "Create your own fantasy Beatles album" essay and evolved into a fake biography. Later, as the book turned into a novel, I needed to make the songs, places and people come alive for those who were not diehard Beatles fans. I struggled to decide whether to explain why *Abbey Road* was the last album recorded but *Let It Be* was the last one released; I needed to describe "Apple Scruffs" to those who had never heard it, needed plot twists that kept a certain level of tension among the band members, needed descriptions of homes, offices and studios. The specifics were hard to come by, but I hope I gave a hint of what life was like back in the 1970s.

The Internet was my first inspiration; the rec.music.beatles newsgroup was full of discussions about members' favorite songs, "what if" scenarios and fantasy albums. Books were invaluable in their information. Keith Badman's *The Beatles after the Breakup 1970-2000* and *The Beatles: The Dream is*

Over chronicled every day in the lives of the four Beatles during that decade and featured quotes, showed the changing dynamic among the four and helped establish the all-important timeline. *Lennon and McCartney: Together Alone* by John Blaney painstakingly described the recording process for all solo Lennon and McCartney songs and helped establish when certain songs were written.

Biographies didn't help with chronology as much as it helped establish the members' personalities. May Pang's *John Lennon: The Lost Weekend* described their relationship in great detail; Ray Coleman's *Lennon* and Barry Miles' *Paul McCartney: Many Years from Now* gave a glossy version of events during the 1970s; on the flip side, *The Last Days of John Lennon* by Frederic Seaman and *John Lennon: The Life* by Albert Goldman painted a different, sometimes controversial picture of the John Lennon and Yoko Ono we hear about.

Geoff Emerick's *Here, There and Everywhere* taught me a great deal about the Beatles' recording process and gave an insider's look into Abbey Road studios. Richard DiLello's *The Longest Cocktail Party* and Chris O'Dell's memoir, *Miss O'Dell*, gave great insight into the sometimes chaotic inner workings of Apple Records. I only wish Mal's book, *Living the Beatles Legend,* had been published.

I offer thanks to my father, Leon Lee, Sr., and my mother, Judith Lee, for being my most ardent supporters. Their encouragement, editing and honest critiquing of the book kept me and the project going. I also thank my sister Susan Hauser for her editing and help with the Britishisms that are spread throughout Mal's narrative; her husband, Steve Hauser, for his legal advice; Lisa Moore of the Moore Firm for reviewing my manuscript; Christina Lingga for designing the book cover; Rebecca Shaw for the layout and interior design; my many beta readers, who discovered inconsistencies and misspellings that I and my editors missed; my wife for her support; and my children for believing that their daddy could write a book.

About the Author

Peter Lee loves music, loves writing and loves to write about music. A former journalist, he maintains a blog, Hooks and Harmony (www. hooksandharmony.com), which is dedicated to melodic pop music very similar to the four lads from Liverpool. He and his wife have two children, both of whom prefer the Beatles and Queen over Justin Bieber and Kanye West.